the curing season

LESLIE WELLS

WARNER BOOKS

A Time Warner Company

Warner Books, Inc., 1271 Avenue of the Americas, New York, NY 10020
Visit our Web site at www.twbookmark.com

 A Time Warner Company

Printed in the United States of America

First Printing: May 2001

10 9 8 7 6 5 4 3 2 1

Library of Congress Cataloging-in-Publication Data

Wells, Leslie.
    The curing season / by Leslie Wells.
      p.   cm.
    ISBN 0-446-52693-2
      1. Young women—Fiction. 2. Physically handicapped—Fiction. 3. Mothers and sons—Fiction. 4. Problem families—Fiction. 5. Rural poor—Fiction. 6. Virginia—Fiction. I. Title.

PS3573.E4926 C8 2001
813'.6—dc21
                                                        00-033001

For my parents, the kindest, most generous and loving in the whole world.

And for my grandparents, who've given me a lifetime of good memories.

I used to think candles were so pretty. Their clean smell, the holy flame. The quiet burn if you touched the wax while hot. The way they kept the image of your fingerprint. We used to dip our fingers into the molten wax, my sister and I. We'd make the shapes of little flower petals, or tears.

Chapter One

In back, the women are laying out the dishes they've brought on the long wooden tables. Steaming hot macaroni, butter lying in golden slabs on top of a melting crust of cheese. Platters of fried chicken, a dish that always gets eaten, every last piece. Creasey salad, dark and bitter green, with chunks of pork mixed in. Dishes of snap beans, again mixed with pieces of fatback, glistening with delicious grease. Homemade potato rolls and flaky pan biscuits. Pickled watermelon and pickled peaches. I look for a bare place to put my two dreary dishes: a bean salad and a dried-out spoonbread. They'll excuse my modest offerings, as they always do.

On the last plank table crowd the desserts. An enormous snowy cake, yellow on the inside, with flaking fresh coconut sprinkled across the icing. Crunchy pecan pies by the dozen. Someone made a cobbler, and its thick pastry only barely covers the bursting blackberries beneath in their beds of sugar, dough, and butter. There's millionaire's salad, although I think this should go on the salad table instead of with the desserts. And peach and lemon chess pie. Someone's even taken the time to grind ice cream, the rock salt and ice still clinging to the outside of the bucket.

Several children have been given cardboard church fans from the funeral home and told to keep the flies off the food. The Jesus on the fans looks sickly, his drooping dark eyes gazing across his folded hands. When the women aren't looking, the children play tag around the tables, ignoring their task.

Joshua is not here; he's with his father and the other men as they greet people filing out of church. I always come out the back way to avoid the grinning line of people, smiling in their stiff Sunday best. Some of them are kindly, but most of them are curious, and I cannot abide that. Since we got to this place eleven months ago, I've avoided the stares and whispers. The people act friendly, and that's enough. They often speak and then forget, bringing their hands up to their mouths. The ones who remember give me a shy wave, as if unsure of how to greet me. Sometimes Joshua calls out hello when he's with me, although I haven't encouraged that. Most of the time we just stick to ourselves.

Aaron is still inside with him. I see the last of the women crowding down the front steps of the church. Mrs. Grey is always near the end of the line, and the pianist, Mrs. Peale. Mrs. Grey invited me, gesturing and pointing, to come to her Sunday school class, which meets during the hour before church starts, but I shook my head. I stay in the church basement with Joshua where it's nice and cool, and meet Aaron after his class is done. Then we go up the stairs and into our pew.

More dishes are filling in the spaces left on the crowded tables—groaning tables, they used to call them back at my home church, Calvary Baptist. It's been so long since I've seen anyone from home. I wonder what Mother looks like now, how WillieEd is doing running the farm. I imagined her life would be easier since Father died, but it seems not.

The one letter from her that found its way to me talked about how lonely she was, the hardship. Imagine missing a man like Father, who made our lives a daily misery. But I guess it's all a matter of what you get used to.

Now she and the children are going it alone. I'm sure Sibby must be married by now. At least I know the church folks would help Mother if she needed food, and Man Murfree across the way pitches in with his tractor when they need it. There's only so much WillieEd can do with a mule. Sibby used to think Man Murfree was sweet on Mother, but I guess that was just a silly whisper, probably started by Alicia Farnsworth. She used to love to stir up all grades of trouble.

As I stand here woolgathering, Joshua comes running toward me, clutching a bunch of dandelions he picked. They're his favorite flower, and mine too. He holds them up smiling, his brown curls twisting at the nape of his neck from the heat. His bright eyes shining, *Mama.* I smile and take the flowers and steer him over to a shady place under a tree, where we sit.

I'm ravenously hungry, but first there's a long prayer by Deacon Sayers. He takes a stance at the head of the tables, close enough so I can see his lips curving around the words.

—Dear Lord, he begins, Bless this glorious day, the Sabbath day on which we praise your name. Thank you for sharing your Son, who shed His precious blood, the blood of the Lamb, for us poor sinners. We pray for those who live in the dark, for those who have not seen your light, the light of the world. We pray for President Truman, that he may make decisions that will lead America toward Christianity and away from the heathenism that has been a plague on the world and our country. We pray that in this time of peace, we will not forget those who gave their lives for their country.

Deacon Sayers had lost his eldest son seven years ago, right before the Germans finally admitted they were licked. I had seen some women talking about it at church one Sunday, shaking their heads. They were saying it seemed like he'd have gotten over it by now. I look at Joshua and cannot imagine ever getting over a loss like that.

—and we pray for those on the Southern Baptist Missions Board, he was concluding, —as they send missionaries out to all parts of the world to make believers in Your name. Help us here in Virginia to support the Board in its efforts to spread Your name to all parts of the globe. Bless this food to the nourishment of our bodies, and we thank You for Your bounty. In the name of Jesus Christ, amen.

The blessing over, people begin to line up at the tables. Joshua is pulling on me to get up; he's hungry, but I hold him back. I won't go until the end, that way there's less notice. I've almost come to hate the kind looks as much as the cruel ones.

Aaron is eating on a bench the men have pulled up under some pine trees. He keeps his hat slouched over his face, chewing mightily. Not a thought about whether his boy has eaten or not. He'll have his seconds and possibly thirds before we even get up to serve ourselves.

At long last the line of women and children has emptied out. I pull Joshua up and we go over to the table. He grabs a biscuit and begins eating it as we go through the line. I fill our plates, avoiding my own poor offerings like the plague. I can't stand to eat anything I've prepared; that's why I've dropped off to nothing. Seems like I don't have a taste for anything but someone else's cooking anymore. And I don't get the chance of that very often.

Joshua is on his second biscuit. I don't want his father to see him bolting his food before we even sit down. I clump over to another shade tree away from the groups of women, and we sit and eat quickly. He looks at me and holds up his plate.

—More, Mama? he asks; I can see his lips moving and his worried look. It makes me sad deep inside for my little boy to already have to worry about things. I glance back at the bench under the pines; the men are laughing and talking. Aaron is picking his teeth with a sliver of haystalk. I motion for Joshua to stay there, and I walk back to the tables, taking it slow.

Several women are at the tables, tickling the last of their appetites with a little taste of sweet potato pie, a spoonful of fried squash, one more bite of ham. I quickly fill up half a plate and walk back to where Joshua waits patiently. I motion for him to eat, and sit in front of him to block him from Aaron's view. Joshua is only three, too young to know table manners, but Aaron expects him to behave, especially at church. Of course, Aaron's religious leanings only began since we moved here. He wouldn't darken the door of a church before we arrived in Tarville.

It's now midafternoon, deadly hot. I feel stuffed and bloated. Sweat runs down my back and pools above the knob at the base of my spine. I raise my apron discreetly and try to fan myself with it, but I can't do it without making too much of a stir. I settle for a large oak leaf and fan Joshua's face. He's fallen asleep and is lying with his head on my lap, eyes blissfully closed, a contented smile on his face.

A shadow falls across Joshua and me. I look up, and it's Mrs. Rattner and Mrs. Willis, two of the deacons' wives. They smile at me, eyes shiny with some secret knowledge. They point to Joshua and mouth exaggeratedly,

—Sweet little boy.

I nod my thanks, my head rocking back and forth on the stem of my neck. With each motion a pounding repeats in my skull. I feel like I'm going to be sick, but surely I can't do that here. Mrs. Willis is speaking to me. I look up at her lips.

—look hot. Some of us are going into the basement to cool off while the men finish their reading.

She gestures toward the steps of the church. While I sat there in my stupor, most of the congregation has gone, and only a few men and their wives are still in the yard. Several of the women are piling the leftover food into boxes, and the others are probably already inside.

—come in with us out of this heat?

I look down at Joshua. He's content, sleeping away. It would be cooler inside for him, but then they'd have me, pinned and needled. The last time I answered any questions I got into a load of trouble. I shake my head no, and point to him.

—Mmhmm, I groan, indicating that I'll stay here and wait for Aaron. The women nod and smile, and turn to leave. Mrs. Rattner looks back at me, and I see her say to Mrs. Willis,

—knowed from the first I saw her she was off-kilter.

My face burns in embarrassment, but the feeling passes, as it has many times before. I've learned to shrug off this kind of comment, letting them think whatever they want.

So it has been for the past year, me not speaking, not hearing a thing except the voices in my head.

Chapter Two

Four years earlier—Gower County, Virginia, April 1948

Footrace after class. Pass it on. Folded into a tiny bit of paper.
I shut it quickly and passed it to the girl with long braids
in front of me, a blush of heat heading up my neck. Maybe
I could get out fast and go down the trail toward the creek,
take the long way home. Unnoticed. Being in the eleventh
grade, I had been allowed three thick books from Mrs.
Spender's borrowing table, and they would slow me down.
But if I left them here, Mary Jane Markley might take them
home to show to her father, who'd surely forbid *Forever
Amber* and might not allow *Jude the Obscure*, either. I'd just
have to take my chances with the books. I wanted to read
them before old man Markley heard about them.

There had been rumblings before about Mrs. Spender's
borrowing table in our one-room schoolhouse. When Carl
Hatting brought home *Origin of the Species*, his mother and
father showed up the next morning at school, screeching,

—Don't ever let Carl borrow from your heathen library
again!

Mrs. Spender explained that Charles Darwin was a scientist, that his theories were going to be taught in twelfth grade anyway by the time Carl got there, but they didn't care. No, he wasn't to bring home any more books. They were Christians, they didn't want their boy's mind filled with the devil's work, science or not. Mrs. Spender never brought that book back into the classroom again. Luckily I'd checked it out a month earlier and had kept it under my pillow so Father wouldn't see it. You'd think Carl would've known enough to hide it when he took it home, but he didn't have the sense God gave a billygoat.

Mrs. Spender asked her last question, and not a hand was raised. That was what happened most of the time. We all had to fill woodboxes, haul water, feed and milk cows, and do a pile of other tasks before we even got to the schoolhouse at eight in the morning. A lot of the kids fell asleep by early afternoon, laid their heads down right on their desks. The schoolhouse got pretty hot in the springtime even with all the windows open, and the heat and the combined smells of sweating children and teenagers who didn't bathe regularly was a pretty potent combination. No wonder they had to put their heads down. I expect Mrs. Spender figured as long as they didn't disrupt the class, it didn't matter.

A lot of us had nothing more in our lunchboxes than frybread and some cow corn to chew on, and that on a good day. At least I had shoes, even if they were hand-me-downs, and even if one had to be stretched and bent to accommodate the sharp inward flex of my right foot. The Amos kids went barefoot year-round, and the Mayhans didn't do much better with cardboard tied on their feet, wrapped around with rawhide. Jim Mayhan had frostbite so bad last winter his little toe stayed permanently black, and bent at an odd angle from its brothers.

I didn't dare raise my hand again, even to rescue Mrs.

Spender, or I'd risk getting beat up once the bell rang. So I
hunched over my books and tried to sneak a look at the
first page of *Forever Amber*. Sometimes I couldn't believe what
Mrs. Spender brought to school. I think she might have just
grabbed whatever was on her shelf at the last minute, not
really paying attention. This was a book I figured I wouldn't
get my hands on until I was eighteen, at least. If I had to
sit up half the night lighting candles to read it, I would.

Mrs. Spender sighed, answered her question herself, then
said,

—All right then. What was the name of Robert E. Lee's
famous horse?

Suddenly twenty hands shot up.

—I know! I know, Miz Spender!

—I know! Let me answer it!

—Traveller!

—It's Traveller, anybody knows that.

came the calls from all sides of the room.

—Who won the battle of First Manassas? she asked.

—We did! We whipped those Yanks! cried Steven Pierce.

—Stonewall got his name there, added Tom Smith.

—And we won Mechanicsville, Miz Spender! and Gaines
Mill! shouted Teak Williams, who normally sat sullen and
never looked up from fashioning spitballs on his desktop.

—What about Frayser's Farm! We won that un, and
Malvern Hill, too! cried Wilma Harp.

Mrs. Spender wore a defeated smile on her pretty face. It
always worked; whenever she couldn't get anyone interested
in the lesson, all she had to do was ask a question about
the War between the States and everyone woke up. Maybe
it was just our corner of southern Virginia, but I imagined
almost every child in the South had learned his Civil War
history at his granddaddy's and daddy's knees. It wasn't some-

thing we needed to learn from schoolbooks; it was part of
what we'd been told since we were little. Most children I
knew could recite the list of the battles the South had won
before they could spell their own names.

Mrs. Spender stood up to ring the handbell she kept on
her scarred pine desk. Everyone flew from their seats and
out the door. I tried to hurry, but it was slow going. My entire leg ached, as it usually did by the end of the day. I said
goodbye to Mrs. Spender, but she had laid her head down
on her arms. I guessed even teachers got plumb worn out
sometimes.

I stepped cautiously to the door and held on to the rough
frame to get my bearings before I negotiated the stoop. These
crazy wooden steps tilted just as you put your weight on
them, always in a different direction from what you expected.
I'd just gotten to the bottom step when Larry Powell sauntered up.

—You a-goin to race? he said, his sulky face twisted into
a smile.

—Not today, I muttered and tried to get by him. He
grabbed me around the waist. Come outside, I thought to
Mrs. Spender. Come out to check on me. If Sibby was here,
nobody would've dared pick on me. But she was home helping Mother with the canning today.

—Hey, y'all, Cora don't want to race us, he cried. Several
other lurkers came up beside him.

—Why not? Ruby Belks called out. —She a chicken?

—Y'all know I can't race, I said, looking them in the eyes.
Maybe if I just gave them what they wanted, they'd leave me
alone. —Y'all better go on or you'll miss the race yourselves.

—Don't worry about us. Come on now, Larry said, pulling
on my arm. —I bet you can race on them old clodhoppers
if you really want to.

Stumbling, I was pulled along down the dirt road that ran behind the schoolhouse, my right leg dragging behind me. The books dropped from my arms.

—Come on, clodhopper. If you can't race, you can at least keep score.

They pulled me along, intent on humiliating me. I allowed myself to be dragged; why try to fight? There were too many against me, and I'd never get away. My face burning, I looked down at my dusty skirt. Mother would have a hissy fit when she saw that; I'd have to try to wash off in the creek before I got home. Clothes aren't made on trees, she'd say, and yank them off of me. I knew it was mainly to protect me from Father, but sometimes I wished she'd take our side. Just once.

The runners were giggling and pointing.

—Look what the cat drug in.

—She aint on my team. You can have her, Teak.

—She aint on my team. Larry done brung her, he can have her.

—Okay, let's get goin, Larry said, pulling a gun from his overalls pocket. —I'm goin to fire this here pistol and the first group's gonna run. Then the second one, and the winners will race each other. You keep note of who comes in first and second in both races, he concluded, giving me a shove.

The entire group, about fifteen in all, was staring at me. I wished I could crawl into a hole and hide.

—Can't any of you write? I said. —I don't have any interest in your race. I have to get home and do my chores.

—You're goin nowhere, Ruby said.

She thrust a piece of torn notebook paper and a pencil into my hands. Larry drew a line in the dust, and seven runners stood behind it. They looked ridiculous posturing and stretching their calves. I wished they'd all fall into a molehill and break their legs. That would teach them. Larry aimed the gun over our heads and fired. I covered my ears, but they still ached with the explosion. The first group tore off in the dirt. Ruby gave me a push.

—You writin? I want to see those names nice and clear by the end of the race.

I arranged the paper against my knee and pretended to write down their names, but instead of Larry's name I wrote *Ignorant,* and instead of Teak I wrote *Imbecile,* and so forth. Ruby kept nudging my arm just as I was starting to write, making the onlookers laugh. Wait til they saw what I'd written; then I'd have the last laugh.

—Thought I heard a gun go off, a voice said behind me.

Everyone straightened up. Clyde, Joab Williams's hired man, strode toward us from the edge of the woods. Joab owned the farmland the school was on. Whispers said he had a teenage daughter so badly retarded she never left the house, and that was why Joab was so interested in educating the rest of us that he donated the corner lot for the school. Who knew if that was true or not? Now here was Clyde, a wary smile creasing his worn brown face.

—We're just having a footrace, whined Nellie Martin, tugging on her rust-colored pigtail. —What's it to you?

—Not much. Clyde spat in the dirt. Being a Negro, he couldn't really make them do anything, but he could go get Joab or Mrs. Spender. He glanced at me.

—Don't your daddy 'spect you home right after school to milk them cows?

—He generally does, I said, relief washing through me.

—Then you'd best be gettin home. I know when your daddy 'spects something, he 'spects it. That your brother's gun, Larry?

—Yeah, what of it?

—Be careful with it. You don't want to go shootin your toes off. Or anyone else's.

He waved and walked off in the direction he'd come from.

—Uppity nigger, said Teak.

—I'm gonna get him and good, said Larry. —Once't my brother hears about this. Nigger has no right steppin into my bidnis.

—Damn straight, said Ruby. —He'd better watch hisself if he knows what's good for him.

I turned away from their ugly words and went back toward the schoolhouse to pick up my books where they'd fallen. I'd always been sensitive to the way colored people were treated, maybe because of my own infirmity. It seemed awfully unfair to me that they were picked on just because they were born with dark skin. They couldn't help it; it was the way the Lord made them, and I didn't see a single solitary reason why they should be kept back because of it. But it seemed that not many people in Gower County thought like I did.

Thanking the heavenly stars that Clyde had come by, I hitched along the woods path as quickly as I could. Maybe I could avoid a beating if I got back and did my chores before Father got in.

Normally I'd be walking home from school with Sibby; my little brother WillieEd's group let out earlier. Sibby and I always had a lot of fun. We'd try to imitate the catbirds' calls, or those of the crows that always lit in Man Murfree's cornfield. We'd laugh and talk about the kids at school, at how Mrs. Spender loved to draw a circle of chalk and have Beckley Hale stand with his nose in it for an hour for misbehaving. Sibby would joke about Mrs. Spender's love life: Do you think she has a secret beau? Widows often do, you know. They're used to having a husband warm up the sheets at night. Sibby would carry on like that the whole way home.

But now, alone without her to lighten my thoughts, my mood grew bleak, and I cursed my clubfoot. Why did I have to be born with this? I knew it was a sin, but I wished it could have happened to Ruby Belks, who was spiteful as the day was long. Sibby used to tell me that Father beat Mother up once while she was carrying me, and that caused the problem with my foot. It was possible; he was capable of anything when he was drinking.

When I got to the creek, I splashed my dirty skirt with a little water to try to clean it off, but soon I gave up and walked the rest of the way home, unhitching the heavy gatepost to let myself into the pasture that was the entry to the farmland we rented from Man Murfree. As always, I had trouble hooking the wire loop back over the top of the post without Sibby to help me maneuver it. Once I'd left it unhooked and several of our cows had gotten out, and I'd really caught it then.

I struggled with the wire for a while, then left it cantilevered halfway on, halfway off the post, hoping none of our cows would see that it was loose and push it open. Cows were smarter than most people thought; we'd almost lost two of them last week when they figured out how to push the stable door open and got foundered on corn that WillieEd had piled up behind the stalls.

Back a few years ago, when we were in World War II, we had to ration the corn we gave to the animals. Sugar was hard to afford, and we had to use syrup to sweeten things. Those who owned cars and tractors would patch and repatch their tires because rubber was scarce. Most of the farmers in our area had stayed at home; apparently the government felt their job was to keep making food for the rest of the country and the war effort, rather than join in the fighting. I guess they figured the soldiers needed to smoke as much as eat, because tobacco farmers weren't called up, either. But many of their sons ran off and joined up, some even lying about their ages and going in at sixteen or seventeen. Almost every family around had a son or a cousin or nephew who'd lost their lives in the war; Man Murfree had lost two of his boys himself.

Since the war had been over for three years, most people had stopped talking about it. Sometimes it was hard to believe there ever had been a war, until you looked at the gaps in the pews at church where once a family had filled the whole row.

Now there was plenty of corn around if you could grow it, and if you could keep your cows out of it. We were all awfully glad our cows hadn't died when they got foundered, as they were our only steady source of cash income. And milking them was one chore Sibby and I didn't mind too much. It was right peaceful, the cows grinding the hard-kerneled corn into sweet-smelling cud between their huge teeth while we sat on little wooden stools, leaned our cheeks into their sides, and tugged away at their teats.

The wild cats that lived in the barn would line up near Sibby because she'd always stop to squirt some milk into their mouths. They'd sit there and lick their faces, then wipe them with their paws, swiping off every drop. If you tried to pet one of those wild cats they'd scratch the devil out of you, but they certainly appeared tame when they were waiting to be squirted. Once in a while a cow would kick at a horsefly, and we'd have to grab the bucket to make sure it didn't get knocked over. But most of the time the milking was uneventful, a nice easy job to do at dusk when the harder chores of the day were done.

By now I had reached the end of the pasture, across the dirt road from our house. I grabbed hold of the barbed wire, grasping the top piece with one hand and the bottom with the other, and carefully climbed through the opening. You could rake yourself mighty good with barbed wire if you weren't careful; Sibby and I both had learned the hard way to go through the fence slowly.

I crossed our dirt road, my feet spewing little clouds of white dust, and went up the hill to the house. I could hear Mother's singing from the open kitchen window. It was a shame with a voice like hers she'd never joined the choir at church. She could sure hit some high notes.

Bringing in the sheaves, bringing in the sheaves,
We shall come rejoicing, bringing in the sheaves.

I took the two stone steps up to our porch and went through the screen door. I put my books facedown in a corner under a gunnysack and went into the kitchen. Mother and Sibby were there, just finishing up their canning for the day, in time for Mother to start dinner. Scarlet beetjuice was spread all over the kitchen table, in puddles on the counter near the sink, and on the stovetop. There must have been twenty jars of canned beets sitting on the counter. Some people, like Mrs. Whitmell, could afford a pressure cooker, but we just boiled the vegetables the old-timey way. Mother sold as much of her efforts as she could, and we ate up the rest.

—I didn't know that many people in Gower County liked beets, I said.

Sibby turned to laugh, up to her elbows in soapsuds at the sink.

—Just because you don't like beets, Cora Mae, don't mean anybody else doesn't, she said.

—What's that all over your dress? Mother asked, frowning at my skirt.

—I fell on the way home, I lied, not wanting to tell her or Sibby about Larry and the others. Sibby would just want to fight them tomorrow, and that would make it even worse.

—I was carrying a few books home for extra credit, I added, hoping this would sound convincing. —Reckon I just lost my balance.

—You look like two miles of bad road, Sibby commented.

—You go through clothes like I don't know what, Mother complained, tiredly wiping her face with the corner of her housedress.

I could remember Mother looking pretty at church when I was a little girl, and I'd heard people say Sibby was the spitting image of Mother when she was young. But now all her good looks were gone; the frown lines had long ago overtaken what smile lines she used to have. Her whole appearance was drab: lank brown hair, threaded with gray, pushed back in a messy bun; a wan face; a plain dark housedress covered in front by a dirty off-white apron. And she was thin, too thin, ever since she'd had Luke.

I had heard some women at church saying she shouldn't have had another baby at her age, but then they noticed me standing there listening and hushed up. I don't know why Mother wanted another baby with the three of us and all she has to contend with, with Father. Sibby said sometimes it's the man that wants the new baby, but I couldn't imagine Father wanting any such thing. He hadn't seemed the least bit happy about Luke's being around, ever since he was born. But maybe there was more to it than we both knew.

—I need this kitchen cleaned up so I can cook dinner. Can you help Sibby take these jars down to the basement, or is your leg hurting? Mother asked me in a nicer tone of voice.

—I can help her, I said.

—All right. I'm going to try to feed Luke before your father gets home.

She went into the back bedroom where Luke was sleeping. I walked over to where Sibby stood sloshing water and canning utensils around in the sink.

—Has he been home all afternoon? I asked.

—No, he hasn't showed up. Maybe the old devil has gotten hisself stewed and won't come home a'tall, Sibby replied, crimping her mouth into an ironic smile. —What happened to you at school?

—Nothing, I retorted, and began drying the dishes that Sibby had washed. —I fell, I added.

—You fell, my foot, said Sibby. —Did someone push you?

—No.

I realized that she wasn't going to let it go, and she'd probably hear about the race tomorrow at school, anyway.

—Larry and Teak and Ruby and some others were running a race. They made me be the scorekeeper for who came in first. That's all. Then Clyde showed up and made 'em all go home.

—Huh. They'd best be glad I wasn't there, Sibby said.

I felt like pointing out that if she'd been there, none of them would have dared to bother me, but what was the use. I nodded as if I was agreeing.

—It was nothing, just a bunch of crazy showoffs, I said. —You know how those boys are.

—Was Bill there today? Sibby asked.

Bill was her most recent crush. Sibby had had more boyfriends than Carter had liver pills; every time you turned around, there was a new one mooning over her at recess.

She was the prettiest girl in school—in the whole county, I'd
heard some say. You might think I'd have been jealous, but
how could I be jealous of my best friend and defender in
the whole world? Besides, if somebody had to be out there
breaking hearts, I'd rather it have been Sibby than old Mary
Jane Markley or somebody stuck-up like her. At least I could
take a kind of secondhand pride in all the boys who'd fallen
to her charms. And I could see why they'd like her, with her
snapping brown eyes that could look almost black when she
laughed; her dark rich hair and eyelashes. And her coloring
didn't come out of a paintbox, like some of the girls' in our
school did.

—No, he wasn't there, I answered.

—His daddy must have kept him out with the haying,
Sibby said. She sighed in happiness that she hadn't missed
a day of school with Bill in attendance.

—How was Mother feeling today? I asked.

—She did fine. I made her sit and rest for about an hour
when we were halfway done, and it perked her up right
good. Now if she didn't have to deal with Father tonight, it
could be a right nice evening, Sibby said exasperatedly.

We finished the dishes and put them away on the shelves.
Then she and I gathered several mason jars of canned beets
each in our arms and went through the screen door of our
back porch and over to the basement steps.

—I brought home *Forever Amber,* I said to Sibby as we
entered the dark basement.

She deposited her jars on a shelf already half full with
other cannings and took mine from my arms.

—What's that?

—Don't you remember hearing about it at Alicia
Farnsworth's quilting bee? It's supposed to be very romantic

and racy, too. Racier than *Gone with the Wind*. I can't believe Mrs. Spender brought it to school.

—Old Spender wouldn't know a racy book if it bit her, Sibby said as we reascended the steps.

—I don't know. If she owns this, she does, I replied. —I'm going to start on it tonight. I'll read you the good parts.

—Okay, Sibby said, but I could tell she wasn't that interested. I guessed if you had real live boys after you, you weren't as interested in the goings-on in books. And Sibby had never been one for reading much, anyway. I was always the bookworm of the family, and she was the flirt.

At times I wished just one boy from school would pay a little extra attention to me, but what with my foot and my being shy, that wasn't likely to happen. Sibby always encouraged me to speak up around boys, but I never seemed to find the opportunity or the words to say. Boys who talked to me at socials tended to be waiting for an opening to speak to Sibby. You might have thought I'd get some of her castoffs, but that never happened. I was plain but not ugly, so that wasn't the problem.

I pondered this as I followed Sibby into the kitchen for another load of beets. Mother was sitting at the kitchen table spooning some mashed potatoes into Luke's birdlike mouth. As I had done so often lately, I wondered if there would ever be a boy for me.

Chapter Three

I met Aaron when I was sixteen, going on seventeen. He came by our farm, looking for work. He came up to our front porch in his dirty overalls and asked Father if he had any need for an extra man on his farm. Father grunted.

—You think I can pay a body to work when I aint making enough to keep the mouths I got filled?

Aaron just glanced at me and smiled. He had a dark shock of hair and heavy eyebrows, and his nose was long with a little hook at the end of it. I thought he was kind of handsome, in a grown-man sort of way, not like the raw farm youths who usually came around. I was sitting on the porch shelling beans, and I figured he didn't notice my foot because I stuck it behind the bucket as he walked up.

—All right, I'll be going on, he replied.

He turned away and headed back down the road, and I imagined I'd never see him again; just another man roaming the countryside. But the next week I was coming back from helping the Strotherses get their hay in (actually I just helped set out the meal, while the other women were in the field. Then I helped clean up after everyone ate. But they were kind enough to let me do it and earn half pay), and all of a sudden there he was walking on the road beside me. I thought to myself, Well, he has to've noticed my foot because he's seeing me walk.

—Mighty nice weather we're having this week, he said.

—I'm Aaron Melville. I don't believe I know your name.

His voice was smooth, educated-sounding. Not like most everyone else from around the county.

—Cora Slaughter, I said, looking down at the dusty road. Grasshoppers sprang out of the weeds and flew in all directions. Somebody said the thermometer at Job's store registered over a hundred, three days in a row the past week. Aaron slowed down to keep pace with me, hard for a person with two normal feet to do.

—I have a job haying with the Bookers, he said. —They seem like all right people.

—They're good folks, I replied. I kept thinking, If you've got a job, why are you talking to me? I couldn't get it out of my head that he still wanted to work for Father.

—What do you do for recreation around here?

I glanced up at him and flipped my braid back over my shoulder so I could see better. I kind of hunch my shoulders, so it's always falling forward.

—We don't recreate too much, I said. —Mainly we just work and go to church on Sundays. Occasionally there's a church social or picnic. Prayer meeting's Wednesday nights.

—No dances around? I hear Gower County has some famous barn dances.

—Some around here do. I rarely go to them, I said, flushing. Did he have a sight problem, or couldn't he see I was lame?

—Aah. Aaron fell silent. We paced along a few more steps.

—Well, he said, I'm going to peel off here. I'm just supposed to be taking a break. Those Bookers work you from sunup to sundown.

—Got to, if you're going to get the hay in before it's ruint, I said. He stopped, and for some reason I stopped too.

—Could I come by to see you Saturday night? he asked.

I looked into his brown eyes, and they almost seemed to glitter. They took my breath away. I'd never been looked at like that, with that kind of intent, as I read it.

—Father doesn't allow visitors, I gasped out.

—Maybe I'll just have to run into you out walking again, Aaron said.

He smiled and hiked down the road. I looked back at him once, his Red Camels covered in hay and dust. He puzzled me. Maybe there was something he wanted from me, but he already had a job. And surely he could tell I didn't have any money. I'd heard of snaky salesmen flattering girls and then taking their family heirlooms, but it should have been obvious from our run-down farmhouse that I had nothing for the taking. What on God's green earth could he want? I puzzled over it as I lay in bed that night, so much so that I couldn't concentrate enough to read more than four pages of *Forever Amber,* which lived up to its reputation.

The next time I ran into him was walking to Job's store for some cooking lard. We'd scraped the bucket in the pantry dry, and none of the shoats were big enough to kill yet. Father hated to buy anything at Job's—he claimed that Job would steal from a blind man—but sometimes he had to send us for something we had run out of. It just about killed him to have to pay for anything except corn squeezins. He'd buy that, whether or not we had food on the table.

I said hello to Job and asked him to give me two scoops. He slid the trowel through the creamy lard and slapped it onto the paper. When I was little I always wanted to taste the lard, since it looked like it would be sweet. Sibby got a good laugh out of it one day when she gave me a whole spoonful to lick. She said I pulled a face sour enough to turn milk.

Sibby always was one for a practical joke, but her jokes were done in fun, never mean-spirited like a lot of kids. One of her favorite tricks was to creep up on me or WillieEd when one of us was taking our weekly Saturday night bath in the tin tub, and pour a jug of cold water right down our backs. She loved to see the looks on our faces when the water hit; she'd double over with laughter at our expressions. WillieEd and I ganged up on her a few times to get her back. It became a real contest to see who could sneak into the room behind the back of the one bathing. It got so you were so busy turning around in the tub to see who was creeping up behind you that you couldn't get much of a bath. Then Sibby turned thirteen and wanted her privacy, and Mother made us stop. But for a while it made Saturday nights exciting.

I paid Job the nickel he asked for the lard and answered his question about my mother's health. She'd been feeling poorly all summer from fevers, and twice I'd snuck out to Job's to beg a powder to help ease her sleep. He gave me two on credit, which I paid back out of what Mrs. Whitmell gave me for helping out, and a third I still owed. But Job was nice about it and never made me feel like a beggar.

When Sibby and I were smaller, he used to call us inside out of the heat and give us a few pieces of hard candy. I always loved the dark store, its two rockers placed by the iron woodstove in the back, the cat curled up on the braided rug, the blended smells of licorice and chewing tobacco and hickory smoke that had soaked into the walls. It felt more like a home than a store to me. I guess that's what Job aimed at, because people from all around liked to come inside and stay for hours talking. Father never did; he didn't cotton to lollygagging, as he called it. Although he considered drinking himself senseless twice a week a worthwhile activity. But it seemed like everyone else in the county enjoyed spending time there.

In the winter, Job would let Sibby and me linger and look at his movie magazines. We'd sit in the rockers and stare at the pictures and imagine the lives of the stars. All the girls at school bought the magazines and passed them around; it was a big topic of conversation, who was getting married and who divorced and which stars were going to be in what movies. Clark Gable was a big favorite; he was Sibby's. I liked Gary Cooper and Humphrey Bogart, but I didn't admit to the latter or I'd be laughed at. Sibby knew, of course, and said she couldn't believe I'd take Humphrey over Clark. But I would, any day. Humphrey's dark brooding eyes captivated my soul.

Whenever we managed to save up a spare nickel apiece we'd catch a ride to Cheatham where the movie theater was and gawk at the big screen, lost in its world for a couple of hours. During the war we'd try to get there early to catch the newsreels, to see how our boys were doing. We always thought we might see someone we knew in a newsreel, but we never did. The soldiers were usually in the background and hard to see individually. Once Sally Bowden thought she saw her cousin Averett riding in a tank, but none of us had seen him. It had been odd at first not having news of the war, but by now we'd gotten used to just seeing previews of the upcoming features before the main attraction.

It was always a real comedown when the movie was over, walking out into the glare of the afternoon sun. Later, Sibby and I would pretend to be movie stars in the barn. She'd be Vivien Leigh and I'd take a turn at Clark, then she'd be Humphrey and I'd be me. I never could quite imagine myself as an actress, so I'd pretend I had somehow managed to get to Hollywood and was working as a secretary on a movie set and got noticed. Mother was always puzzled that we'd volunteer for such a hot, itchy job as pitching hay in the barn, and then she'd wonder what took us so long. She'd have been amazed at how we whiled away those hours, reenacting scenes from *Gone with the Wind* or fresh from our imaginations.

After I got my lard and answered Job's questions about my mother, I headed for the door. I did glance at *Movie News* on the way out. I was interested to see a photo of Joan Crawford on the cover, smiling ever so sweetly. Those movie stars surely led the life of Riley. Mary Jane Markley, who somehow snuck the magazines past her watchful father, said some of them had ten servants living right in their houses, mansions with a hundred rooms, and special dishes for their dogs to eat off of and special servants just to feed and brush the dogs. She probably made half of it up, but those stars did seem to live on easy street, I reflected. I went out the door and there was Aaron, almost seeming like he was waiting for me.

—Hello, stranger, he said.

I was still standing on the stoop, so for once I could look down into his face instead of always craning up at people. His dark eyebrows drew together in a way I thought very manly.

—Hello.

I couldn't think of anything else to say, and blushed. I'd always envied the girls whose words flowed out like honey.

If I was a man, I'd want to be with that kind of woman, someone who could talk the birds out of the trees.

—Buying a few sweets? A ribbon for your head for Sunday school? He seemed to be laughing at me, something I'm sensitive about. I stepped off the stoop carefully, shook my head, and went on by.

—Wait a minute, can't a feller have a conversation? Where are you going now?

—I've got to get back home. Father wants his dinner, and we were out of lard.

—Plumb out of lard. Imagine that.

Something in the way he said it seemed funny, and I laughed, and he laughed.

—Can I walk with you a ways? he asked.

I glanced around anxiously. If anyone said anything to Father, I'd be in trouble.

—No one's here to report on you, Aaron said. There was the slightest hint of a hard edge in his voice.

—I guess a ways. You don't know my father. Nothing's worth getting his ire up, I said. —Not even a walk down the road.

—I've known fathers like that. They aint all they're cracked up to be. Some of 'em's bark is worst than their bite.

—Not mine. I wish that was true. His bite is a six-foot-long belt with a metal clip that sings. You feel the echo in your skin for months.

—I see. Do you object to having such a strict household?

—It's all right, I said proudly, not willing to admit anything to a rank stranger. —Others have worse. We have food to eat and clothes on our backs. We aren't freezing to death in the winter. My mother and brothers and sister are there.

—I see.

Every time he said this, I felt he was laughing at me. Suddenly I was annoyed.

—What are you following me for? I asked. —What do you want from me?

—Me? Aaron pointed to his chest as if in surprise. —I want to be your friend.

—I have enough friends, I lied. In truth I didn't have any, not the kind of giggly-close girlfriends Sibby had, unless you counted Ann Hodges, and that was only because she was blind and had to sit out everything too. Over the years we'd run out of polite conversation and now sat silently by while the others had gunnysack races, danced, or did anything social.

—Well, maybe I want to be more than your friend, he whispered, now close to me.

I was shocked; a shiver went up and down my arms. He touched my shoulder lightly and left in the other direction. I thought about his comment all night long, turning it round and around in my head.

Then I didn't see him for two weeks, and I thought I'd go crazy. You'd think a girl would have better things to do than to moon over some stranger, but no one had ever taken much of an interest in me except a kindly one, and I was tired of that kind of interest, tired of watching the other girls get all the attention, even fat old Sally Hicks. Part of me was excited that a man might look at me that way, and part of me was afraid. What would Father say? I couldn't imagine it.

In the back of my mind, I kept thinking Aaron was playing with me. Maybe a group of boys from another county heard about the clubfooted farm girl and put him up to it. Maybe it was a mean dare. Such things had happened to me before. I'd learned never to trust anyone who seemed friendly unless they had gray in their heads. And even older people could have their barbs.

I'd just told myself for the hundredth time to stop thinking about him when he showed up at a barnraising for John Mellers. John's old barn had finally fallen in due to years of rain and sleet and being hammered by the walnuts off the old trees surrounding it. A huge nut burst through the roof one Saturday morning when John and his oldest son, Paul, were milking the cows, and knocked John plumb out. Paul had to run to the creek twice for buckets of cold water before he came to his senses. After that John swore he was going to reroof the barn, but of course he didn't, what with his hogs getting out of their pen and trampling his henhouse and eating his best layers, and then their littlest having croup all winter. So finally the whole thing caved in and John said just as well. He announced at church that they'd feed anyone who'd come to help raise a new barn that next Saturday.

I went just to get out of the house—I took every opportunity I could to do that—and to represent the family in case we ever needed help. It was a good thing to pitch in because you never knew when you might have a cow stuck in the creek or a barn cave in from snow or such. Father never did a man's work in the community, but one of us, Sibby or Mother or I, always tried to attend such events. I think people knew about Father and his drinking and forgave us that because they always pitched in and helped us in the times we really needed it.

—How are you, Cora? asked Mrs. Mellers as I stepped onto the porch. She was carrying a heavy covered dish out to the plank tables in the yard.

—Good, thank you. I brought some of Mother's cornbread.

—That's awfully nice, honey. You can bring it right out

here; we're getting ready to serve dinner. They've been at it since six this morning.

I followed Mrs. Mellers to the table, placed Mother's dish there, and went back inside with her to help carry more food. There was a huge bowl of delicious-smelling fried chicken on the kitchen counter, and an enormous platter of ham biscuits. My mouth started watering.

—Get you a few ham biscuits before these men tear into everything, Mrs. Mellers said, smiling. —Otherwise you'll be eating table scraps. I had me a plate a few minutes ago. Go on, she said when she noticed my hesitation. —In fact, sit a spell and have a plate. You'll be plenty busy when we start serving the boys.

She bustled through the door to the back screened porch and outside to the tables. Suddenly I was starving. I filled a plate to the brim with ham biscuits, baked beans, potato salad, and snap beans flavored with fatback. I poured myself a big glass of iced tea and sat down at the kitchen table. I looked around at the steaming dishes, sniffed the good smells, and dug in. Everything was delicious. I fantasized for a moment that Mrs. Mellers was my own mother, but that felt too disloyal to Sibby and Mother, so I stopped. Then, biting into a chicken leg, the fragrant juice from the meat running down my chin, I thought, no, but I could imagine being engaged to Paul, their oldest son.

Although I didn't know him well—he was a few years older, and had been away for two years after joining up—he'd always been nice to me. Once, when a group of us children were playing in a neighbor's barn, we decided to see who could jump off the highest hay bale. The bales were piled almost all the way to the roof—some sixteen feet—and it was a game we often played, since it was exhilarating to fall into the huge pile of loose hay on the barn's floor.

I was used to flinging myself off the bales, since it was one of the few rowdy games I could fully participate in without falling behind or getting hurt because of my foot. But for some reason, Paul wouldn't let me go; he was afraid I'd hurt myself, he said. I'd wondered ever since then if he didn't have a secret crush on Sibby. Maybe he'd wanted to impress her that day with his concern about my safety, since he knew that she was protective of me. At any rate, it was unusual enough behavior for the other kids to tease him all afternoon about it, saying he must be mooning over me.

Paul didn't even act bothered by this, and eventually the others stopped and we went outside to play kick the can (a game I had to sit out, but they let me call the fouls and decide who was being too rough). Ever since then, I'd had the nicest impression of Paul. Maybe he'd become interested in me this very afternoon, seeing how helpful I was to his mother, how much she liked me, and how sweet I could be. Or—a more likely scenario—maybe he'd get engaged to Sibby. Then I could come to live with Mrs. Mellers and help her out, as I'd be almost kin. That, I decided as I got up to get one more ham biscuit, would be the perfect ending.

It was with this in mind that I went out to serve food to the hungry men who were just coming into the yard from the pasture, where the skeleton of the barn was already visible. I can't say that Paul seemed to pay special attention to me when I served his plate, beyond inquiring politely about Mother and Sibby. But Mrs. Mellers, Alicia Farnsworth, Mabel Blackstone, and Evelyn Winters were very kind to me and urged me to rest after the first group was served.

—Sugar, why don't you sit awhile. It's hot out here, urged Mabel.

—Hot enough to fry an egg, said Evelyn. —Let's all sit for a minute.

We settled into the yard chairs that Mrs. Mellers and Alicia dragged up from near the back porch. I appreciated Alicia bringing me a chair, and also the fact that she didn't make a fuss about it and thus call attention to my leg.

—I told John that old thing was going to fall in on him and leave me a widow if he didn't get it fixed, Mrs. Mellers commented, fanning herself with a corner of her apron. —Crazy fool almost let it cave in on him. If something had happened to Paul, I'da knocked John in the head myself. I'm not gonna have a child survive a war and then get kilt by a barn caving in.

All the women murmured their agreement, and I joined in. I'd noticed lately that the women at this kind of gathering had started including me and Sibby in their conversations, unlike a few years ago when we'd just been part of a passel of kids underfoot. It was nice, this new inclusion, and I was eager to learn from these women things I figured I couldn't from my mother, with her worries and cares. At times they'd laugh over a ribald joke, or make a veiled allusion to something about their husbands that I couldn't quite make out.

Deep down, I knew I'd never belong to these groups other than as a spectator, as I doubted I'd ever be married and able to participate in the conversations about childraising, husbands tramping in mud from the field after the kitchen floor was just mopped, and such. Even so, it was a thrill to be included in my youthful state. If I went on to be a spinster, at least they looked kindly on me and probably would let me continue to sit in without really contributing.

Maybe I'd wind up sewing and ironing like old Edwina, I continued my reverie, the community spinster who lived in a one-room cabin on Man Murfree's property. He let her live there, and she helped him with his laundry and cook-

ing since he was a widower. Edwina also went to other farmers' houses whenever a baby was born, there was a death,
or some crisis occurred, to help with the washing and cooking and cleaning. She wasn't usually paid money, but people gave her food and old clothes and occasionally a pig or
a chicken. Some rumored that she had a hundred dollars
hid away in a sack, but most of us doubted that.

Her grandfather had been in the War between the States,
and once Sibby and I were talking to her about it after Silas
Crowell's son got himself killed in France after lying about
his age and running off to join up at sixteen. A lot of the
local farmboys had volunteered for World War II, and it
seemed like every other month someone got the dreaded
telegram. Edwina and a group of us girls and women would
go over to the house of the family whose son had been killed
and do anything that needed doing. We saw a lot of Edwina
in those years; it seemed she was always the first to hear
and the first to arrive. This time, when Sibby and I went to
the Crowells' to see how we could help, Edwina was already
there, as usual.

She was pressing clothes with an old hand iron, and Sibby
and I started in folding. We talked about the war for a while
in hushed tones, and what had happened to Cal Crowell.
Then, having read up on Civil War history, I asked Edwina
what her grandfather had said about that war. Edwina looked
at me from around the edges of the bonnet she always wore
and spoke in her trembly, old voice.

—It was a turrible time, she said. —Turrible.

—What did he tell you about it? I asked, eager for more
details.

Edwina shook her head and went back to her ironing.
Every few minutes she'd look up at me and intone,

—Turrible,

without adding another word. Finally Sibby had to leave the room, she was laughing so hard. From then on, every time Sibby or I asked the other how something went, the answer to the question was, —Turrible.

—Someone's head is off in the clouds, Alicia commented, leaning over to ruffle my apron. I smiled, embarrassed. Alicia was a notable gossip, and I wouldn't want her inferring anything personal from my dreaminess.

—I was just wishing days like this could last all year long, I said. —Eating like this, and the company.

I smiled and the women smiled back, nodding in agreement. It was such a nice change from the usual routine farm work.

—Your sister couldn't come, Mrs. Mellers said, not a question.

—No, she had to help Mother today. She hasn't been very well since the baby.

—And I feel bad I haven't been over to check on her in a long time, Mrs. Mellers replied. —I promise I'll get by as soon as I get my squash in.

Evelyn and Mabel nodded.

—Child, I haven't seen the light of day since my twins came along, Mabel said.

Mabel, mother of six, had had twins the last go-round, making eight children all under the age of twelve. The other women nodded sympathetically, and I nodded too.

—How long was your labor with the boys? asked Alicia, although all of us already knew. We'd heard the story before, but we all wanted to hear it again.

Mabel sighed, and her big stomach under the apron repeated the movement as an undulating echo. She settled herself back into her chair.

—Forty-six hours, she breathed with a grimace. The doc-

tor was away tendin to the people that got burnt up in Say-
erstown, that boardinghouse fire. He didn't get there til after
the boys came.

—How'd it start? Evelyn prompted. —First two times I
went into labor, I was out picking corn. Got to be where
Tom'd tell me, Woman, go get us some corn, you're long
overdue for that baby.

I laughed along with the others. I knew Mabel's story almost by heart, but every time I heard it my stomach seized
up in anticipation and fear. It was like those times at the
movies where you knew the villain was going to kill an innocent victim and you were afraid to watch, yet you couldn't
wait to see it happen.

—Mine came all different times, different ways. I told you
all about my water breakin at the mill, Mabel said. —Mr.
Sawyer's poor little Wesley, just eleven, saw all the water
gushin out of me and turned and ran. He told his dad, Mrs.
Blackstone's done carried in a big cistern under her skirt and
it's done spilt!

Mrs. Mellers held her side as she laughed, and Alicia hid
her mouth behind her hand. I smiled, wanting her to get on
to the interesting part.

—But with the twins, I just had me some faint little tweaks
and pains at first, like the devil pokin me with his pitch-
fork, but from inside, Mabel continued. —That went on for
about four hours, then I had the sharpest, awfullest pain I'd
ever felt with any of 'em. Liked to've knocked me into Sunday.

—Uhmm-umph. Evelyn drew out her grunt sagely.

—I told James to run and fetch Sam from the field. I figured I'd go quick, like the last time. By the time Sam got to
the house, I was pacin the kitchen, prayin. In between

prayers, a few choice words would slip in. Lord forgive me, but I was gettin it in my back.

—That back labor's the worst, Alicia chimed in. —I had that with my second.

—Mary and Otis ran and told Sam before he could even get in the door. Mama's cussin! Mama's cussin! Sam figured he'd find me on the floor, but there I was, just walkin round and around that kitchen. He'd sent James on to Zola's to fetch her. Zola Hardaway's my second cousin, Mabel added. —Zola delivered two of her sister's babies, and I always had her with mine. Seems like we never got a doctor in the house til after I'd spit the baby out.

Evelyn hooted. —Nina Herrick says it's bad luck if the doctor gets there in time. The one time he did come before she had the baby, it had colic for six months.

—I never once't had a doctor present, added Mrs. Mellers. —Not with Paul, nor Corinne nor Bobby. I wouldn't know what it was like to have one.

—We had Dr. Withers for all of ours, Alicia said, somewhat prissily. —I can't say as I thought he did much good though.

Mabel snorted. —There's no doctor in this world that could've helped me none. By the time I passed twenty-eight hours, I just knew. I'd spent all night long thinkin the baby had to be almost here. I'd thrash around on the bed, then get up and pace. Thrash and pace, thrash and pace, all the livelong night. Every once in a while I had to let out another choice word. That made Sam laugh, since I never cuss, but I told him if he thought it was so funny he wouldn't be gettin near me for a year after this. He got right solemn-looking then, and said he'd go fetch me some iced tea.

The women laughed knowingly. I blushed, wondering at their familiarity with all these bodily functions, with what men did in the dark. Sibby and I had discussed this many times at night in the room we shared. She knew, she said, where *it* went, and you were supposed to get used to it and even like it after a while. It made both of us feel a little queasy to think about such things, but yet it was fascinating. How on earth could you get to like *that*?

I couldn't imagine what men and women said to each other while this was going on. Sibby said they probably kissed, but I couldn't imagine something so romantic accompanying such an ignoble act.

Of course, Sibby, who had actually been kissed several times, said kissing wasn't all that romantic. She'd supplied me with the details every time it had happened to her: Travis Williams's buck teeth had cut her upper lip; Wade Biggers had tried to jam his tongue down her throat, and almost strangled her; Jimmy Peates had dry lips and pursed them just like old Miss Simms, our Sunday school teacher, when she used to kiss us on the cheek every summer after we finished Bible school. In fact, Sibby had said she'd rather have a kiss from Miss Simms than from Jimmy Peates because at least Miss Simms smelled nice, like old lady powder, while Jimmy stank like he hadn't bathed in a month of Sundays.

—The next day, Mabel continued, —I was bleedin like a stuck pig, but still no baby. Just the pains, stronger and stronger. They'd slack off for a time, then come back even harder. But I never got the urge to push. I had started to be afraid I was never going to get the baby out, that I was going to die. Dear God, just don't let me die still pregnant, I prayed. I just want to get this out of me and then go on. I admit, that wasn't a very Christian thing to think, she apologized, —but that was all that come to me. I was way past thinkin about the baby and namin it or any other pleasure on earth.

—That's all right, Mabel, Evelyn added. —God is a man,

He never had to go through labor. If He had, He never would've made women the way He did.

—Oh, Evelyn, Alicia said, wide-eyed, but the rest of the women giggled.

—Go on, Mabel, said Mrs. Mellers. —The men'll be here in a few minutes; I can see them lowering that last beam.

—Well, the sun set and still I was painin with no end in sight. Zola and her three and one of her sisters had been camped out in my house all day long. With my six and her three children runnin through the house, it was startin to get on my nerves. I'd stay upstairs as long as I could because I didn't want mine to see me in that condition, but I had to come down some just to get some air. This was in August, she added, and we groaned collectively, imagining the heat upstairs under the tin eaves of her roof.

—Sam had gone on back to the south forty; he had to get the last of the tobacco picked or we wouldn't have anything to feed the ones we already had. I thought, If this sun sets on me still in labor, I'm just gonna keel over right here and die.

—I remember that feeling, and this was after twelve hours of labor, not two days'orth, commented Evelyn.

—Well, to make a long story short, I finally fell asleep Sunday mornin at around two o'clock. I hadn't slept since Thursday night, because the pains started that next day. I had Sam bring all the children up to say goodbye to me. I really thought, This is it. I'm goin to meet my Maker. And I have to tell you, I wasn't sorry. I would've shaken the hand of Old Spite if he would've made that pain go away. Sam was cryin, the older kids were cryin because they knew why they were comin upstairs to see me. The babies started cryin because the older uns were. It was awful. Poor Zola was cryin, and then hers started in. I thought, At least I'll be missed. At least I'm not goin out of here with nobody that loves me, like some do.

Who would cry if I died? I asked myself. Sibby, WillieEd, and Mother. That was about it. Maybe a few people at church. It was a sobering thought.

—Then I fell asleep. When I woke, I was already pushin. The pushin woke me up! I hollered for Zola, and she and Sam came runnin upstairs. She grabbed one leg and shouted for Sam to grab the other. First out come Zeke, then out come Zachariah. I figured if I named 'em both with Zs, the last letter of the alphabet, then I wouldn't have any more. That sounds like crazy logic, but I was desperate. Zola got 'em cleaned up nice and put one on each breast. And did those boys suck! They were hungry after fightin one another all that time to see who got to come out first. I just rested. I was glad to be alive. And don't you know, 'long about noon, Doc Pickens showed up, lookin pleased as punch with hisself. Didn't so much as blink when Sam told him I'd had forty-six hours of labor and twin boys. He patted my head like you would a cow, and said, You done good, Mabel. I wanted to take the iron pot that Zola had used to boil water and bean him in the head.

Mabel laughed, the other women laughed, and then we all sighed. The second group of men were coming up the hill to be fed.

—Men just don't know their knees from their elbows, Evelyn snorted.

—Well, Mabel, how long was it before Sam got near you again? Did you make him wait a year? Mrs. Mellers asked, winking at Evelyn.

Mabel chortled. —Don't you know that man wanted to resume relations after a month? I fought with him about it for eight weeks, then I gave in. But I don't know what I'd do if I got in the family way again, she said with a worried look. —I pray every night that it won't happen. With eight mouths to feed plus the two of us, we've got our hands full. I never want to go through what I did with the twins.

—You know what they say, always an easy labor after a hard one, Alicia pitched in.

As the men came over to the table, exclaiming over the bountiful food, who should approach but Aaron. I was surprised he'd show up at the barnraising, since it was made up of people in our farming community who'd known each other for years. Aaron was all grinning and filthy, with wood chips and sawdust clinging to his hair and clothes, but he looked fine to me. Instinctively I moved to the far end of the table, away from the other women. I didn't want Alicia or any of them to notice me talking to Aaron. I figured that was my business.

—Well if you aint a sight for sore eyes, he said right out loud. I looked to see if someone was standing behind me, and he laughed.

—I'm talking to you, Cora Slaughter, he said. His teeth seemed enormous in his wide mouth. They almost scared me, they were so big and white.

—Hello, Aaron. It was the first time I'd said his name out loud, though I'd practiced in silence night after night.

—Where's Father? he asked, and I didn't like his disrespect, although I had to smile a little.

—He couldn't come. Would you like some of these beans?

—Heap me up a plate, and two–three biscuits, too. Work like this gives me a real appetite.

He said it slowly, smiling at me like he wanted to eat me alive. I glanced around nervously, but no one seemed to notice our conversation.

—It's going to be a nice big barn. John's needed a new one for some time, I commented.

—I don't care about the barn. Haying's going to be done soon, and I need some new work. Figured someone might notice a good worker like me in this crowd and hire me on. I'm saving up to start my own clerical situation in Unionville next spring. I was clerking at a store there til February, when they had to close because business was bad. I'm not cut out for this farmhand stuff, but a man's gotta do what a man's gotta do. I'm much more satisfied behind a desk.

Now that he said it, I could picture him sitting at a desk with paper and pencils, all ready to do his figures. Now I knew why he didn't seem to fit in with the other farmboys. He seemed more refined than the others, although with the dust and dirt all over his overalls, you had to look hard to tell. But at that time I was looking hard, and I thought I could see it.

—I imagine clerking is hard work too, all those numbers. Adding up those columns in school makes me dizzy, I said.

Actually, this wasn't true; I was quite good at math. I was just repeating a line I'd heard Betsy McGuire use when she flirted with the boys after choir practice. Mrs. Spender had even wanted to send me to college based on my math and reading test scores, but of course we didn't have the money. Father laughed out loud when I told him.

—What's a cripple like you going to do at college? he had said.

Sometimes I was surprised that Father was still able to figure out ways to hurt my feelings.

Aaron laughed. —I don't imagine you'll have to stare at a lot of numbers, he said. —That's a menfolks thing. I don't know why they bother teaching suchlike to girls anyway. You womenfolk need to know how to mend a sock, put food on the table, and have babies. That's what comes in handy for the women.

I looked at him. He was smiling at me again, with a certain meaning in his smile. Every time he spoke to me, he seemed to be implying things I couldn't believe he'd mean. Yet when I'd see him again, it would start up all over again. I shook my head and handed him a fork.

—Eat your fill of beans, there's plenty here, I said.

—I will, and I'll be back for more, he replied, and headed off to sit with the men under some shady oaks.

After another hour I had to sit down to rest my leg. I ate a couple more ham biscuits, and suddenly Aaron squatted beside me. I could smell the tinge of his sweat, he was that close.

—That was good eating. What dish did you bring? he asked.

I hesitated to tell him I couldn't cook worth a durn.

—I was going to make biscuits, but I didn't have time, I lied. —So I just brought some of Mother's cornbread, and came to help serve the food and clean up.

—I'd love to try some of your homemade biscuits. I can tell by those hands they'd be soft and sweet.

I looked at my hands. They looked ordinary to me; in fact they were rough and scratched from chopping firewood for the cookstove. I never seemed to do it without getting at least one splinter that was hard to dig out. But his pretty words made my heart shake.

—I do fine with any kind of bread, I said, wondering where these fictions were coming from.

—Ever make spoonbread? My mama used to fix that every once in a while, when she got in the mood. We'd have creamed potatoes, chicken with brown gravy, and some kind of fancy green beans she dished up. I miss all that. Aaron sighed.

—Where are you from?

—Potters Creek, he said. —My daddy had a big farm there until he died, then we had it hard. My mama had to sell the farm lot by lot. Finally we lost all but the patch of land the house was on, and I had to go to work at the feed store. When they found out I was good with figures, well, they promoted me right away. I bought me a wool suit and moved to Unionville three months later, got me a job in the post office. Then I moved on to clerking and did that for a few years.

All this sounded pretty good to my young ears. And the story about losing the land gained my immediate sympathy. It wasn't until later that I learned none of it was true.

—I'm sorry to hear about your mama's farm, I said. —Where is she now?

—Living with relatives, Aaron said.

That seemed to be all he wanted to volunteer.

—Were you in the war?

—No, I managed to avoid that. The post office needed workers to help with the home effort. Some of that mail was highly classified, let me tell you. Even in Virginia, you'd be surprised at how many spies were around. You could nary trust your own brother or sister. Aaron frowned, his eyebrows drawn together.

—Do you have any brothers or sisters? I asked, anxious to learn more personal information about him.

Aaron laughed. —Five, but none of them's any 'count. Left mama as soon as they could walk off the place. I'm the only one who still helps her out when I can, and lately it hasn't been what I'd like to send her.

What a nice man, I thought, to take care of his poor mama.

—Guess I'd better get back to work, Aaron said. He stood up and brushed off his Red Camels. —Some of the fellers asked me to go to Jebson's still after we're done for the day, but I don't have time for that kind of mess. When am I going to see you again?

I blushed and looked down at the cracked toes of my shoes. So he didn't drink, either. My mind worked over the possibilities.

—This Sunday after church I'll be walking home alone. I stay to help wash the Communion glasses every fourth Sunday. I'd have some time then.

Aaron reached down and pulled me up by one hand so I wouldn't have to struggle to stand.

—I'll be waiting for you a little piece up the road from the church, he said.

Chapter Four

All the rest of the week I had my mind set on seeing Aaron, and I was clumsier than usual. On Friday I dropped a whole load of wood on the steps and got cussed out and kicked in the behind as I was picking it up. Father threatened to get his belt on Saturday when I stood up too quickly in the kitchen and knocked over the butter churn. My arms were aching from the endless churning, and my foot loses sensation at times. I just couldn't catch the churn before the still-liquid butter ran out onto the floor. Luckily Sibby distracted him with a note from a man who wanted him to come for a taste of his grain liquor that night, and he left without remembering to whip me.

After Sibby and I cleaned up, the empty Saturday night stretched out ahead of us endlessly. Father was mercifully out for his taste; Mother sat in her corner and read the Bible by the light of a flickering kerosene lantern while Luke slept in his cardboard box stuffed with an old rag blanket. Man Murfree was the only farmer around who had a Delco plant, and once in a while we kids would go over there in the evening just to gawk at his electric lights and running water. He was always real nice about it, inviting us inside and showing us how the light switches worked. He always told us to bring Mother over sometime to see his electricity, but she would never come.

On slow nights like this I longed for something other than a kerosene lamp to read by. After a time the type would start to break up and crawl across the page before my tired eyes, for all the world like hatching bluebottles. But the way Father's farming was going, and with him drinking up what little money he did bring in, it would be a June sweetening before any of us saw anything more electric than a lightning bolt.

For a time the only sound in the room was the pinging of the tin roof as it cooled from the blistering late-afternoon sun. WillieEd picked at his toenails with a whittling knife, a shock of dark brown hair falling into his eyes. I put down my book—Sir Walter Scott's *Ivanhoe*—and helped Sibby darn some of Father's socks. Mother got up out of her chair and put the Bible back in its place on the table.

—That's enough work for today, girls, she said. —The light's not strong enough to half see. Why don't you get out your dolls and play?

Sibby and I ran to the corner where we kept our old corn-cob dolls and brought them over to the light. Much to our surprise, Mother actually sat on the floor with us and helped us repair their smudged faces with burnt wood from the stove, drawing new eyebrows and eyes with a charred twig. She even made the dolls talk to each other in high, silly voices, which left Sibby, WillieEd, and I speechless with laughter.

At times like this, when Father was out of the house and Mother seemed to take hold of herself, we could be positively happy. Everything was so peaceful with Father gone. But then he'd return, and Mother would shrink back into her former self. She seemed more like a shadow than a real person around him. I guess she was so afraid of saying the wrong thing and setting him off that she just figured she'd be quiet most of the time. But those little glimpses of Mother on evenings when he was away showed me that there was more to her than we probably realized.

Luke woke up, and Mother went to rinse out some of his things while Sibby rocked him and WillieEd shook a little wooden rattle he'd carved for him. Luke generally didn't cry much, which was a good thing given Father's loathing for noise (unless he himself was making it). Luke had been a sickly infant, and Mother still watched over him with a hollow-eyed stare. But he looked to me as if he was quite healthy now with a good appetite for bread sopped in milk and anything else Mother could sneak him from the table. Once he got his hands on a piece of pork that fell from Father's plate and sucked on it happily for over an hour.

—Aint good to encourage a taste for meat in the child, Father grumped. —We aint goin to have a lot of that around if this year's anything like the last.

Mother just grimaced and kept spooning up her mash.

I spent the first part of that night tossing and turning in bed, hearing Father let himself in very late and bumble around in the kitchen. A jar of something crashed to the floor (which Sibby or I would have to clean up in the morning, depending on who arose first) before he finally stumbled up the steps and into their bedroom across from ours. I burrowed under the quilt, trying not to hear him start in on Mother, but I was never able to block out the sound entirely.

—Get up, you ugly rib of Adam! Get out of that bed! Come see to your man, you lazy dadburn lie-abed!

I heard something thump, and then the sound of her being dragged across the floor. Sibby sat up in bed, listening.

—hurt your foot? Let go my hair and let me see what you've done to yourself. You're tired, get into bed and I'll bring you some coffee, came Mother's attempt at mollifying him.

—I said, get up woman! You're pure-tee lazy, no two ways about it!

Something pounded against the wall. Sibby leaped out of bed.

—Sonofabitch, she said. —I'm going in there to see about Mother.

Now I knew I had to go, too. I wanted to burrow farther under my quilt and not move, but I knew I had to help Sibby. She pushed her way into their room, and I trailed reluctantly behind.

—Now see what you made me do!

Father was screaming, hopping around on one foot. Whatever he'd broken downstairs must have been glass, because a piece of it was embedded in his heel. It was a wonder he'd made it up the steps with such a shard in his foot, but he must have been so drunk he couldn't feel much. Blood spurted everywhere as he hopped about, but he still had hold of Mother by a hank of her hair. A great ugly bruise was spreading across her cheek, and her left eye was beginning to swell shut.

—Father! Sit down and let me get that glass out of your foot, shouted Sibby.

She pushed him back on the bed as I teased Mother's hair out of his hand. When he was drunk he was much more pliable than sober, but sometimes he'd remember our interference and we'd all catch it worse the next day. He shouted blue blazes as Sibby pulled the shard from his heel and bathed and swathed his foot with a clean rag. Mother sat limply on the bed, staring vacantly at the floor as I dipped the hem of her nightgown in cold water and held it to her face. At times I felt like we were the parents, and Mother and Father the children in this household.

I went out to get WillieEd, whom I found hesitating in the hallway, his eyes enormous. I couldn't blame him for not wanting to confront Father in this state.

—What happened? he whispered. —Is Mama all right?

—It's all right, he's cut his foot, I said. —Come help us get him situated.

WillieEd followed me in and grabbed hold of one of Father's legs, while I maneuvered the other and Sibby got him under the arms. Before Father's head even touched the pillow, he was snoring. Sibby offered Mother her bed, saying she could bunk in with me, but Mother declined and gently laid herself down next to Father. Hair straggling over her shoulders, stick-thin in her faded gown, she looked like a girl wizened before her time. I doubted if she'd sleep a wink all night for fear he'd awaken.

Looking at her ruined beauty, the pretty young mother of my childhood a foggy memory, I swore I'd never be anything like her. Back then, I didn't understand how or why she stood it.

Sunday dawned bright and new. My right foot had fallen all the way asleep during the night, as it often did, and before I got out of bed I rubbed it hard with both hands, trying to get some feeling back into it. I usually avoided looking at my clubfoot, creased and striated as it was, like a glutted sluggish earthworm curled in upon itself. I had to walk on the outside of my foot, as the inside was twisted up. The part I set my foot down on was a hard rind, and often the skin flaked off and peeled. The inner arch never touched ground, and was soft and pink as a baby's skin. When I was a little girl I used to stroke this part with wonderment, amazed at its delicacy, but lately I avoided contact with my foot unless it was aching so badly I had to rub it. Nowadays I tried to wrest it into its sprung shoe as quickly as possible, so I wouldn't have to look at it.

I took care going down the stairs, as it was still very hard to navigate on my foot. I cleaned up the mess in the kitchen (Father had broken a jar of stewed tomatoes), swabbed off my face with cold water from the tin bucket, and tried to rebraid my hair before everyone else got downstairs. Father stayed abed as he usually did after his Saturday night sprees, and when Mother came down, she silently put out cold bread and a tiny slab of butter for our sustenance. She didn't like to use the stove in case the squeaking iron hinge woke him up, as Father awakened after a night of drink was an ugly sight to behold. Mother put on some face powder to cover up the bruise on her cheek, bundled up little Luke, and made Sibby change into her other dress before we headed out the door to walk the two miles to Calvary Baptist Church. Since WillieEd had turned twelve, he claimed he didn't have to go, and Mother had given up on trying to make him.

Reverend Davis's sermon seemed to go on forever. I never heard a longer message in my life. Finally it ended, but then three people accepted Jesus Christ as their Personal Lord and Savior, which as a Christian person I should have been happy about but on that particular day I could have cried. With Communion and a special offering for the Lottie Moon mission, followed by a sermonette about Christ on the Cross after all that, it was one o'clock before I was able to collect the glasses from the emptied-out pews and take them down-

stairs to the quiet, empty kitchen and begin to scrub them
out.

Normally I loved to drain the tiny cups of their last drops
of purple grape juice before I washed them, feeling the glow
of the sweet liquid on my tongue, but today I didn't bother.
I did gulp down the leftover squares of bread, even though
it was the Body of Christ. I was so hungry I figured God
would forgive me. I didn't want to faint out on the road and
have Aaron think I was sickly on top of lame.

It must have been after two before I finally finished drying the last little cup and set it back into the round tray.
Gripping the iron rail, I pulled myself up the basement steps
and let myself out the back door.

I went along as quickly as I could. It was another stulti-
fying day, the cicadas increasing their racket the higher the
sun climbed. I hoped we wouldn't have an Indian summer
because Mother suffered so much in the heat, particularly
since she'd had Luke. Thinking of her pregnant reminded
me of Aaron, and what he might have in mind. I couldn't
help imagining some romantic beginning, him coming along
on a horse-drawn wagon maybe, pulling me up beside him
and giving me a romantic, Clark Gable–like kiss. A dizzy
boiling began in the pit of my stomach every time I thought
of it, and I knew that this would send me accursed down
to hell if I died on the spot. But there was no sign of lightning in the sky, so it looked like I would survive the day
and would live to repent my wicked imaginings.

Aaron did meet me on the road past the church that day,
just as he said he would. While he didn't sweep me into any
horse-drawn wagon, he did take my arm to help me around
the deep ruts (which no one had ever done), making my
skin tingle at his firm touch. I was sweating and panting
from the effort of keeping up with him, because even though

he tried to slow down for me, he still was walking far too quickly. Finally he convinced me to rest in the shade of a tree, away from the boiling hot sun. We stopped at a large oak in the middle of a field of rye, and sat under it. I remember being there, the sweet-smelling rye blowing around us in the wind, feeling like I was the happiest person on earth.

—You get done with your business at the church? he asked me as I caught my breath.

—Yes, I washed all the Communion cups and threw away the leftovers (a half-truth, as I threw them away down my throat).

—They pay you for this?

I laughed. —No, I just do it. It's a way of being useful.

—Hmph. I don't believe I'd spend my time washing up alone in a church if I didn't get paid, he said. —When I was clerking in Unionville, now that was a job. Soon as I get a little cash saved up this winter, I'm going back and get another office job.

This was a variation of what he'd said earlier at the barn-raising, and it sure sounded good to me. I had had it with Father's meanness. I was also sick of the gore and muck of the farm, where I had to listen to pigs squealing as they got their throats cut, to see a chicken running around the yard spurting blood from its neck, its useless foolish head gasping in the dirt. Away from possums split end to end, lying in the fryer on the oven, their feet slopping over the edge of the pan. From fish eggs stomped on to hear them pop. From squirrels skint on the front porch and the dogs fighting over the tufty scraps.

I had an idea that I wanted to go someplace where I didn't have to see my meals murdered before I ate them; where the food was far, far away from the living animal it once was.

I'd read an article in one of Job's movie magazines that talked about vegetarianism, and I liked the idea a lot, even though I would have missed ham biscuits. I imagined that in a place like Unionville a woman might eat only vegetables and get along quite well. I said as much to Aaron.

—Well, I don't know about all that. I do like a fried pork chop occasionally. Although I certainly don't like seeing the hogs getting kilt. But I'd rather be around men who can talk about more than the weather and the crops, men who read newspapers. These local hicks (I blushed, because what was I if not local, and a hick?) don't care about anything they can't see past the ends of their noses. All they can talk about is how much they're gonna get for their tobacco come fall.

I sat forward eagerly. —That's why I've tried to read so much; I think it's good to be informed about things. I'd like to have an office job myself, someday, if I could make it to a city like Unionville. I've thought I might be able to earn a living typing correspondence, or some sort of work like that. I'd like to teach in a school, but I don't know if I'd be able. At least I've read everything I could get my hands on. The lending library comes to town about every two months and I check out the maximum number of books, and my sister, Sibby, lets me check out books on her card since she's not much for reading. And our teacher Mrs. Spender used to bring her own books to school until they made her stop. I got quite a lot of reading done that way, *Walden* and *Origin of Species* and *Pilgrim's Progress* and *The Inferno*.

I didn't mention *Forever Amber,* which was by far the most interesting book I'd ever gleaned from Mrs. Spender's lending table, because I figured it would be unladylike.

—Those are good books for beginners, Aaron replied in an airy, knowledgeable way. —I have a lot of books that I left behind in Unionville. You could read some of them if we ever swung back in that direction. Things much more advanced than *Pilgrim's Progress*. I could teach you a little about accounting too, enough so you could do the monthly bills and grocery figures. That would leave me time to do the office work and relax after I got home. When you've been dealing with figures all day, you don't want much to do with them in the evenings.

—I'd imagine not, I agreed, stunned by this sudden turn of conversation. I was thrilled to hear he was thinking of bringing me to Unionville at some point. It seemed that somehow the discussion had turned into what *we* would be doing in the near future. Did this mean Aaron was thinking seriously about our being together—for life? It seemed soon for that—we hardly knew each other—but I could garner no other meaning from his words. All I could understand from it was that he wanted to marry me.

—Would you stay in clerking? I asked.

—Probably for the time being, Aaron said, hitching up his galluses a bit. He frowned slightly. —My aim is to have my own business of some sort in two–three years, either a store or a loan office.

My mouth must have gaped open. I knew Job, of course, who owned his own store, but no one else in my immediate acquaintance had more ambition than to pay the rent on their land or to get the tobacco in before it was ruined by the sun or the rain or hail or insects. Security was only as good as the next crop, which meant every year a family might be on the verge of going hungry.

—Why, that sounds like a fine plan, I said, smiling at him.

Aaron reached over and put his hand on my arm. —I'd like for you to be a part of all that, Cora, he said.

It was silly, but I had an image of me in a pretty gingham dress with a white apron, sitting down to a kitchen

table surrounded by three little smiling children, Aaron at
the head of the table blessing the steaming hot food. It was
probably from one of those *Saturday Evening Post* covers that
I used to look at in Job's store, but at that moment it was
real to me.

—I'd like to be, I whispered.

I couldn't tell if he'd heard me or not. After a moment he
said he'd best get going, and I said I'd better, too. My heart
sang when Aaron said he'd try to meet me on the road leading up to our pasture one day this coming week. But although I waited for him beyond what was seemly every day
after school, he never came. It would be several weeks before I saw him again, and I almost went out of my mind
with longing.

Chapter Five

Finally school let out for the summer, and all of us from ages eighteen down to five went home to help with the backbreaking work of getting in the tobacco. The children whose families were lucky enough to own a few acres or more of land would help their parents; poorer children like us would hire out to labor in other people's fields.

Sibby and I usually hired ourselves out to Man Murfree, since Father rented our house and land from him, and since he was kind to us. Then once we'd picked for him, we'd go to other farmers in our area. We worked alongside the colored people, because that was who mainly did the picking and handing, at least in Gower County.

Out in the field, a boy would lead the farmer's mule, hitched to a tall wooden crate called a slide, between the rows of tobacco. Sibby and I would walk barefoot behind the slide along with the Negro pickers, constantly bending to pull the leaves as fast as we could. You always pick tobacco from the bottom up, because that is how the leaves turn yellow—bottom ones first. And you pick several times in a season.

Picking is hardest when you're stooping down in the heat.

It isn't unusual for someone to keel over right as they reach for a leaf. Once or twice I've felt dizzy myself, and had to sit at the edge of the field until I overcame my lightheadedness. Most pickers hate to stop because they are docked for pay for every five minutes they aren't working. Of course I was always the slowest picker due to my foot, and Sibby made a great effort to pace herself to stay back with me. She had a reputation as a good fast picker, but she wouldn't hire on unless the farmer hired me too.

Picking tobacco was suffocatingly hot work. To shield our faces from the sun, we wore broad straw hats that were tattered from years of use and stiff inside with dried sweat. The gum from the tobacco left your hands black and sticky. It was very hard to wash off; it stuck to your hands, even after many soapings. We used to go to the branch and try to scrape it off with sticks under the water, but usually that only made your palms raw; they'd still be tarred with gum.

After the slide was full of leaves, the boy leading the mule would fling himself onto its back and ride it to the packing barn, pulling the slide behind it. There, the women would hand and string the tobacco on sticks under big shady trees. Sibby and I would pick as long as we could stand it, then we'd come in from the field and hand.

Sibby would place a tobacco stick on top of the slide. We'd reach into the slide, grab three of the broad leaves, and hand them to the stringer, who'd wrap the end of a piece of twine around them, then wrap the twine around the tobacco stick. She'd move down the piece of twine a little, wrap three more leaves that one of us handed her, and loop that around the stick. You got into a nice rhythm with handing, and it was easy compared to picking—which was why it paid so much less. But it was good to be able to work where I didn't have to struggle to keep up.

The colored women were very friendly to us, and it was interesting to hear their conversations, which, like the white women I had listened to, focused mainly on problems with their men, their children, keeping a house clean, and money. Hattie and Marcelle were the oldest, in their mid-fifties probably, and they supervised the rest of us and made sure the stringing went quickly and smoothly. Hattie was heavy-set, her skin a pretty shade like the caramel creams I bought at Job's store. Marcelle was string-thin, and one of her eyes constantly watered so that a lot of people called her Cryin Marcelle, but I never did.

Hattie and Marcelle had the best singing voices, and we loved to hear them belt out *Just a Closer Walk with Jesus* or *When the Roll Is Called Up Yonder* in plangent tones. Sibby had a beautiful voice, and she'd join right in, but I never could carry much of a tune, so I'd just listen. The bare unadorned singing out there under the huge shade trees always sounded so much better than our prissier church choir with its piano accompaniment.

—That's some nice singin you done, Sibby, said Niecey, Marcelle's oldest daughter.

—You mean my caterwaulin? I sound like an old crow next to you all, Sibby laughed.

—Lawsy, did you hear 'bout Mary and Johnell? Hattie asked Marcelle.

—Naw, what they up to now? Marcelle responded.

—You know they had their sixth in February. Now Mary's set to have a seventh.

—Sholy you're kiddin.

—I'm tellin you straight.

—Where on earth they gonna put that new baby? They's livin on top of each other now.

—I don't know. I went by to see Mary, and she said she

wisht you could just sit on an egg and hatch a baby like a chick. And Johnell say, if they was eggs, I'da stepped on a few of mine befo' they hatched!

—Lawd, did you ever, Marcelle chortled, holding her sides, her eye watering down her cheek. She always cried more when she laughed.

—Whew, I got to have a drink, said Hattie, wiping her face with a rag she pulled from her dress sleeve. She unscrewed a mason jar of water that she kept cool under a tree and took a few deep draughts.

—Y'all hear what T.C. did over Memorial Day weekend? piped up Carol, Niecey's cousin.

—Naw, do tell, responded several voices.

—Mr. Oliver sent him into town to fetch some nails he needed to fix his wagon. You know how he always sendin T.C. into town to fetch stuff for him, Carol added. —Lettin him drive his truck, and T.C. think he's big as Ike doin that.

—Mmmhmph.

—Well, that blamefool got drunk as a skunk in town, clumb into Mr. Oliver's car and drove back, weavin all over the road. Like to hit Judy and Ann walkin, they had to jump into the ditch when he come by. They say he got his head stuck out the window, and drivin in broad daylight with his headlights on. Well, Mr. Oliver is comin up the road in his car and he see T.C. comin. He stop and flag T.C. down. T.C., he say, What you doin drivin all over the road like that? Man, you gonna hit somebody! Don't you think you oughter pull over and sleep awhile? T.C. say, Naw, Mr. Oliver, I'm fine. See, I've got my headlights on. Nothin's gonna happen to yo' truck. Onna count he'd heard on the radio you supposed to put yo' lights on over Memorial Weekend, for safety.

We all laughed appreciatively.

—And you know Mr. Oliver like his taste of drink too,

added Hattie. —He and T.C. gets drunk together lots of times. I've seen 'em sprawled out by Mr. Oliver's barn.

Suddenly in the midst of the hot sunshine a sprinkling of rain fell. Niecey went to stand close to the tree trunk, but the rest of us looked up gratefully at the cooling drops.

—Whee, you know what that mean, cackled Hattie, lifting the front of her housedress with her fingertips. —Devil's beatin his wife.

—Lawd, here's another stick finished, said Marcelle. —Junior! Come on over here, take this stick to the barn.

And so the afternoon would pass companionably.

Once the stringer had tied off, a young boy took the stick swaying with tobacco leaves into the barn. The men would place it high up in the rafters, where it would be cured. You cured tobacco for seven days, and had to constantly feed wood into the concrete firebox outside the barn and then check the temperature on the inside. You had to be careful not to scorch it, and not to let the fire go out, because the curing had to take place continuously, all day and all night. Since the farmers were paid according to the quality of their tobacco at the big warehouse auction in the fall, the curing was the most important part of the whole process.

You could always tell when it was curing season because the farmers and their wives and children would walk around hollow-eyed from lack of sleep. It was like having a brand-new baby every summer, one farmer's wife told me. I knew what she meant, because Sibby and I had to spend a lot of time taking care of Luke in the middle of the night when he was a baby and Mother was so exhausted.

So Sibby and I would hire out to watch the fires, to give the farmers and their wives some rest. We'd sleep on cots right outside the barn door and take turns waking up every two hours, all night long, to check the fires that cured the tobacco leaves. I was a little afraid of sleeping outside in the dark, but as Sibby said, it was easy money compared to picking, especially when you took turns, as we did. And it was good to be away from Father, on our own. We'd bring black-eyed peas with us and cook them on the hot flue eyes that covered the pipe that went from the firebox into the barn.

Those nights were heaven, eating those tasty dried peas with the crickets and frogs singing out for all they were worth. Sibby would entertain me with ghost stories for hours on end as we sat by the light of the kerosene lamp, and I'd jump every time I heard an old hoot-owl, or a dog go panting by in the dark.

Once the tobacco was cured, it was put into a cool, damp underground pit beneath the barn. The tobacco stayed there for two days until it got in order—until moisture got back into it so the leaves were flexible again, instead of crumbly and dry. Then it was taken out of the pit, and Sibby and I would help cut the twine and take the leaves off of the sticks.

The farmer's wife would sort it into three grades: excellent leaves were entirely golden, good had some brown and some gold, and poor was mostly brown. We'd help her sort it into big piles on plank tables and then tie it into twists. The twists went into large, flat baskets to be loaded onto a truck and driven to the warehouse for the auction. Sibby and I always felt a sense of accomplishment when the last load was sent off—as if the crop were partly ours.

Tobacco is hard, hot work, but I always liked the summers best when I could get paid and feel useful. It was one of the only times I felt I was contributing to my upkeep. None of the colored workers ever commented on my foot; they were very kind to Sibby and me, maybe because we were often the only white children who were working alongside them. The women would invite us to share their lunches under the shade trees when it was time for our break.

Some of the farmers' wives fed all the workers their noontime meal. If lunch was provided, the colored people would eat outside on the back screened porch if there was one, or else under trees in the yard. They were never invited inside with the whites, who ate in the kitchen. Sibby and I always preferred to eat with the colored people. We hated when we had to eat with the farmer's family because the other kids always looked down on us for hiring out to pick. I remember one particularly nasty boy who liked to come up behind me and say,

—Y'all aint much better than the niggers, is you? Maybe y'all is part nigger. Lessee if you hidin nappy hair up under them braids.

And he'd yank on my braid so hard my head would spin. I never let on to Sibby because I was worried he could best her in a fight. She got into enough battles on my behalf as it was. Our clothes were always more ragged than those of the farmers' kids, and inevitably one of them would mock our threadbare shirts or my bad foot. When that happened, Sibby would wind up in a fistfight with the one who'd made the comment, and they'd meet in a gully after the meal and light into each other. I told her time and time again not to pick fights—just to ignore their comments, as I did—but she wouldn't.

—You think I'm going to stand by and let some cracker make fun of us? she'd say. —You've got another thought coming. I'm gonna tear him up!

I'd be upset when she came back all scratched and torn, but she always said she made the other kid look worse than she did.

Sibby was the one who got us the tobacco work, since

she was determined to be independent of Father. The problem was, she always spent her money the minute she got it. I tried to save my earnings, since I assumed I'd be on the farm forever. I knew my marriage prospects were nil, and my imaginations about going off on my own seemed likely never to get off the ground. I dreamed of teaching or becoming an office worker in a city somewhere, but how to accomplish that with the pitiful amounts I was able to save?

Mrs. Spender was encouraging; in fact, she told me over and over that it would be a shame if I didn't go to college. That spring before I met Aaron, she had made me stay after class several times to talk to me about where I could go. She even said there were places that gave out scholarships to good students like me, and that she'd write letters on my behalf. But I never could figure out how I could afford to go, even if I got a handout; I'd still have to feed and board myself. Making thirty cents an hour picking tobacco wasn't going to get me anywhere. And as Father had made clear, he certainly wasn't about to help me.

I tried to hoard my puny savings, but the movie magazines at Job's store beckoned. I couldn't take them into the house, but Sibby and I would hide them behind a loose plank in the barn wall and read them whenever we had a chance. Sibby didn't even bother trying to save her earnings. What she didn't give to Mother, she spent on candy, a hair ribbon, the movies. She always said if she had a quarter on the day she was going to die, she'd go out and buy herself an ice cream sundae and go see *Gone with the Wind* one more time.

Occasionally we'd plot ways to make money so we could leave the farm, run away to California or somewhere exotic, but I had a feeling Sibby wasn't going to have to rely on her savings to get out of the house. Half the boys in the county had already tried to come courting, and it would take just the right one who wasn't scared off by Father to take her away.

Chapter Six

Sibby met Charlie at a barn dance the same summer that I met Aaron. She'd dragged me along as she often did, insisting that I could at least talk to people and enjoy the refreshments. On such occasions, my thoughts always pulled me in opposite directions. I knew I'd have no problem moving around to a slower reel, because Sibby and I had practiced dancing together many times in the barn when we knew no one would see us. Yet I disliked the humiliation I always felt at these socials; I knew that the other girls only came over to talk to me just to pass time until some boy asked them to dance. And no boys ever approached me at all, except to ask me if I knew where Sibby was. Yet I always kept the secret hope in my heart that someone would come along who'd overlook my foot and who'd take an interest in me—in the real me, not just my external attributes, or lack of them.

This particular night, I'd stood before our half-fogged-over wall mirror, trying to see myself between the patches of rust that had eaten away at the peeling silver paint. Sibby forced me to hold still as she tied a pink ribbon in my hair, which I thought looked ridiculous. I took the opportunity to compare our mirrored reflections. My hair was dark brown, like Sibby's, but didn't have the wave in it that hers did, although she always claimed if I didn't wear it in a single tight braid all the time, it would have more curl. My eye color was a curious blue, one I thought washed-out, but that she always claimed was the color of cornflowers. Whereas she had nice ruddy coloring, my face was pale, and I thought my nose was too long. I'd always admired the way hers turned up pertly. Sibby told me I was pretty, but I'd take her looks any day over mine.

—Done, she said, fluffing out the ribbon on either side. —Now just take that apron off, and you'll be beautiful.

—I think I'll leave it on, I replied. —My dress has a tear in the seam.

I hated wearing a dress without an apron because I thought it made my limp more pronounced, but Sibby knew all of my tricks.

—You'll look silly in an apron at a dance, Cora. Come on, you look just fine in that dress. The ribbon perks you up right nice. You'll have fun, don't be a stick-in-the-mud.

I could do nothing but go along with her. When Sibby made up her mind to something, she was as stubborn as a mule. She used to call me Caspar Milquetoast when I didn't want to accompany her in one of her schemes.

So, off we trudged to the social. At this point it had been three weeks since I'd last seen Aaron, and a week since I'd stopped waiting for him on the road, but I still hoped there was just a miscommunication and I'd run into him and things would be like the way they were the day he met me after church. One reason I agreed to go to the dance was that Aaron might be there. Of course, he might be there with another girl, as I well knew, but I told myself at least then I'd be able to forget about him.

The dance was being held in Jonas Smith's barn, two miles

off, and I dreaded the walk because I knew Sibby would be in a hurry to get there and it would be hard going for me to keep up. Luckily, every once in a while I'd spy a big black walnut and point it out to her, and she'd have to stop to find two rocks to crack it. Sibby had a weakness for black walnuts. So while she was searching for the rocks, I'd have a chance to rest up a little and catch my breath.

—Land sakes, Cora, I know you're just finding walnuts to slow us down, she laughed, but she stopped to crack them anyway. —Now I bet I've got pieces of nut all in my teeth.

She bared her teeth for me to check.

—Only a little on the bottom, I said.

She broke off a straw and poked furiously at her teeth. —Now?

—All gone, I said. I knew she couldn't stand to face a boy with nuts in her teeth.

—Now, when we get there, you go around and socialize, she said as we walked. —Don't stick up in a corner with Ann Hodges. She's only holding you back. Come on out of your shell and talk to people. You're really interesting, Cora, with all the books you've read. It's just that people don't know it.

I sighed. Sibby had been giving me pep talks since we were little. She always made it sound so easy, until I entered the room and saw all those blank faces looking at me. I imagined them sneering at my foot, or worse, pitying me. It got to where I couldn't talk to anyone without picturing what they were thinking about my foot. It seemed like it just wasn't much use.

—I'll try. But you know what'll happen. People will be polite, then when it comes time to dance, I'll be left behind. Nobody wants to drag around the floor with someone with a limp.

—Maybe not this time. You wait and see, Sibby replied.

I looked at her profile. How could boys not like Sibby? Her nose turned up perfectly, her black eyes sparkled, and her mouth was naturally rosy, unlike girls like Mary Jane Markley who had to paint themselves. Any boy would be thrilled to be looked at by Sibby. And she was a good dancer, to boot.

I could hear the first strains of the fiddle, floating over the rustling ears of corn in the field next to the road. The barn was just around the bend, but I was in no hurry to get there.

—Jeeesus wept, Peter crept and Moses went fishing! Come on, Cora, we don't have all night! I hear the music starting! Sibby urged.

—You go on without me. I'll be there in a few minutes, I said.

—No, I'll stay with you. Isn't it exciting? I just know you'll have a good time tonight.

A juicy smile of anticipation burst upon her lips.

Finally we came to Jonas Smith's big old barn. He had a couple of socials there every year, since he had three daughters who loved to dance. His oldest had gotten married to a farmer she met in this very barn, so there was a reason behind the parties. The other two, May and Willa, were snooty girls who prided themselves on being able to sew the latest patterns. Tonight they were wearing new cotton frocks with big flowers appliquéd on them, and big yellow bows on the back of their heads. They greeted the line of newcomers, flashing big smiles to the boys and sizing up the girls' outfits. They looked down their noses at Sibby's and my washed-out dresses, but they spoke politely enough.

—How are y'all? they said. —Have some refreshments before you start dancing. Mama made a good coconut cake.

—Thank you, Sibby said. —Thanks for having us.

I followed behind her, saying hello. When we'd passed them, she whispered to me, —May would be almost pretty if she wasn't big as the side of a barn. But I'm afraid Willa couldn't do a thing with her plug-ugly self if she had *two* fancy dresses on.

—Hush, they might hear you! I whispered back.

She just laughed at me and dragged me by the hand over to the refreshment table. I took the paper cup of lemonade she gave me and we helped ourselves to the coconut cake.

Sibby's eyes were already roving around the big room, and I took the opportunity to look for Aaron. Bales of hay were piled up everywhere so people could sit, and the fiddlers were tuning up their strings. Several boys and girls waved for Sibby to come over, but she just waved back and stood by me. I saw no sign of Aaron, but it was early yet. Maybe he'd show up later in the evening.

—You can go on over to Betty and them, you don't have to hang around me all night, I said to Sibby. I knew she was dying to join her friends.

—I'm fine right where I am.

She took a tiny sip of her lemonade. It was funny to see her try to drink like a lady, when at home we'd have water-gulping contests and wind up with our whole shirtfronts wet.

—If anyone wants to talk to us, they can come right over here, she added.

Soon two boys approached us; Tom Givens and a fellow I didn't recognize.

—Hi, y'all, Tom said, addressing us both but looking only at Sibby.

I'd gotten so used to this kind of one-sided salutation that it rarely bothered me anymore.

—This here's my cousin Charlie Walpole, from Mattox County, Tom continued.

—Hi, Charlie, Sibby said, her face lighting up with her smile.

—Hi, I muttered, figuring no one would notice what I said. To my surprise, Charlie smiled at Sibby and then looked right at me.

—Nice to meet you, he said. —I hear the fiddlin's going to be mighty good tonight. I hope I can tempt you two out onto the floor at some point tonight. At different times, of course.

Sibby raised her eyebrow at me and smiled. —That would be just fine, she said. —And Tom, you owe me a dance from last time when you stayed out on the floor with old Aubrey Whitelain. She knew she was stealing a dance from me, and she just kept you out there. I had to sit the whole dang thing out.

Charlie smiled at her. —I can't imagine you having to sit out much if you didn't want to, he said.

—See you girls later, said Tom, and they left out a side door.

I knew they were going to drink out of their flasks; Tom's flashed silver in his overalls bib while he was standing there. I didn't approve of it, and Sibby knew that. But she just laughed when I commented on their drinking.

—Long's they don't act like Father when they're drinking, I don't mind, she said. —I wouldn't mind a nip once in a while myself.

I gasped, and turned around to see if anyone had heard her. Sibby laughed. —Shut your mouth, Cora, you're catching flies. I think that Charlie fellow is a fine piece of work. I may give him a good spin out there on the floor, if these geezers ever get their fiddles tuned.

Just as she spoke, the fiddles whined loudly and sprang into a wild country jig. Nelson Ridout came and grabbed Sibby's arm and had her out on the floor before she could say goodbye to me. I didn't blame her; I knew she loved dancing more than anything. If I could have flown around like she did, I would have loved it, too.

I walked over to the side of the room and sat down on a big bale of hay. The stalks pricked my legs through my skirt uncomfortably and when I shifted, I spilled some lemonade on my dress. I gulped down the rest of it just to get rid of my cup.

All the boys started coming up and asking the girls to dance. One by one, they trailed out onto the floor. I sat watching, as I always did. Usually there were three or four girls left out with me, and we would gather together at the refreshments table and make spurious conversation, trying to ignore the fact that there was a dance going on. But tonight for some reason, maybe because the fiddlers played as if they were possessed, every single girl but me was asked to dance.

When Nanny Williams left her seat to go out onto the floor, I knew I was doomed. Nanny was the only one, other than Ann Hodges, whom I could count on never to be asked. Fat and ungainly, with moles all over her face, she and I had commented on the weather and church business so many times through these affairs that I felt I could recite the color and placement of each mole in my sleep. For Nanny to be asked was the last indignity. I was the only girl in the whole teeming place who was sitting the dance out.

To add insult to injury, I saw Wade Beacham walking around partnerless on the floor, talking to his friend Jared Opsher. Jared was reeling Pam Tucker around in a wild fling, and carrying on a conversation with Wade at the same time. Wade had to see me sitting there, had to be aware I was the only girl left out. In fact, I was sure the entire dance floor saw me sitting there, as isolated as the last burr clinging to a prickle tree when the wintry winds begin to shriek. I was sure they were thinking to themselves, poor old Cora Slaughter, can't get somebody to shuffle around the floor with her, when even the worst of the wallflowers have been plucked from the vine. I wished Aaron was here. Surely he'd have come over and walked me around the dance floor, even if only out of pity.

I sat as if paralyzed on the hay bale. My whole face felt hot, and I was sweating under my thin cotton dress. I wanted to get up and walk out, but if I did, wouldn't it draw more attention to my pitiful state? I hoped that if I sat there, frozen, people wouldn't see me even if they looked my way. For a few minutes I prayed for Wade Beacham to come over and end my agony, but I saw him glance in my direction once and determinedly go back to talking to Jared as he flung Pam around the floor. He saw me; he was just not going to help me. My eyes darted around looking for Sibby, but she was now at the far end of the room dancing wildly with Tom's cousin, Charlie. She wasn't going to rescue me; she only had eyes for him.

The song seemed to go on endlessly. I looked over at the ladies serving lemonade, hoping one of them would notice me and come over to help me, talk to me, get me out of there. But no one did. I didn't know how they could not see me, sitting alone as I was, but no one came to save me, not even the adults. It seemed like the longest dance in the world. I wished that I could disappear.

Finally the music stopped. The minute couples started milling around and coming off the floor, I pushed up from the hay bale as fast as I could and went outside. I didn't realize I'd been crying until the cool night breeze hit my cheeks.

I swiped at my face, flushing with shame. What a complete embarrassment I must be to Sibby. All I could think of to do was to start walking home. That way I wouldn't have to see everyone else avoiding my eyes for the rest of the night.

The dirt road shone white under a full moon. I trudged along, kicking up dust with every footstep. Crickets sounded in the ditches, then fell silent as I approached. A few steps later, they'd start up again. Even the insects want to avoid my company, I thought in self-pity. The sweet smell of the hay tickled my nose, and I blew it on my pocket handkerchief. The mucus was black with the dust I'd inhaled. I wondered if it was streaked down my face, as well.

I hadn't gone far when I heard laughter and footsteps behind me. Embarrassed that it might be someone from the dance, I moved to the side of the road and hoped they'd go on by without paying me any mind. But soon I heard my name being called.

—Cora! Land sakes! Wait for us!

It was Sibby. I looked back and saw her and Charlie coming along behind me. I came to a stop and waited. Sibby came huffing up.

—Why on earth did you leave? I went to bring you some lemonade after that first dance and I couldn't find you anywhere. Willa said she saw you light out onto the road.

I hoped that Charlie couldn't see I'd been crying.

—I didn't feel like staying, I tried to say in a carefree voice. —I was tired of that music. It was so loud, I was getting a headache.

Sibby looked at me closely. —All right, I'll walk on home with you. Thanks, Charlie. I hope to see you again sometime.

—Oh, I'll see you two girls home, he said. —I prefer your

company over all that's in there. I'll double back and catch Tom at the end of the dance.

Sibby and I exchanged glances. Father might be home, and if he was, we'd better not show up with Charlie in tow.

—Tell you what, Sibby said. —You can walk us to the pasture gate. Our father doesn't like us to entertain at home.

—All right, Charlie said evenly. He seemed to take everything in stride; me leaving the dance, our father not wanting company. Nothing seemed to ruffle his feathers.

All the way home, we talked and joked. A big-bellied moon followed us high over the rustling cornfields, making the slender stalks shiver with light. Charlie talked about wanting to raise cattle, and Sibby got me out of my mood by poking fun at May's dress. I was laughing so hard by the time we reached our pasture gate that I almost forgot my earlier humiliation. We stopped to say goodbye to Charlie.

—I enjoyed it, Charlie said, shaking Sibby's hand and then mine. —Since I can't come calling, when can I see you again? he said, this time addressing his comment more to Sibby.

She told him what days he could walk her home from her tobacco-picking job, and they parted with plans to see each other again that coming week. Walking through the pasture in the moonlight, she told me all about Charlie; that he was finished with school and was helping his father farm.

—They have a hundred twenty acres in Mattox County, and he'll come into sixty of it when he gets married, she said.

—He told you that already? I asked.

—Not only that, Sibby said, smiling. —He told me he's going to marry me, come hell or high water.

I stopped still in my tracks. For a moment I could not move. The thought of Sibby leaving home filled me with despair. How could I go on if she wasn't there to take up for me at school or worse, in our house? I stared at her, scarcely breathing.

—When? I asked.

—When what?

—When are you going to marry him?

Sibby laughed. —Oh, that's just crazy boy talk. He probably says that to all the girls, she replied. —I wouldn't let it bother me for more than a minute.

But the rest of the way home, all she talked about was Charlie. How he wanted to get out of tobacco eventually and raise dairy cows, feeling that tobacco was a doomed enterprise in the long run. How he had two younger sisters, and how he wanted her to meet them soon. How he thought his parents would like her. And so on. I listened with half an ear, feeling desperate. Despite what she said, I knew this was it. Sibby had never acted this way about a boy before. She would be eighteen in November. I knew she'd be out of the house in less than a year.

Chapter Seven

With all this on my mind, I went to work at Mrs. Whitmell's place. Sibby was still picking tobacco at a neighboring farm, but I had grown so dizzy in the record-breaking heat that she had asked Mrs. Whitmell if I could help out indoors for a few weeks. I hated to leave her doing the hard work, but I really needed a break from the hot sun. I didn't know how much longer I could hold up with the pain in my foot and no sign of a cool breeze.

Mrs. Whitmell was a kind, fat lady from our church. Her husband had died several years ago, and her two sons were running their big farm. She loved to cook, but given her size and the heat, she sweated immensely and had trouble getting all her ingredients together. In particular she did not like going down her basement steps, so I was kept busy going up and down them, bringing her the jars and bottles she needed.

Unfortunately, I never learned anything about actual cooking, since she did all that herself. But she loved to talk and I liked to listen, so we made good companions. At times when she was overcome by the heat, she would sit in a kitchen chair with her blouse unbuttoned, her enormous bosoms glistening with sweat above her brassiere, and I would fan her. When it got too hot in the kitchen, we'd go out on her front porch and drink huge glasses of iced tea. It was a pleasant way to earn money, the only drawback being that my foot ached horribly if I had to go down the basement steps too many times. But I didn't complain for fear she would hire someone else in my place.

On my way home from Mrs. Whitmell's, tired but happy with my quarter in my pocket, I tried to imagine living at home without Sibby—no one else to help Mother, no one to draw Father's ire away from me and WillieEd. I worried about whether Charlie was serious about marrying her.

They'd only just met, but things had happened quickly before in Gower County. One of the girls in the upper class at school had met a boy from Cheatham and had married him the following weekend. One of Mother's cousins had run off with a traveling wares salesman she had met just the previous week. Her family had never gotten over the scandal of it; they didn't even allow her name to be uttered in their presence. I wondered if Sibby would do anything so precipitous. I would try to pry it out of her tonight to see what her plans, if any, were.

I was so deep in thought that I did not hear the footsteps behind me until they were almost upon me. I whirled around and there was Aaron, almost as if he had materialized out of the hardbaked red clay.

—I didn't mean to surprise you, he said cheerfully.

I couldn't believe I'd finally run into him again. I had begun to think he'd wandered off looking for work in some other community. I guess absence does make the heart grow fonder, because he looked even better to me than he had the other times I'd seen him. Again I marveled at how his dark eyes seemed to glitter in the late-afternoon sun.

—I called out, but you didn't hear me, he continued.

—Thinking about the dinner you're going to fix when you get home?

I didn't know where he'd gotten this idea that I was such a cook, but I wasn't about to dissuade him. My heart was beating so fast at seeing him again that I felt as if a big hand had grabbed it and was rhythmically squeezing it. I only wished I looked less bedraggled; I knew an afternoon in Mrs. Whitmell's kitchen had left me worse for the wear.

—No, I, uh . . . I was thinking about a book I read this week. A novel. It was written by a woman named George Eliot, isn't that funny? But she took on a man's name since back then women weren't supposed to write books . . .

I faltered when I noted his look of disdain.

—You don't like novels? I asked. I had assumed he was quite a reader, from the way he talked. But maybe he did not like fiction. I could see that a man might not; might prefer works of math or science, for instance.

—Not much. I don't like to sit around and read. Drives me stir-crazy. I'm a man of action, myself.

I puzzled over this. —But you must have had to have studied a lot to get so good at numbers, I said. —Did you tire of books after you learned all your arithmetic and accounting?

Aaron laughed, and I caught a whiff of something on his breath. Surely not, I thought; he told me he doesn't drink.

—I tired of books, that's right, he said. —After I studied arithmetic.

He laughed again. I didn't know what to say to this, so I lowered my head and looked at the cracks in the dry road as we walked. There were so many grasshoppers jumping in the fields that at times they would spring out at me and stick in my skirt. I'd brush them away with my hand, and Aaron would chortle.

—Don't like bugs, do you?

—Not much, I replied. —Do you?

—Not much. The worst are lice. Takes a long time to get those buggers out of your head.

—My little brother had them once. Someone had them at school. Horrible things. I shuddered.

—What do you like, aside from books? Aaron asked. —Got many boyfriends around here?

—Oh, I don't have any boyfriends, I said shyly. I thought it was an odd question for him to ask.

—Oh, I bet you do. You young girls always have boyfriends, several of 'em, he retorted, grinning into my face.

—You're not all that much older than me, are you? I asked, trying to turn the conversation around. I knew he was grown, but I thought he was maybe twenty-two, twenty-three.

—How old are you, fourteen? he asked, ignoring my question.

—No, I'm sixteen, I replied. —I'll be seventeen in a few months.

—I see. Big girl, he said.

—How old are you?

—Too old for you to ask, he said, scowling.

I felt embarrassed. —I'm sorry, I just thought—

—Never mind. Never mind how old I am. I'm old enough to know better, that's how old I am, he replied with a leer.

I didn't know what he meant by that, and I didn't think I wanted to know. Somehow I couldn't get the conversation to go in the right way, the way it had gone the other times I'd seen him. Maybe he'd decided he didn't like me anymore. But why would he walk along the road with me? He could have spoken and gone on ahead. For anyone to walk at my pace was an effort.

—Does your leg hurt you much? he asked, almost as if he'd read my mind.

—A little, I admitted. —I had to go up and down Mrs. Whitmell's basement steps a few times today, fetching things for her, and it always hurts after that. But I can't complain. She's a nice lady and she pays me.

—How much does she pay? he asked.

I thought this question a little rude, and hesitated.

—Oh, come on, I'm not going to tell your Sunday school teacher, he said.

—Five cents an hour, I whispered. Suddenly I was ashamed. I knew it was less than half what others earned, but I was grateful for anyone to hire me.

—And she feeds me, too, I added.

Aaron seemed to light up in a rage. —A measly nickel! You slave away at her house and she pays you a nickel an hour! That cheap miser! You have to tell her to pay you more, or you won't work for her. I've never heard of such a lying fool in my life! A nickel! She should be hung!

I was astonished at his outburst. I didn't know why he cared so much. Could it be because he cared for me? Otherwise, why would it bother him if I was underpaid?

Aaron seemed to calm down. —You are being taken advantage of. Do you understand that? he asked, turning and glaring into my eyes. He took my chin in his hands and held it tightly, too tightly for comfort. I nodded, hoping he would let go. I could feel the pinch of his grip after he released me.

—Good. You do that.

He seemed to feel we had arrived at an agreement about my wages, and his mood lightened. —I see we're at your father's road. Since I know he doesn't want the likes of me on his property, I'd best be going.

—It's not only you, it's anyone—

Aaron held up his hands. —Don't bother, I know when I'm not wanted. When will you be venturing out again?

I thought quickly. —I have to go to the Boswells' farm to clean up their kitchen and do some ironing tomorrow morning.

—I won't be around tomorrow morning, he said. —Maybe I'll run into you later this week. He saluted and walked off.

Tiredly I opened the pasture gate and went through it. As usual, I had trouble hitching the metal wire back over the wooden post. Finally I got it hooked and continued through the pasture, picking my way around cow piles. Most people hated the way they smelled, but I didn't mind. Cows were more pleasant to be around than most people I knew.

I puzzled over Aaron's strange behavior the rest of the way home. He seemed happy to see me, but then his responses to my attempts at conversation were bizarre. I was sorry that after waiting to see him for more than three weeks, we'd had such a bad encounter. I wondered if I'd simply caught him in an off mood. Certainly that seemed the best explanation for it. And his disgust at my pay seemed overwrought. Why should he care so much what I earned? I could not figure it out, unless he was merely angry at an injustice to me. I was happy to think that was the reason, and comforted myself that he must care for me if that were so. Perhaps, I told myself, I would be out of the house before Sibby was.

That night, after we were in bed, Sibby talked of Charlie. He'd walked her from the Myersons' farm where she was picking this week, and they'd talked about so many things: the kind of family he wanted (a big one), what his sisters were like (talkative), his theories on farming (people were going to get tired of smoking eventually, and tobacco prices would drop). I must admit that for the first time ever, my mind wandered while Sibby was confiding in me. Finally she grew quiet, and I said,

—He sure does sound nice. Do you think you two will get married?

—I hope so, Sibby replied. —I've never met anyone like him. He's so polite, so steady. And I think he's really handsome.

Charlie was good looking, but I thought Aaron was much more striking, with his dark hair and eyes. I hadn't mentioned Aaron to her before; for some reason I'd held back. But now I brought him up.

—What did you think of that fellow that came by looking for work a while back? I asked, then held my breath.

—That scruffy man with the dirty overalls? I didn't think much of him, she sniffed. —Why?

I was too embarrassed to go on.

—Why? she pressed. —Did you see him somewhere else?

—I just thought he was kind of interesting looking, I said. —I saw him walking on the road, and he was friendly.

—Watch out for those types, Sibby said in her older sister voice. —Those traveling, I need work today and I'm gone tomorrow men. No telling where he comes from.

—Actually, he said he's from Potters Creek, I replied in what I hoped was a diffident tone.

—Hmph, Sibby sniffed. —I don't know anyone from there. I kept quiet after this.

—You sure you just ran into him once? Sibby asked, now curious.

—Yes, I lied. —I imagine he's gone from the county by now. I'm tired, Sibby, Mrs. Whitmell wore me out today. I'm going to sleep.

—Good night, she said, but she was sound asleep long before I was.

Chapter Eight

The next time I ran into Aaron was several weeks later, when I was coming back from mending clothes at the church. We pulled our chairs together in a circle, said prayers, and then sewed. Some made quilts, and some mended things. I always had the family's mending to do, since Sibby wasn't patient enough to sit long for sewing, and Mother couldn't see to thread the needle anymore. I'd take a basket of things and pull my chair back a little so everyone wouldn't see how threadbare our undergarments were. I liked to sew and listen to the other women gossip. I enjoyed the companionship, and it was an excuse to be away from the house.

Walking home with our basket of clothing, I was unprepared to run into Aaron, but as I walked by a packing barn there he was, lying under the shade of the tin roof, picking his teeth with a wooden toothpick he'd whittled. It occurred to me that he had a lot of free time for someone who was working, but then the thought passed. Maybe they'd given him an afternoon off, or he had finished early. He got up from his bed of grass when he saw me and sauntered over.

—Let me take that for you, he said, hefting the basket under his arm.

It wasn't heavy, and I said I could carry it, but he insisted. I was embarrassed that he might see our undergarments in the piles of clothing, but he didn't look.

—Are you heading back home? he asked. —You look mighty tired today.

My spirits sank, as I thought I looked better than the last time he'd seen me. At least I wasn't sweating in the church basement the way I had at Mrs. Whitmell's.

—No, I'm fine, I said. —I was mending some things at church with some other ladies.

—You're a woman of many talents, he said.

I looked up at him to see if he was laughing at me, but he didn't seem to be.

—Not really, I replied.

His mood seemed normal today, unlike the last time I'd seen him. He seemed to be in a quiet frame of mind; thoughtful, even.

—Why don't we sit down and rest awhile? he asked. —You look like you could use some shade. Let's head over there toward those trees.

He pointed to the far side of the field.

I knew I should go home to see if Mother wanted me to do anything, but it was so tempting to sit with Aaron. Our last meeting had gone so badly, I wanted to somehow make up for it. And he smiled so nicely when he asked me that I had to say yes.

—Just for a while maybe, I said. —It would be nice to rest some before I go home.

I followed him across the field, stepping carefully through the tall green grass so I didn't lose my balance. He was whistling a strange tune that I'd never heard. I asked him a few questions, making an attempt at conversation, but he kept on whistling, and I told myself he hadn't heard me.

—Let's sit here, he said, and leaned back against a tree.

I sat beside him, smoothing my skirt down to my ankles. I remember that it was a comfortable spot, and when we sat, all the birds stopped singing for a moment, then started up again. It was such a pretty sound, and I commented on it.

—Not as pretty a sound as your voice, Aaron replied. —I was thinking about your voice just the other night. It's nice and soft, not loud and irritating the way some women sound.

—Thank you, I said, surprised. No one had commented on my voice before. I had never thought it was particularly soft, or particularly anything. Aaron smiled, and I felt my insides melt. He looked so handsome sitting under the tree, the wind blowing his thick hair back.

—I think you have a nice voice, too, I added quietly.

—Do you? Aaron said, and he scooted closer to me so that he was sitting beside me. —I'll give you something else to like about me.

He took my shoulders and hugged me to him. I clasped my arms around his neck, tears brimming in my eyes. This is it, I thought. This is the love of my life; I have found him. I pulled back, expecting Aaron to let go. But instead of releasing me, he pulled me to him again.

After that, things happened quickly. Before I knew it Aaron's mouth was covering my mouth, his hands were moving all over me. Finally I was able to push him away and sit up.

—Someone might see us by the road, I said, brushing grass off of my skirt.

Why I said this instead of protesting his actions, I don't know. It was the first thing that popped into my head. Aaron looked at me and laughed.

—Not where we're going, they won't, he said.

He pulled me up, and we started walking down the road.

—Where are we going? I asked.

I knew I really had better start home, but it was so enticing to be in his presence again, and my stomach was still doing flips over his kiss. To tell the truth, I think I was afraid if I didn't go along with him he'd revert back to his odd manner of the last time I'd seen him. I wanted more than anything to keep him in his current buoyant mood. He didn't answer my question though; he just started whistling again. Eventually we set off down a smaller dirt path. Against my better instincts I kept going along with him. I told myself that I knew him, that it was all right. And I was hoping he'd want to kiss me once again before I went home.

We came to his house, as he called it. It was really an old cabin he slept in, one side stoved in and the other half looking like it could collapse at any minute.

—That's where you live? I asked, pulling back. He'd caught hold of my arm somewhere on the path off the main road.

—Yes, that's my humble abode. Come on, I'll show you. Aint much but it's all I've got for the time being.

I guess curiosity overcame what good sense I had, and I allowed myself to be pulled along by the arm into his shack. When I saw his living conditions, I felt an overwhelming sympathy for him. All he had was an open fire that he cooked on with a griddle, a pallet of rags, and one change of overalls hanging from a knob on the wall. A broken piece of mirror for shaving. And that was it. It occurred to me later to wonder why, with all his book learning, Aaron was reduced to living like this, working for hire in other people's fields. Maybe he was sending all he earned home to his poor mother. I turned to him to express my concern.

—You can't stay here much longer, I began. —It'll get cold in a few months. You have to find somewhere better to stay.

—You worried about me, is that it? he asked gruffly.

—Well, I—

As I started to explain, he grabbed me and kissed me again, harder than before. Before I could catch my breath, he was kissing my neck and pushing me farther into the cabin, away from the door. I stumbled over the pallet, and he pushed me down onto it.

—No! I can't stay here, I have to go—

—You'll stay, and you'll like it, he growled. Before I could protest again, he started yanking my skirt up over my legs.

—Stop! Stop it! I screamed, trying to pull my skirt back down. It only ripped, which seemed to spur him on.

—Don't be a little tease, he said, pulling on my under-drawers.

I screamed and fought him with all the strength I had, but it was not enough. He pushed me down onto the pal-let and had at me like a savage. I had never before been kissed, much less had relations with any man, and it was painful, to say the least. I was sobbing and sore when he was finished.

—What did you think we were coming back here for? To have tea? he asked. —Don't pretend you didn't want it too.

Seeing that this only increased my tears, he tried a more tender approach, reaching over and stroking my arm.

—Come on now, it wasn't that bad, was it?

I was crying and shaking, so horrified at the entire turn of events that I couldn't begin to reply. Where was the Aaron I'd spoken to these past weeks, who'd held my hand to help me around ditches, who seemed so concerned for my wel-fare? I hurt in places I didn't even know I had. I was bleed-ing and bruised, and too ashamed to ask for a rag to clean myself up. I sat there crying for some time.

—Girl, you need to get a grip on yourself, Aaron said. He

left the cabin in disgust and didn't return until some hours
later.

While he was gone, I tried to figure out what I should do.
At first I thought I'd go home and tell Sibby what had happened, and get her help. But the more I thought about it,
the more it seemed I ought to wait and see what Aaron had
in mind. Surely he must be planning to marry me. Maybe
he had just been overcome with passion. I'd read books that
implied this happened to men—that this kind of thing was
beyond their control. Maybe it would be all right. I had in-
vested so many hopes and dreams in Aaron Melville—it was
just too hard to let go of them all at once.

I decided that I couldn't go home in this state of disarray,
my skirt ripped and filthy with my blood. I could just imagine walking in the door and seeing the dismay in Mother's
eyes, the rage in Father's. Sibby had warned me against Aaron,
and I had foolishly ignored her advice. Until I could return
home with a marriage certificate, I couldn't face them. I decided to stay at the cabin and talk to Aaron when he got
back, in a more reasonable frame of mind, I hoped. The
more I thought about it, the more I felt sure we would go
to a preacher the next day to set things straight.

That's what we'd do, I decided. I pictured myself finding
a creek in the morning, washing off and rebraiding my hair,
fixing my skirt so the tear didn't show. Aaron would get
cleaned up too, and we'd hold hands and walk together to
the nearest church. Not Calvary, I thought; I didn't want Reverend Davis to see me like this. There was a little church a
couple of miles off with a younger preacher whom I thought
might be more sympathetic to a couple who'd obviously had
relations before their union was blessed.

My body finally stopped trembling as I imagined the simple words being read from the Bible, Aaron's chaste kiss on my cheek once the preacher had wedded us for life. Then we'd walk back to my house and make our announcement to my family. No one would be pleased; I couldn't pretend that they would, I reminded myself. Least of all Sibby. But there wasn't that much they could say. People ran off and got married all the time, didn't they?

When Aaron stumbled back into the cabin, it was pitch-dark. He seemed cheerful, and in my naïveté I thought he was just in a happy mood, since he'd told me he didn't touch liquor. Now I know that he was merely drunk. I hadn't known where to find a candle, and he made a great fuss about lighting a kerosene lantern so he could see.

—Don't want to be sitting around in the dark, girl, he said. —Now, have you stopped all that crying? A woman crying turns my stomach.

—Yes, I said. —What are we going to do?

—Do? said Aaron. —I'm going to go to sleep. I have to work tomorrow, early. Tobacco don't wait for any man, he said, and laughed.

—I meant, when are we going to see a preacher? I insisted. —We could find someone tomorrow if we get out early. There's a little church a couple of miles down the road from here—

Aaron looked at me and frowned. —You must have found my secret stash, he said. —You aint thinking too clearly. No one I know is seeing any preacher about anything. I make it a habit to avoid preachers of any sort.

—B-but we have to get married, I blurted out. —Now that we've done this thing.

—You can stay here with me, Aaron said a bit more gen-

tly, —for the time being. If you can't go home. I can understand that. But no one is getting married, least of all me.

—But what about what you were saying about us going
to Unionville? And teaching me accounting? I thought you—

—We may well go to Unionville, and then we may not,
he said. —I'll have to see how things shape up. If I go, you
might come with me. And you might not. We'll just have to
see.

With that, he flopped down on the pallet and fell to snoring. It must have been one or two o'clock in the morning.
There was no way I could go home now; Father would have
thrown me out. I sat up all night looking at the dirt floor,
wondering what I had done.

Chapter Nine

After that first night with Aaron, things seemed to happen in a blur. I stayed with him in the cabin, afraid to go home. No family that I knew of would have admitted a daughter back into its fold after she'd spent a night out with a man unless they got married immediately. Try as I might, it was beyond me to come up with a giant falsehood about where I'd been and why I was so bedraggled.

After a week went by, we had to move to where Aaron could find some work. He admitted that he'd been fired from his tobacco-picking job, he couldn't find work anywhere in the area, and he was flat broke. He had to leave, and I insisted on going with him.

What was left for me in Gower County? My name was ruined; Father wouldn't have allowed me back into his house, and I couldn't imagine the shame of facing Mother and Sibby. I was sure that Sibby knew I'd run off with Aaron, and that by now she'd told them of our conversation about him. I may as well have slept in a ditch if I stayed here. And as foolish as it may seem, I was still in love with Aaron. I just couldn't believe he wasn't going to marry me eventually. So I tagged along.

Trudging down the road, Aaron led me from farm to farm, from community to community. Everywhere there was the same story: they'd already hired their pickers for the tobacco crop. Maybe if someone quit . . . but no one ever did. There simply was no work to be had anywhere, according to Aaron. I was able to get an occasional day's worth of work helping a farmer's wife, but more often than not they'd take one look at me limping in my dirty clothes and say they didn't need any help.

At night we would sleep in barns or even an open field if we couldn't find shelter. There was of course little opportunity to bathe; I had to make do with splashing off in a creek whenever we came to one. At first I tried to convince myself that this was romantic; two lovers out on the road, us against the world. But after a while the novelty began to wear thin.

When Aaron was around, he was fairly convivial; once in a while he would talk about Unionville and clerking opportunities and what we would do when we got to the city.

—Heard about a good situation in Cheatham, should be opening up around November, he said one night after we ate potatoes that we'd roasted in an open fire in a field. We were lying together on two old feedbags that he'd found in a barn and that we carried with us for bedding. I was propped up on my elbows, staring into the embers of the fire, and Aaron lay back looking up at the stars.

—That sounds good, I said cautiously, having heard this kind of talk before. I was getting a little weary of the romantic life on the road by now, and was ready for Aaron to find some steady work so we could sleep with a roof over our heads.

—Yep, fellow tells me in good faith that he saw it in the papers, Aaron said in a satisfied way.

Of course, I knew that seeing something in the paper and actually getting a job were miles apart, but I so badly wanted to believe what he said that I let myself feel happy about it.

—Wouldn't that be nice? The two of us cozy in a little house somewhere, you working in an office? I murmured, watching a blazing twig of hay burn bright red, then gradually molt into gray ash.

—I guess it would. You my girl? he asked, teasingly.

—You know I am, Aaron, I said shyly, savoring the shape of his name in my mouth, my right to say it any time I wanted. I started to tell him how much I loved him, but when I looked over at him again, his mouth was open in a snore.

In moments like these I would experience a surge of optimism; a feeling that things would work out for me yet. Many times, once darkness fell, Aaron would throw himself upon me with such frenzied vigor that I felt he must love me. He was not tender, and most of the time I was left aching and sore, but I told myself that I was simply not used to lovemaking and that the physical aspect would get better with time.

After these heavings and mutterings in the dark, he would collapse and roll away from me, and then I would try to talk to him about his past life, or what had happened that day, or our future together. Most of the time he fell asleep quickly, but if he stayed awake, we would have a short conversation that I would run over and over in my mind the next day, turning it into lovers' talk.

—Did you have any luck with the farmer you met in town? I'd ask.

—Not much.

—How about the man that told you to come back next week? The man from the feed store?

—I aint heard back from him yet. Something'll turn up, we won't starve.

We, I'd repeat to myself the next morning. He thinks of us as *we*. I'd nearly faint in gratitude, feeling that he cared for me.

Or I'd ask him about his family. Generally he'd just laugh and say they were best left alone, the whole bunch of 'em. I gathered that unlike what he'd told me, he was not sending his mother money and that there was no affectionate memory on that front. When I prodded him more—for, after being alone all day, I was dying for some companionship, for some conversation—he'd grunt and say they never had a pot to piss in (his words) growing up. When I asked about his father, he replied that he never knew the bastard. His brothers and sisters appeared to be scattered to the winds. Aaron had no idea where they lived or what had become of them.

About this time I discovered Aaron's true age. I'd assumed he was about five or six years older than me—twenty-two or -three—but it turned out he was twenty-nine. A notice slipped out of his pocket when I was folding his extra pair of overalls; he'd applied for a job with the post office in one of the towns we'd just passed through, and on it he'd filled out his name, age, and other information. I wish he'd got the job, I thought in passing, but then the fact of his age hit me. I'd had no idea he was twelve years older than I was. All kinds of thoughts ran through my mind. What had he been doing all this time? He'd been old enough to work for over thirteen years and still had no roof over his head. I puzzled over this and tried to pry more out of him in our evening conversations, but he would not elaborate much on his past.

*   *   *

Perhaps the most telling thing that happened was one day when we stopped to wash off in a small river. I was sitting on the bank soaking my feet, and Aaron pulled his shirt off and was splashing himself. I noticed a long line of small dark points on his back, and asked him if a spider had bitten him the night before. Aaron laughed and said

—No, that aint from any spider. One of my mother's man-friends didn't like having a little kid around. So he took a fork and heated it up and held me down and poked it into my back. That's what those are.

Horrified, I tried to ask him more, but he laughed in a way that quelled me.

—My mama had lots of manfriends, he said brusquely. —I don't know what was worst, the ones that liked me or the ones that didn't.

After that, I didn't try to ask him much about his family.

Along about September, it became obvious that he wasn't going to get any tobacco work. It was then that Aaron started to drink openly, during the day. The first time I realized he was drinking, I was waiting for him in an old stable that was half a mile down a dirt path than ran alongside a corn-field. I'd been there the whole hot afternoon, and was hoping we could get out and walk and feel some cool air on our faces that evening before the sun set. Yet it got later and later, and still no Aaron. Finally a shadow at the door made me jump; it was he. He stood there in the doorway, and I knew something was wrong from his rumpled appearance. I stood up and went over to him.

—Are you all right? I asked. But when I got closer, I could see him sneering at me.

—Are you all right? he mocked me in a high-pitched, prissy voice.

I turned and went back to where I'd been sitting. I realized he'd been drinking, and I derided myself for not understanding it earlier. Suddenly the blinders were removed from my eyes. This was why he couldn't find work; he'd been getting drunk most afternoons.

I turned away from him, but he came pawing at me. I pushed him back—which I was able to do only because he could barely stand, he was so intoxicated—and went over to sit by the window. Aaron lay down on the floor and mumbled to himself for half the night, cursing and moaning. He'd struggle up and strike out as if he were wrestling with someone, then fall back down onto the dirt floor.

—Leave me alone, you bitch! he'd scream, then he'd mutter something incomprehensible. —Don't you touch me! Don't come near me!

At last he lay still, and I went over to stroke his head as he slept. I was beginning to have some sense of what Aaron had endured as a child, and it was terrifying. We hadn't had it easy in my home, but Father's whippings almost seemed inconsequential compared to what Aaron seemed to have suffered at the hands of his mother, and his mother's boyfriends, of which there had been many. Now that he was unconscious, a surge of protective sympathy went through me. I looked down at his handsome (to me, then) sleeping face and imagined the boy he once must have been. It was easy to love him when he was still and quiet like this. If only he'd been as easy to love when he was awake.

On that night, and many times in those first few months, I longed to go home to the comfort of my own bed, but the thought of Father's wrath stopped me. And I'll admit, I did have my pride. The thought of Mary Jane Markley and all those girls I'd gone to school with hearing I'd run off with a man and, worse, come hobbling back home unmarried, was more than I could bear. I knew they'd figure I'd been

so desperate for male company, I'd taken up with the first
no-count who'd given me half a look. The poor gimpy girl
couldn't get anyone but a field hand, and even then he de-
serted her. I could just imagine their whispers and knowing
smiles.

But I guess the main reason I stayed was because I was
still in love with him. I'd had the idea of Aaron Melville—
and of someone to love, at last—in my mind for so long, I
just couldn't give him up.

Finally, in late October, after nine weeks of roaming the countryside, Aaron got taken on to milk cows and slop pigs at a
big dairy farm in Shoah. We were allowed to sleep in a small
barn in the back of the property. I tried to keep his clothes
mended, and went up to the house every day to offer my
services. Eventually the farmer's wife got used to me coming
and let me do a little cleaning and sewing for her. For pay
I was given food, which was good because we had nothing
to cook with in the barn, not even a pit to make a fire in.
I'd bring something home in a pail from the farmhands' lunch
for Aaron's dinner. He would wolf it down, but I would eat
nothing, having eaten earlier at the house. Then he'd go out
drinking with some of the hands.

I was very lonely, but happy that we weren't walking the
roads anymore. Aaron still had his moments of high optimism where he'd talk about going to Unionville and clerking, but I had realized by then that they coincided with his
drinking. It was around this time that I learned the queasy
feeling in the pit of my stomach every morning wasn't hunger.
My monthlies were never regular, but I'd gone twelve weeks
without having one at all.

Aaron came home that night, and I gave him his supper.
I was awfully nervous about telling him my news. I knew

better than to hope he'd be happy about the baby, but I also hoped that knowing we had a child coming might help him settle down and stop drinking. And maybe he'd finally agree to marry me, too.

—Mighty good succotash, he grunted after swiping his plate with a piece of bread. —Too bad they're so stingy with the meat.

—I think it's nice of her to feed us at all, I commented. —She knows we don't have anything to cook with.

Aaron eyed me in mock surprise. —You lookin down your nose at the circumstances here?

—I'm just grateful for the handouts. We need them. And we're going to need them a lot more in a few months, I said. When he didn't pursue this, I added,

—Aaron, I'm expecting.

His mouth set in a grim straight line.

—Well, is that the truth. Guess I didn't think someone as stick-thin as you'ud get knocked up. Guess that was my mistake.

—I didn't think it would happen either. I guess I thought you were taking care of things so this wouldn't happen, I said sharply, to cover my disappointment at his response.

—You thought I was taking care of things. So it's my fault, huh?

—No, I'm not saying that. It's both our faults. It's no one's fault, it just happened, I stammered. —Maybe it will be nice, I mean, to have a child.

—You plannin on keepin it? Aaron asked in a disbelieving tone.

I felt a chill go through me. I couldn't believe he'd suggest otherwise.

—I couldn't give a baby away, I said. —I couldn't do that to my own child.

—You sure it's mine? he asked, cocking an eyebrow.

—How could you say that! You know you're the only man I've ever— I gasped, so angry I couldn't finish.

He shook his head and stood up. —You women. Never know what's the truth, comin or goin.

—That's not so and you know it, I said. —We're going to need to save up some money now, for the doctor, I added. —And for a place to stay. We won't be able to sleep in barns like this once we have a little one.

—Reckon not, Aaron said, looking around the barn as if seeing it for the first time. —It would get pretty drafty in here in the winter.

He turned to head out the door. A pang of loneliness hit me hard. I'd hoped that for once he'd stay home, with the news I'd just given him.

—Can't you stay here tonight? I couldn't help myself from crying out.

—I'm just goin out with the boys awhile. I'll be back later, he said.

But it was almost sunrise before he dragged himself back home, and almost noon before I could get him into any shape to go to work.

As the next months wore on, Aaron stayed away more and more, often not coming back to the barn even to eat dinner. I'd sit alone on the dusty hay bales and eat the meal I'd brought back for him, wondering what was going to happen once the baby came. At times I was thrilled at the thought of having a child; a tiny person of my very own to love, and who'd love me back. But more often I worried about how we'd provide for someone so helpless and dependent. Every time I attempted to talk to Aaron about saving some money, he'd just reply that he didn't have anything to give me. I knew he was drinking it all up, but whenever I looked through his overalls pockets, I couldn't find any. The only thing I could figure was that he took his weekly pay right to the man with the still the minute he got it.

That winter was bitter cold, and at night I'd put on every piece of his and my clothing that I could find, along with old burlap feedbags discarded in the barn. I'd burrow down into the haystack enveloped in all the old clothes and bags, wishing I had a book to help me while away the hours. In the morning my limbs were so stiff it would take fifteen minutes of gingerly walking about before my toes would stop being numb.

And I was so lonely. Time and time again, I thought about returning home. I'd debate the matter in my head, late into the night. The thought of facing Father's wrath and Mother's shame was something I didn't know if I could bear. But Sibby would stand by me, wouldn't she? However, if she was about to marry Charlie, as it looked like she was when I left, I didn't want to ruin her chances by showing up pregnant, with no husband in sight. Perhaps I could say Aaron had died or run off, but he was capable of showing up in Gower County again looking for work. It was such a small community; word tended to get around fast about anyone who got themselves into trouble. Any self-respecting man like Charlie would shy away from a family like that, I knew. I had ruined my own life; I didn't want to go and ruin Sibby's, too. And so I stayed.

As I got bigger, it became more difficult for me to get around. Both my feet throbbed now, swollen as they were. At night, pains shot up through my legs like fiery knives. I wondered if this was the normal condition of pregnancy, or a special curse sent down upon me for my sins.

The farmer's wife was kind and let me rest when my legs ached, but I knew once the baby came we wouldn't be allowed to stay. From what I gathered, Aaron had fallen behind in his work. I believe she had convinced her husband to keep him on only for my sake, until the baby was born and I got my strength back.

There was an early heat wave in April that scorched the earth. Lying there in the dusty barn, staring up at the night sky through the chinks in the logs, I could hardly breathe from the weight of the baby on my chest. At that point I began to wish for it to be over. I still hadn't been to see a doctor, but from what the farmer's wife had said, I assumed I'd have the baby in May. She told me of a midwife who would assist me when my time came and who'd accept payment later. I knew that was my only hope.

I was terrified of dying while having the baby, as so many women did in my community when I was growing up. Mabel's forty-six-hour labor, and other women's birthing stories that I'd listened to first- or secondhand, gave me the shudders. My own mother had had a doctor when she'd had me, and even so had almost died in the process.

When Luke came along there wasn't enough money for even a midwife, so Mother had suffered through it with only Sibby and me. We'd kept a bucket of water boiling on the fire and put hot rags on her forehead and belly. When she finally gave birth to Luke eighteen hours later, I thought she had indeed died, there was so much blood. But Sibby, who'd been through it before with one of our cousins, said she knew Mother would be all right. I wished I could just go home and let Sibby tend to me, but I felt that I couldn't. I had all this on my mind as my time with the baby approached.

The night I began having my pains, Aaron was nowhere to be found. I was leaving the farmer's house when a grinding ache began in my lower back. The wife guessed what it was and sent for the midwife. She told me to go on to the barn and lie down. I remember staring up at the huge dark rafters, dotted with dried-up wasps' nests, clenching my teeth against the pain, wishing one of the beams would fall on me and put me out of my misery.

The midwife came, and the farmer's wife showed up later with hot water and rags. The farmer's wife held my hand, gave me a stick to bite down on, and wiped my forehead with wet rags. The midwife massaged my stomach and told me not to push the baby out yet. Even when I screamed at her that I had to push it out now, she wouldn't let me.

I thought I would die from the pain, it was so horrible. It scissored across my huge belly as if some great hand was breaking me in two. In all the times I'd felt Father's belt cut into my back, I had never imagined an agony this fierce. I imagined how sorry Aaron would be that I'd died in my birthing bed. How sorry that he hadn't been there to make sure I was all right. But then the thought of dying without seeing his face again made me want to struggle to live.

Finally the midwife said I was ready, and my body started pushing for all it was worth. At first it was an immense relief, and I thought the baby was about to come out. But after a while, I was exhausted, and there was still no baby. Now the midwife was screaming at me to push, and I was screaming back that I was too tired. The farmer's wife took one of my legs, the midwife took the other, and they held them up in the air and made me increase my exertions once more.

When the baby came out of me all bloody and silent, I could hardly sit up to look at him, I was so tired. The midwife wiped him off and laid him on my bare chest while she made me force out the rest of what was left inside me, then cleaned me up. The baby gave me a shy glance and began to suckle lazily. I felt a tremendous surge of something that

I now know was love. I could hardly take my eyes off him to tell the midwife to come back for her payment next week, as I'd extracted a promise from Aaron to have some money saved up by then. But the farmer's wife interrupted me and told her she would pay the bill herself. I gasped out my thanks, tears starting in my eyes. I was ashamed to have turned into such a beggar.

Aaron stumbled in the following afternoon, stinking drunk. The farmer's wife, who'd stayed with me the entire time, took one look at him and left in disgust. The baby was crying softly. I tried to hush him, as Aaron always had a splitting headache when he'd been out all night long. I suckled him and pressed him close under the rag blanket and got him quieted down. Aaron took a look at me and said,

—You look like something got sent for and didn't come.

He stumbled over to a pallet he'd made up of old rags and fell down in a stupor.

I needed food, and help getting up to bathe off some of the blood that was still seeping out of me. Every time I shifted, more blood would spurt out, and I felt I would die from the cramping in my womb. But Aaron was in such a stupor that I couldn't get him to wake up. In the early evening I finally managed to rouse him by calling out as loudly as I could, but as soon as he'd taken a few steps he tripped and fell, senseless, onto the floor. God knows what would have happened had not the farmer's wife come to the door at that moment.

She took a look at Aaron and told me to hold still and wait. She went back to her house and hitched their mule to a wagon, then helped me and the baby get into it and took me to her own house. She let me lie in one of her beds and nursed me for a week until I was able to walk and take care of the baby.

I felt as if I'd dropped into heaven. It was so good to be inside a house again with clean sheets and no filthy smells. The farmer's wife was an angel. I can never think of her without tears coming to my eyes. If it hadn't been for her, I think I and the baby would have died. Not once in that time did Aaron come to see how I was doing or to see his son.

At the end of the week, I was much recovered and able to care for the baby, whom I had named Joshua. I had always loved the story of the battle of Jericho in the Bible, and the little song we used to sing about it at church.

The farmer's wife sat me down and had a long talk with me about what I should do in the future. She finally got me to admit that Aaron and I weren't married. Upon hearing that, she said I should take Joshua and go to a big city and get a job doing typing or some skill where I didn't have to be on my feet. She said I was young and smart, and had a lot of energy despite my clubfoot. Someone would give me work, she said. She even gave me the name and address of a cousin of hers in Cheatham, and said I could call to see if there was any office work among his acquaintances.

But I thought I should remain with Aaron. I was afraid of striking out alone with a baby; afraid I'd wind up in some county home for indigent mothers. I'd heard that unmarried women who weren't living with their manfriends often didn't even get to keep their babies; they were taken away from them and sent to orphanages. All of us girls had listened to stories about those places, growing up; in fact, many mothers used it as a threat to keep their daughters in line: *If you get into trouble, I'll send you right to the county home. You'll wish you never met that boy!* And then the litany: *You'll embarrass us in front of everyone. We won't be able to lift our heads when we pass our neighbors. You'd better watch yourself around him if you don't want to ruin your life, and our lives too.*

Going home seemed too risky. Father was entirely capable of sending me to one of those places, or at very least of setting me right back out on the road again, even with a newborn.

At the time, staying with Aaron seemed better than winding up a walking testament to shame. And I already loved my baby son so fiercely that the thought of losing him was unthinkable. I'd rather lose my life than have him taken away from me.

So I thanked the lady and said I had to stay where I was for the time being. She gave me a long look and told me to call upon her if ever I got into a bad fix again. She gave me some food for the next few days and said goodbye. I think she knew somehow that Aaron was planning to leave, and that that was the last time she'd see me. Maybe Aaron had told one of the hands, who had told her husband.

I trudged home slowly, carrying Joshua in a small quilt the lady had given me, the food wrapped up in a bundle. When I walked into the barn door Aaron was stuffing his belongings into a towsack.

—Where are you going? I asked.

He put down the gritchel. —I thought you were gone, he said. —Thought you'd taken up with the farmer lady.

—She helped me, I replied, a lump rising in my throat. —You were nowhere to be seen. Your own son, a week old. He's beautiful, and you've barely even taken a look at him.

Aaron seemed to soften. He came over and looked down at the baby sleeping in my arms. —He's a tiny little bugger, aint he? he said. —Got my coloring.

—He does, I said proudly. —I've named him Joshua. Want to hold him?

—No, I might drop him, Aaron replied, seeming embarrassed. —I've never held a baby. When he's older, maybe I'll give it a try.

He put down his bag. —Reckon we'll head out first thing after sunup, he said. —I'll go out and get us something to eat.

After he left, I eased myself into bed, nursed Joshua for a while, and then fell into an excited reverie. This indication of interest in the baby had given me hope. I thought that maybe once Joshua had grown some and was more of a little person, maybe when he could talk, Aaron would become even more interested in him, teach him to hunt, let him help him in the fields. If only we could make it to that point, I told myself, things would be so much better.

Chapter Ten

The first time Aaron hit me, it had been three weeks since he'd had even the lightest of jobs. He'd been on a real bender, out drinking every night until the early hours of the morning, and then sleeping it off until late in the day. One such afternoon Joshua, who was then about six months old, was sleeping on a little pallet that I'd made him. We were staying in another half-caved-in shack on someone's land, probably a place that colored people had lived in and abandoned years ago. Aaron had just awakened and was in a terrible frame of mind.

—Whyn't you fix me something to eat, make yourself useful? he asked.

I'd spent all afternoon scavenging vegetables from other people's gardens, hoping no one would see me, carrying Joshua from spot to spot as I added squash and tomatoes and potatoes and turnips to my gunnysack. My leg was aching, and I was hot and exhausted. I was also exasperated at his laziness.

—Why don't you fix yourself something to eat? You haven't worked in weeks, and when you do earn some money, you drink it up. I'm not fixing anything for you.

—Oh you aint, huh? Aaron pulled himself up, came over and pushed me, hard. —There's more of that for you if you smartmouth me, he said nastily.

—Whatever happened to that clerking job you told me about? I asked. —Like the one you said you had in Unionville? If you have all that book learning you told me about, why are you doing this kind of farm work anyway? I spat out.

Aaron's face twisted, and he grabbed my hair. While I was trying to pull away, he slapped me with the flat of his other hand, again and again.

—You stupid bitch, he said, flailing at me. —There never was a job in Unionville. I don't see you earnin your keep! Don't you speak to me like that, you bitch!

By now we were outside. I tried to get away from his blows.

—Stop it! Stop, Aaron! I yelled, but he hit me until I fell, then kicked me twice in the back.

—That'll teach you how to speak to me, he said, and stalked away.

I lay there on the ground for a few minutes until I heard Joshua crying in the cabin. Then I got up and limped inside. Aaron had shoved me against things when we'd had arguments before, but he'd never hit me like this. As I cradled Joshua in my arms, I suddenly decided to try to return home. Perhaps Father wouldn't try to send me away if Mother and Sibby interceded on my behalf.

I placed Joshua on his blanket and began putting our few things together in an old feedbag. I heard a noise behind me and whirled around; it was Aaron. I cringed, expecting him to swing out at me again. Instead, he knelt in front of me on the floor and buried his head in my stomach, weeping. Then he looked up at me, his bloodshot eyes watering.

—Sorry, he croaked out. —I'm sorry I hit you. I won't do it again, Cora. Don't go, I need you.

At his words, my resolve melted. I put my hands in Aaron's hair and held him to me. At that moment I felt he truly needed me. Aside from Joshua, he was the only one who ever had.

—I won't go, I said, blinking back tears. —I know you didn't mean it. But you have to stop drinking, Aaron. I'm afraid you're going to hurt me, or Joshua.

—I'd never hurt the baby, he said, slurring his words.

I helped him into bed, and soon he was fast asleep. I picked Joshua up and crooned to him, feeling relief. I didn't want my boy growing up without a father unless he had to. If Aaron would just stop drinking, or even curtail it some, we would be fine.

We moved around from place to place all that summer. Aaron would get work in someone's fields, and I'd feel optimistic again. Then, despite his protestations to me that he hadn't been drinking, after a couple of weeks he'd lose his job again when he didn't show up for work. Or he'd argue with the farmer who'd hired him over how best to till a field, how to pick tobacco or beans, when to get the hay in. He always knew more than anyone else, even though he didn't have a roof over his head or clothes to wear. According to himself, he was the smartest man he'd ever met.

He once came to blows with a colored field hand who insisted he rest the mules when they were blowing hard and dripping with sweat in the parching heat. It turned out that Aaron had set up a meeting at a still, and he wanted to get the ploughing finished by four o'clock. But the colored man knew the farmer didn't want his mules done in, and he made Aaron let the mules out of their traces. He took them down to the creek to drink, and then tied them under a shade tree to rest.

Aaron cracked the man over the head with a sharpened hoe when his back was turned tying up the mules. The man staggered and then spun around, still standing. Apparently he was very strong because, despite the deep gash in his head, he thrashed Aaron to within an inch of his life.

Ever since then, Aaron has had it out for colored people. He'd start cursing when one walked by us on the road or showed up to work in the field. I hated his attitude, but the one time I tried to talk to him about it he laughed in my face. I never knew what he would do if a Negro was around, and it was hard to avoid toiling side by side with them if you were picking tobacco in our part of Virginia.

Toward the end of summer, Aaron began to make an effort to work more steadily, perhaps realizing we'd need a sturdy roof over our heads come winter. After a few months when he'd had regular work, we were able to rent a halfway decent little two-room house, and I managed to scrape together enough money to buy a few cheap dishes and some household items. That whole following year, he seemed to be more able to balance drink and work so that he wouldn't get fired. I think he knew that he had to do better with a child depending on us.

Occasionally when he was drinking he would hit me with his fists or kick me, but I had learned to gauge when he was going to find liquor—on Wednesdays and Saturdays, for the most part—and I'd stay away from the house with Joshua, going on vegetable-foraging missions, until eight or nine o'clock at night. At times I'd consider going back home to Mother and Sibby, but Aaron seemed to sense when my resolve to leave was strengthening and he'd choose that moment to say something sweet or act tender. He could still sway my emotions enough to make me feel he loved me deep down; to make me feel he needed me.

Now that Joshua could walk, Aaron seemed more interested in him. Once in a while he'd bring home a baby rabbit or squirrel from a nest in a field where he was plowing, and Joshua would delight in stroking the small furry bundle. The next day he'd cry when we had to let it go back to the woods, and Aaron would promise to find another.

At dinnertime, when Aaron would sit down at the table, Joshua would come over to him and pluck at his clothes or grab his hand. Aaron would wrestle with him a bit or jiggle his arm.

—Daadaa, Joshua would say, wearing the big grin that melted my heart.

—Whodaa? Aaron would say, making Joshua laugh.

He never stayed around for very long to play with Joshua, but every time he'd show the slightest bit of interest in him, my hopes would rise.

I was happy to have been in one place for a whole year and not moving and shifting about constantly from place to place. I had learned to throw a few meals together so Aaron didn't complain as much about my cooking, and Joshua was a pure pleasure to me. I had never thought I'd have a baby, me with my clubfoot, so I felt doubly blessed. When Joshua opened his sleepy eyes in the morning and smiled at me, I felt my spirit soar. And his soft little voice learning to say *mama* was the sweetest sound in the world. His efforts at crawling, and later walking, made me so proud. At last I was a mother, something I'd never thought I could be. With this realization my heart would swell in my chest like a dove stretching its wings.

Around this time, I got my first letter from home. I don't know how Mother tracked me down, but it was addressed to the farmer's wife at the house where I'd had Joshua, and it had been written over a year ago. Somehow the letter had made its way here to me. Mother's note said:

Dearest Cora,

I regret that I must tell you by mail that your father has died. He suffered a stroke while walking home in the hot sun on September 28th and fell where he stood. He was not discovered until the next morning by one of Man Murfree's hired men. We have had his burial and are now mourning his loss. It has been ever so hard since he has gone. We are struggling to keep body and soul together, and we all miss your father terribly.

I hope that you are well, and that you will come home to see us. I trust that you have not gotten yourself into any trouble. Remember that the Good Book says,

For this my son was dead, and is alive again; he was lost, and is found.

Now that your father is gone, we dearly need help with the farm and Luke. There is more work than your sister and I can manage, even though WillieEd does what he can. I hope you will take this into account and return home soon.

Mother

With trembling fingers I unfolded the second note, wadded into a corner of the envelope.

Dear Cora,

I'm writing this fast as Mother forbid me to write you. The old devil has gone and good riddance. Things would be fine if you came home, no matter what you have done. Mother cannot manage for herself and I don't know how much longer I can stand it here. I miss you every day

—S.

I reread both letters again and then crumpled them into my apron pocket. Father dead and gone for over a year! I couldn't believe it. What a wonderful freedom for Mother, even though I couldn't tell it from her letter. But she would never write something like that; she'd feel it was un-Christian to say anything bad about someone who'd died, particularly her own husband. I wondered what Sibby's note had meant. *Things would be fine, no matter what you have done.* . . . The more I thought about it, the more her words rankled. And Mother quoting the prodigal son at me. It seemed as if they all believed I'd come crawling back, begging for their forgiveness.

Yet they had no idea what I was doing; for all they knew, I could be earning good money as a secretary or a teacher somewhere! It hurt me that they imagined me in some pitiful state, although in reality that was closer to the truth. Then it occurred to me that if they'd addressed the letter to the farmer's wife, they must have heard something about me living in the barn with Aaron. Maybe they even knew I'd had a baby there. Perhaps one of the farmer's hired men had been in Gower County, and had talked about us to someone Mother or Sibby knew. I cringed at the thought of how that tale must have been told.

I pulled out Sibby's note and read it once more. Why would Mother have forbidden Sibby to write to me? And what did she mean, she couldn't stand it anymore? It sounded as if Mother and Sibby were getting on each other's nerves. I could see the two of them arguing, Sibby chafing at the bit to go out with Charlie, or perhaps other boys if she'd tired of Charlie by now. With Father gone, I imagined Mother would have a time reining Sibby in. But what did Sibby think, that I was going to come home and simply take her place so that she could cut loose and get married? I had my own family now, my own child. For the first time ever, I was indignant about something Sibby had done. Why would she assume I'd want to give up my life and come back home to be a nursemaid to Mother, WillieEd, and Luke—so she could begin her own life?

The more I thought about it, the angrier I got. Finally I tore a corner from a bag of flour and wrote on the back of it:

Dear Mother, WillieEd, Sibby, and Luke,

I was glad to hear from you, and of course sorry to hear about Father. I imagine this has been a very trying time for you.

I am doing well and plan to pay you a visit as soon as I can.

Love to everyone,

Cora

The next time I walked to town with Joshua, I posted the letter. Only after I had mailed it did I realize they would know where I was living from the postmark on the envelope. Oh well, I told myself, if they want to track me down here, so be it. They could see that I was doing all right and had a fine son. Depending on how things were going with Aaron, perhaps then I'd decide to come back home with them.

For several months after I'd sent the letter I expected Mother or Sibby to show up at my door, and whenever mail came, my heart pounded. But no one came to our house, and no letters of pleading or rebuke arrived.

It was when we'd been in our new home for about a year and a half that I made my mistake. Joshua was a little over two, and I was just so proud of him, it loosened my tongue. I was in the general store buying some cornmeal and a few other items that we needed when a lady approached and asked me all kinds of questions about Joshua—how old he was, where we lived, what his favorite foods were, and so on.

I guess it was out of pride, because unlike my normal reticence, I answered her questions and even gave her more. I told the lady where I came from, how my family hadn't seen Joshua yet but I hoped someday they would, that Aaron's family was from Potters Creek. I didn't go into a lot of detail about Aaron; I just acted like he kept so busy working that we hadn't had time to go see either of Joshua's grandparents.

The lady was so curious and friendly that it was hard to resist her. In the end she asked if she could visit us. It was then that I came to my senses and said my husband was so busy, I didn't think we could have company right now. But I appreciated it. In a very kindly manner she said that she understood, and went on her way.

Later that week I discovered my mistake. Two government men came to the house when Aaron wasn't there and told me they were doing a census. They asked me a lot of questions about where Joshua was born, how old he was, where Aaron worked, where my parents lived, and so on. Something about their manner bothered me, but I felt I had no choice but to provide them with answers. The men finished with their questions and gave me a sealed letter for Aaron. Then they left.

It turned out Aaron had applied for the dole, saying his wife was crippled and mentally unstable to boot, and couldn't take care of our son. He'd said that both our parents weren't living, so he had to stay home to take care of Joshua, and therefore couldn't work. He'd been using the dole money to buy drink, and then occasionally working for a local farmer for extra cash to keep us fed.

Apparently it was his saying that I was unhinged that tipped the government man in Aaron's favor. He felt sorry for him, and decided to let him collect a check every other week, rather than just once a month as was usual. The lady I'd met in the store was this man's wife, and he'd described Aaron's plight to her. When she met me and I used Aaron's name and told her where we lived, she realized that I was the person her husband had described, but that I was certainly not insane and could take care of my child quite well on my own. That shot down all of Aaron's lies. The letter explained all this and stated that he shouldn't expect any more checks from the government, and that he now owed back all the money he'd collected so far, for many months.

At the time, I didn't know what was in the letter, as I dared not open it. I had no idea what the men were there for, or how it would affect us. Had I only opened that letter, perhaps I could have just run away with Joshua then and saved us so much trouble later on.

When Aaron came in that afternoon, I handed him the letter. He read it quickly and began shouting.

—Goddammit! What did you tell them? You've messed up my dole money, you idiot! Did you tell them I was able to work? Who have you been talking to?

Suddenly I put it all together. For a moment I saw the

woman's hateful, smiling face. I hurried Joshua out into the yard and then went back inside to face him.

—It was an accident, I began, trembling. I'd never seen Aaron so furious. —A lady in the store was asking me some questions about Joshua, and I—

—You what! Aaron grabbed my shoulders and shook me, hard. —You told her what!

—I—I told her that he was two years old, where we were from. She asked what you did, and I told her farm work. She just asked a few questions!

He started slapping me back and forth across the kitchen.

—I didn't know! How was I supposed to know you were on the dole! I screamed, trying to avoid his huge hands. But he was everywhere. He bloodied my mouth with his fist, then grabbed the broom handle and hit me about the head with it. I yelled at him to stop, but could not escape him in the small room. I didn't want to run outside because I didn't want Joshua to see him hitting me.

—You idiot! You've ruined it now! How did you think I could afford this house, pitching hay? Now you've gone and ruined it! he screamed.

Joshua was crying outside the door to come in, but Aaron did not relent. He grabbed the iron skillet from the stove and hit me with it, then pushed my hands into the hot embers in the oven. I screamed again that I hadn't known, trying to get my hands free, screaming how could he blame me when he didn't tell me? But Aaron just cursed at me. Finally I broke away from his grip and ran into the other room. He cornered me, knocked me down to the floor with a cuff that swung my whole body around, and started kicking me. I tried to stay conscious so I could get Joshua inside when it was over, but at some point I eventually passed out. I believe he kicked me for a long time after that.

When I awoke it was the middle of the night. I felt as if I was on fire. My hands had blistered terribly, and my whole body seemed to be an open running sore. I was lying naked in the middle of the bed, and Aaron was sitting beside me. I tried to close my eyes again quickly, but it was too late; he had seen me open them.

A candle was burning on the floor next to the pallet, and tallow was smeared all over the bedcover. I guessed that he'd been burning me with the hot wax.

—I have a little surprise for you, he said, slurring his words. At some point he must have gone out to get something to drink.

—Where is Joshua? I croaked. My bottom lip was cut, and I tasted the warm curdle of my blood.

—Never you mind. You just think about what I'm doing now.

He reached down to the floor and held up the candle. I was so broken and tired I almost didn't care what he was doing. I only wanted to know if Joshua was indoors, or roaming around frightened outside in the dark.

—Where is he? I asked, starting to rise. I had to stop to catch my breath.

—You're not going anywhere, Aaron said, pushing me back down onto the bed. —You just hold still. I'm going to take care of your running off at the mouth right here and now. Now if anybody asks you any more questions, you aint going to even hear them.

He picked up the candle, grabbed my head, and twisted it to the side. Pain shot all over my face, and blood from my cut lip ran down my neck. I lay still, awaiting a blow. Instead, a searing began in the middle of my head, and I realized he was letting the hot wax drip into my ear. I screamed and tried to get away, but as always he was much stronger than I.

The sensation in my ear was unimaginable. He held me there for some time, writhing, and then turned my head to the other side. I screamed again as the hot wax dripped into my other ear, scalding what felt like the center of my being. I screamed and cried, but now I could not hear myself. I could not hear a sound I made, and eventually I stopped making any noise altogether.

The next morning we left the cabin and eventually wound up right outside Tarville, a dusty little town about ten miles from the North Carolina border, where we are now. Every so often Aaron checks my ears, and every few weeks he pours candle wax into them again to make sure I cannot hear. Once in a while, when he is digging out the old wax and putting in the new, I hear noises, but I cannot tell if they are coming from me or from outside of me. I have no idea if I have any hearing left, or not.

Sometimes he fashions the earplugs from wax ahead of time and lays them on my pillow. He knows I will put them in because it is much less painful to push the soft, malleable wax into my ears than to have the scalding tallow poured in straight from the candle.

—Your silencers are waiting for you up there, he'll grin.

He told me before we left that I was not to speak to anyone in the place we were going to, nor act as if I understood what anyone was saying, even if I could hear a little bit. I remember him mouthing the words slowly, the grits he was chewing like white ashes on his tongue.

—What about Joshua? I asked, unable to believe what he was telling me. —Can't I talk to him?

Aaron shook his head. —Far as I'm concerned, you're a deaf-mute now, he said, again speaking slowly so I could read his lips. —And the boy can just think that too. I don't want his head filled with any foolishness of yours.

—But how long are you going to do this to me? Why don't you just let me go back home? You don't need to keep me here, I said, trembling and crying.

—I'll keep you as long as I want, he replied. —You're going to stay put right here and see after me as long as I want you to.

—It was only an accident. You don't have to plug up my ears. I wouldn't do anything like that again.

—I'm makin sure of that, Aaron said. —You won't have the chance to.

The first few times he filled my ears with the hot wax, I tried to plead with him, but he has completely turned against me. Something in his mind has twisted, and cannot be made straight. To his way of thinking, I am now not to be trusted, one of the worst qualities in a woman, he says. He won't listen to me begging him to stop, and when I try to talk to him, he hits me and tells me to shut up, that I got myself into this situation and I'll remain quiet as long as he likes me to.

I hope that one day he will tire of me completely and let me leave with Joshua. But for some reason he wants to keep me here, under his control, where I am available to him for cooking and bedding and for venting the rage in him that drink unleashes.

Chapter Eleven

—The men are coming at seven o'clock, Aaron says, facing me squarely and moving his lips carefully to be sure I can read them. While at first it was hard to read lips, now I am very good at it. But I always act slower than I really am around him because I don't want him to know how well I can interpret. Even half of a sentence is usually enough; most people around these parts are slow talkers anyway. The wax he puts in my ears keeps me from hearing anything, and I don't get much chance to work on my lipreading except at church, since Aaron doesn't say much to me. But Joshua is three now and is speaking more, and that's good practice.

It's after five, and I've got the corn boiling, the potatoes stewing in lard and stinking with onions the way Aaron likes them, and a piece of pork that came from God knows where hissing in the fryer. Aaron's made his usual pronouncements about what a bad cook I am, how I can't do anything right and how I'd better not ruin this piece of meat or he'll knock me into tomorrow, even if the men are coming. Nary a one of them hasn't given his own woman a black eye or two, he says, and I'd have to agree with that.

This is a rough bunch, not like the men from church.

They show up in their overalls, smelly and hot, and start drinking before the food's set down. I often wonder what the churchfolks would think if they knew Aaron belonged to this group, but maybe they're members of their own secret sects. I have to believe any other gathering would be better than this. But that's Aaron's specialty, to pick the worst of the lot and throw in with them.

Aaron seems more jittery than usual, so tonight's meeting must be important in some way. I can't imagine what these grown men see in getting together once a month just to gab, for all the world like a group of gossiping women. There's Ed Bean, whom I disliked from the start because of the way he eyeballed my walk, and Larry Thrush and Catwaller Jones. There's Merris Coombs, who always has fishhooks stuck into his overalls bib, and Timothy Wellridge and Perkinson Bailey. Thomas Jones, Sam Jones, and Carlson Wellridge. And a few more stragglers who come and go in the dark and whose names I don't know.

I hate these meeting nights because if it's at someone else's house, Aaron comes home in a black mood and takes it out on me. If it's at our house, I have to cook for the lot of them. Not being much of a cook, it's hard to know what to make or how to time it. If the food gets done too early and becomes cold or gets burned, Aaron is furious.

He seems to want to impress these men in the worst way, worse even than the men at Christ on the Cross Baptist that he worked so hard to join. The letter he pretended was from our "former church" to move our membership was a good one, I have to admit. Even if he did spell *exemplary* wrong. I didn't point out his mistake, but no one at Christ on the Cross seemed to notice it. They embraced him as a fellow pew-warmer on the spot, just like he was their long-lost brother.

I believe Aaron thought he'd have it easier if he joined a congregation when we moved to Tarville. Maybe he thought they'd be handing out jobs where you didn't have to sweat. But if he did, he was mistaken. He gets hired to hand and pick, like anyone else on two feet when tobacco's in season, but nothing much beyond that for the rest of the year.

I poke the piece of pork with a fork tine once more and then go into the back room, where Joshua is playing with his pinecones. I stretch my arms out to him, reach under his arms, and lift him onto my hip. This motion almost makes me lose my balance, but I like holding him, and I'm going to do it for as long as I'm able.

—Hmm*hmm*hmm, I hum, my voice going up in the middle and then down again, which is his signal that it's time to go to bed. I carry him up the plank steps just as he begins to protest, so Aaron can't hear. I don't want anything to set him off tonight.

As I reach the top of the stairs, a wave of heat stifles me like a heavy blanket thrown over my head. Even though I keep the windows wide open, it is hot as hellfire up here. Joshua clings to me, clutching my neck with both arms. My shoulders sweat from the contact with his skin. I breathe in his little boy scent, holding him tighter. He looks into my eyes and smiles.

—Mama, he says. —Not time for nighty yet.

He still waits for an answer sometimes. I just smile and kiss his forehead.

—Hmm*hmm*hmm, I hum again, and set him down on his pallet to change him into his nightshirt.

—Not time, Mama, he says again, tugging at my sleeve.

When we first moved here it took him weeks before he'd stop looking at me for an answer, but now he mostly talks to me from habit, knowing I won't reply. These are the times I long the most to speak.

—Hmm*hmmhmm,* I hum insistently, slipping his arms through the sleeves.

The cloth is worn soft from so many launderings, and is frayed almost bare at the elbows. I'm going to have to come up with something else for him to sleep in once the summer's over. The wind blew mightily through the chinks in the wall last winter. I can't imagine how I'll get anything from Aaron to trade for wool for new long johns, but somehow I'll have to manage it. Aaron is still insisting Joshua wear things he outgrew last year. I've cut and mended and added on, but at a certain point he'll have to have new clothes or he'll be walking around in rags.

Joshua stops struggling and lets me pull the shirt over his head. I settle him on the pallet with his favorite wooden stick, the one I dyed red with berries, and let him chew on that, rubbing his back until he falls asleep. When he was younger I'd make him a sugar teat with a lump of sugar in a rag, dipped in milk, for him to suck on, but it's been a long time since we could afford sugar. I always like to make sure he's fast asleep before I go downstairs. Another way Aaron claims I'm coddling him, but I don't want Joshua waking up and coming in on some of our nighttime scenes. I hope I'll be able to put that off as long as possible.

I stumble going down the steps and stand still for a minute, making sure I didn't wake him up. Joshua doesn't appear in the doorway, so I know he's still dead to the world. I continue clumping down until I make the bottom rung, and there's Aaron frowning at me.

—tough as shoe leather, he says, indicating the pork.

Now I'm in for it.

—Hahahmm, I moan, and take a step toward the stove.

Maybe I can soften it up with some water and salt. How I wish Mother had taught me something about cooking! A clout to the back of my head sends me crashing into the hot stove. I hit my chin on the pot cover and grab hold of the oven door to balance myself. The heat sears my hand. I had to use a lot of wood in the old iron cooker to get it hot enough for the pork.

Slowly I straighten myself and open the pot. I have to hold on until I regain my balance, even though it burns. I know it will antagonize Aaron more if I turn to look at him. He likes it when he can hit me from behind without my knowing when it's coming. I try to stiffen my back in case he decides to get me in the spine, a favorite place for his well-aimed kicks, and brace myself against the stove. Nothing comes and I uncover the pork and clump over to the bucket and get a dipperful of water, go back to the stove, and pour it into the pot. The meat does indeed look vile, and if I cared anything about the coming company I would be embarrassed. But I do not.

The room feels empty. I turn around and see that some of the men have come into the yard, and Aaron has gone out to greet them. They are slapping each other's backs in a vulgar way and seem to be congratulating themselves on something. I shudder to think what that might be. Maybe Merris Coombs caught a big catfish down by the river. I know from my covert lipreading that he prides himself on finding the best spots to fish.

I pour the boiled corn into a chipped bowl and stir the potatoes and onions one more time. At least this seems to have turned out all right. If they drink enough before they eat, they won't notice that the pork is tough. It could be pig slops as far as they could care, once they've gotten far enough along into their jars. It has always surprised me that such a

clear and innocent-looking liquid could cause so much meanness and crazy behavior. But I guess that's one reason they
like it so much. Father certainly did.

I dress the pork up with some turnip greens, and it looks
edible. I dab a little more water on it with a dishrag and rub
on more salt to flavor it. I take the dish outside to a plank
balanced on two rocks, which is the table they will serve
themselves from. More men have come, and they are standing around in groups unscrewing their mason jars. Good, let
them drink themselves silly before they start to eat.

I turn to go back into the kitchen. At least I can't hear
their gibes, although I can imagine what they are saying about
my limp. I'm sure Aaron has made it known to them he
married me purely out of pity—another fiction of his that
I've seen him mouth at Christ on the Cross—so they'd feel
no compunction about mocking me. I'm sure he's told them
all kinds of spiteful things about me, that I'm a bad wife,
can't cook worth heck, possibly that I'm crazy. I know I
sound and probably look crazy too. It's been a long time
since I've seen my face, but I imagine it's not a pretty sight.
Aaron has a prohibition against mirrors, which actually suits
me fine. And of course, I'm not really even his wife.

I go back into the kitchen and pick up the bowl of corn.
I hate making so many trips outside, but with my unsteady
gait I can only manage one dish at a time. No one tries to
speak directly to me, which is good. Aaron is involved in
what looks to be a heated discussion with Sam Jones and
another man, one I don't know. He's waving his arms about
and opening his mouth wide, teeth flashing in the waning
sunlight.

Soon they'll light a fire in the pit in the yard. They will
sit on the ground holding their plates in their laps and drink
until they drain their jars dry. Then the discussion will be-

come even more animated. Sometimes two of them get into a fight, but they are always pulled apart by the rest. I wish someone would smack Aaron good upside the head, but so far that hasn't happened.

I make it back up the steps and into the kitchen for the last dish, the potatoes reeking with onion. I'm so sick of the sight of the food that I don't even bother scooping a little into a bowl for myself. I'll go upstairs with a piece of bread and a raw potato; that will be enough supper for me. I pick the heavy platter up and sidle over to the door. This one is tricky, but I manage to make it down the steps without spilling any of it and over to the plank.

When I look up, I accidentally meet Ed Bean's eyes.

—help you with that, he says.

I set the platter down, his hands holding the other side of the plate, and straighten my back without looking up at his face. I'll pay later for any kindnesses any of them show me, so I don't want to encourage it. I used to be afraid of Father, but I must say Aaron far outdistances him in imagination and cruelty.

I make it back up the kitchen steps without incident and without anyone noticing me. I look out the dirty windowpane and see them hunkering over the food, filling their plates greedily and sitting down on the grass. Aaron drags a couple of pine branches over to the pit and lights them. I hope the sap spits in the heat and pops on their bare arms. Soon he'll have a roaring blaze going and their real meeting will take place. At times I've been tempted to try to decipher what they're saying purely out of curiosity, but the punishment would not be worth the prize if I got caught spying.

I cut myself a dry piece of bread and begin to peel a potato. I feel the floor vibrate behind me, and suddenly there's a hot body leaning into my back. I catch my breath and whirl around. It's Sam Jones, groping at me with his huge meaty hands.

—shouldn't wear such a purty dress if you don't—

—Mmm! I protest as loudly as I can. I try to push him away, but he comes back at me, scissoring my bad leg between his legs. I can't help crying out in pain.

—real wildcat underneath them—

I realize I haven't dropped the paring knife. I twist my wrist around and scrape it along his arm. He opens his mouth wide and jumps back. Suddenly Aaron is at the door, squinting his eyes at me.

—the salt? he says. He looks at Sam. —Need something? All the food's out there.

Sam shakes his head and blunders out the door. Aaron comes over to me, but I scurry around the table to avoid his cuff and grab the salt cellar out of the pantry. I thrust it at him and he grabs my wrist hard.

—around. May need more—

I shake my head adamantly and point upstairs. I don't want to stay down here any longer. Aaron gives me a hard stare and takes the salt out of my hand. He whirls around and darts out the door. Hands shaking, I grab my piece of bread, leaving the half-peeled potato on the table, and go up the stairs fast despite the pains shooting all the way up my leg.

I'm being forced into a huge dark gunnysack. There are scratchy branches in the sack, the pine needles scraping against my legs. I fight the men who try to put me in the sack, but it's no use; I feel their hot breath on me and see their grumbling. They are angry because the pork was tough. They want to hang me over the fire in the sack, cook me, and then eat me. I twist and turn, but the drawstring is drawn tightly around my neck. I see the faces of Sam Jones, Ed Bean, and Merris Coombs, who has a fishhook stuck in his tongue. I struggle and then I awaken.

Aaron looms over me in the dark, pushing into me. His hands squeeze my neck, tighter and tighter. A high thin scream comes out of my mouth. I can't get my breath, I claw at his hands, but they continue squeezing the breath out of me. His heavy weight on my chest, thrusting, thrusting. His toenails scratching my legs. He stops for a minute, grinning at me insanely, and releases my neck.

I take in big gulps of night air, sweet and cool. He grabs my face roughly and turns my head to the side. He pokes a finger into my ear, then turns my head to face him again.

—Sometimes I wish I couldn't hear everything, he sneers.

—Lot of things just aint worth hearing.

I try to breathe softly, hoping he'll get off of me and go to sleep.

—You got your breath? he asks, his lips slurring over the words.

Slowly I nod my head, afraid to take my eyes off his face.

—Good.

He smiles, and suddenly his hands are around my neck again, tighter than before. The thrusting starts. I am choking, I am drowning. This time I struggle desperately until at last I pass out.

Chapter Twelve

I awaken before the sun comes up and go downstairs to light the oven. Aaron will sleep until noon if I'm lucky, and I'll be able to feed Joshua breakfast and get him out of the house before Aaron comes down with his thundering headache. If I knew drinking something gave me a headache like that, I'd avoid it like the plague. But that's too much common sense for Aaron and most men I've observed.

I step out into the dewy yard. Nettie, our old mule, nickers at me in hopes of something to eat, but we haven't had any feed for her for months, and she's had to make do with grazing weeds at the edge of the field. I stand next to her, scratching her behind her ears for a few minutes before I gather up several pine branches and take them into the kitchen. I poke them into the oven, scrape a match on the iron cooking surface, and light the fire.

I back into the table and accidentally knock a spoon off of it. Then I stand looking at the stairs for a few minutes until I'm sure I didn't wake him up. Even when he's not suffering the ill effects of drink, I try not to awaken Aaron before I've got things going. He hates coming down to a cold kitchen with no fire and no bread frying. In the better times we had eggs and an occasional piece of bacon, but it's been a long while since we had that. Our one chicken doesn't lay, or if she does, she hides them where I cannot find them. My mouth waters as I conjure up these delicacies, and I deride myself for even thinking about them.

I chew a hard rind of bread and begin scraping off the dishes from the night before. The plates are filthy, having sat in congealed grease all night. If I can get these dishes washed and set out to dry, get Joshua up and dressed and give him a piece of frybread, and put Aaron's breakfast in the frying pan for him, then we can leave the house in peace long before he wakes up.

I go out the door again and grab the bucket sitting by the back steps. I got dressed upstairs in the dark, so I haven't yet seen what's making my legs so sore. It's still very gray outside, but when I reach the rise a glimmer of sun haloes the far hill and I pull up my skirts to see. I can't hold back a shudder as I view the bite marks going up and down the inside of each of my legs, the tender skin chewed and rechewed so it's raw and sore.

I imagine this took place after I blacked out. It infuriates Aaron when I'm not awake when he's choking me. Usually I try not to faint, because if I do I'll be in more pain the next morning. One night after I passed out he took a piece of burning tinder from the fireplace in our bedroom and scored it up and down my feet so I could not walk the next day or the next. The blisters oozed and burst, oozed and burst, for weeks afterward.

I pull down my skirt and limp along the path to the spring. My neck is still sore; I can just imagine what it looks like. When I get back to the house I'll tie a piece of rag around my throat in case I run into anyone. Not that I really care anymore what anyone thinks. But Joshua might see the marks; he's getting to the age where he notices things.

Going along this path reminds me of the trail to the creek that I used to take through our woods back home. Same cold tin pail in my hands, morning light flickering on the leaves, branches tickling my face and arms and making them wet with dew. Sibby and I had so many good times at that creek, skinny-dipping in the sweltering summers. There was a big old muscadine vine that hung right above the widest part of the water. We'd make a dam with rocks and mud and strip off our clothes, then swing from the vine out over the water and splash into it. Falling buck naked into the cold water was a delicious shock.

More than once, walking home from school in April when it was already hot, we'd stop and hike up our skirts and wade in. Occasionally Sally Bowden, who lived on a neighboring farm about two miles down the dirt road from us, would accompany us. She'd always have to stop at the creek to scrub off the lipstick she'd put on at school. None of our parents would have tolerated our painting our faces, but some girls dared it once they were on school grounds, knowing Mrs. Spender didn't care.

Sally would scrub and scrub at her mouth, splashing it with creekwater. The smears of crimson made her look like a circus clown that had been left out in the rain. I had never dared to paint my mouth. When I first met Aaron, I had contemplated going into Job's store for a tube of lipstick, but never got up the nerve. Now the idea of wanting to please him in that way seems like someone in another life, and I guess it really was.

I reach the spring before I know it. I wade in and dip my bucket into the deepest part. Thin gray minnows swirl into the pail as I fill it with the icy clear water. I scoop them out with my cupped hand. The motion sends me back to when Sibby and I used to spend hours at our creek catching crawdads. We'd bring a couple of our mother's big mason jars down with us, then squat on a rock in the middle of the creek and watch carefully. After a while, you'd see a little claw or a whisker poking out from under the rock. Then an arm. Finally the whole crawdad would appear, slowly edging out from his protective cave.

You had to be very patient; the minute he saw a shadow, he'd dart back under the rock. Finally when he was out in the open water, moving quickly across the smooth sandy bottom, we'd submerge the jar and scoop the crawdad into it with our hands. One day we caught twenty-two of the little creatures. They looked just like miniature lobsters, and many times Sibby bemoaned the fact that you couldn't eat them. People did in places like Louisiana, I'd read, but our variety was too small—only a couple of inches long.

One day, I caught the best one either of us ever had: a huge black crawdad, double the size of any we'd ever seen. We named him Granddaddy and let him go reverently at the end of the afternoon. We always let the crawdads go; we wanted to keep the creek well stocked, and there was nothing to do with them at the house, anyway. But they provided hours of pure entertainment for us.

I smile at the memory, then sadden when I think of how long it's been since I saw Sibby. I heave the bucket and struggle uphill with it, then back down to the house. With my limp it is impossible not to spill some, but I get back to the kitchen with most of it intact. Thankfully Joshua is still upstairs, asleep. I put the bucket on the stovetop to heat and dip a rag into it to wipe some of the blood off the inside of my legs. My skirt is covered in beggarlice from the woods, and I pick them off and throw them outside.

Later, after I've washed the dozens of dirty dishes and fried some bread in lard, I go upstairs to awaken Joshua. He stretches, eyes still closed, and I stroke his warm back until he peeks at me. It is already hot in the dark little room, and I carry him naked but for his drawers downstairs, where he lets me dress him without protest. He wants two pieces of frybread, so I have a dry crust. Aaron always likes his breakfast just so, three pieces of frybread and a cup of chicory waiting so all he has to do is pour in the hot water. I set out Aaron's plate and cover the fry pan and wash Joshua's plate and his face and then pull his hand to indicate we are going outside. Joshua's expression brightens. He loves to do anything out of doors. He follows me out of the house and into the woods.

We take our time going to the creek, Joshua pulling on muscadine vines and examining various stones and gathering pinecones to float in the water, and me having to stop and rest whenever my foot hurts too much. I am one big ache with my throat still feeling choked and my inner legs bleeding from the bites and my clubfoot aching the way it always does in the morning. But even with the pain, it is good to be alone in the woods with a few hours of freedom before the day gets hot enough to smother. I hope that Yellow Scarf will be there today. The thought of seeing her spurs me on again whenever I falter.

The sun is shining through the trees, and the creekwater swirls clear, showing the pretty brown sand at its bottom. Some women have dammed up the other end with logs so that this part is nice and deep for bathing. I draw in my breath when I see a movement through the trees, but then I see an ocher blur and know it is Yellow Scarf and her children. I call her that in my mind because she usually covers her head with a yellow rag. I wave and they wave and we all approach the water.

Yellow Scarf sits down on the bank and digs her toes into the mud. Joshua peels off his shirt and runs over to her boy, Tyree, and girl, Yvonne. I have learned their names from watching Yellow Scarf as she calls out to them. Soon they are splashing around happily, Joshua's skin glistening white in the water, the others' brown faces and arms made darker by being wet.

Yellow Scarf is the only person I have run into in this new community who doesn't seem bothered by my infirmities. She seems to accept me with nothing but friendly incurious interest. And there is added safety in the fact that since she is a Negro and lives in the Bottoms, no one Aaron knows would hear that I take Joshua to the creek to bathe. He'd have a hissy fit if he knew I spent time around any other women—particularly a colored woman. Ever since my mistake with the government lady where we used to live, he's made sure I never have a chance to communicate with anyone else. Not that you can do a lot of communicating when you can't hear and you're forbidden to talk.

Joshua and Tyree are running up the bank and swinging on a grapevine, dropping off into the water. Yvonne opens her mouth in a giggle of delight whenever one of them splashes her. I lie back on the warm sandy bank and let the sun soak into my body through my thin dress. Yellow Scarf smiles at me and does the same.

—Nice mornin, she begins, turning her head toward me so I can see her face. She seems to know I can read her lips and interpret her words, even though I do not reply. I nod in response to her greeting. We have fallen into this pattern of communicating, where she talks and I either nod or hum acknowledgment.

—Squash are comin up fine. I got me about a dozen tomato plants gonna be ripe soon. You ever plant tomatoes? They're easy. They spring up like weeds once you get 'em going. I like me some fried tomatoes, little pepper and salt. John say I salt ev'ything, and I do. I even like salt on my cucumbers.

I nod, smiling in agreement. I've salted cucumbers, too. The bite of the salt goes well with the cool, crunchy green taste.

—You ever salted a watermelon? They's good with salt. Not cantaloupe, though. But a nice melon's tasty with a little salt. Your boy like melon?

I shrug, indicating we haven't had any. When she smiles, her face warms up and she is pretty, I think.

—have to bring you some of my melons. I got some Sugar Babies you'd think you'd died and gone to heaven when you bite into 'em. Yvonne! Don't you splash your brother, hear me? I'll tan your hide! she shouts at her little girl, who is romping around with the boys. —Kids, she sighs. —These chirren don't know how easy they have it. When I was their age, I was pickin cotton in the field, day in and day out. I remember gettin home and bein so tired, all I could do was lay down and cry.

I nod, thinking about that. I'd had my share of hard chores growing up, as we all had, but I had worked in the fields after I was thirteen, and only as a summer job when school was out. I wish I could share my experiences picking tobacco with her, to compare it to cotton, which I'd heard was harder, and to let her know I'd worked hard as a child, too. But I don't dare let Joshua see me talking.

—didn't want my chirren to have to work like I have, Yellow Scarf is saying. —I want to give them a better life, somehow, but we got to get out of the Bottoms to do that. If John gets steady work this fall we could move. I've got a cousin

down to Dry Fork that knows of a house we could have for
not much. Comes with five acres, not too rocky. I've got a
mind to go, but John don't want to leave his mama. I say,
Bring her with us! We'll have room, if we can get this house
my cousin told me about. But he say his mama don't want
to move, she been here all her life. I say, Man, you want to
get eaten alive every summer when the skeeters hatch? Just
cause you been doin it since you was little don't mean you
have to keep on doin it!

She shakes her head, tsk-ing. I see motion above me and
look up at a mockingbird that lands on a branch above our
heads. She sees my neck, which I'd forgotten to cover, and
her mouth opens wide. She motions toward my throat, her
pecan-colored forehead wrinkled in consternation. She moves
closer to me.

—Your man do that?

I nod.

—You gonna stay with him? she asks, frowning.

I nod again, and shrug.

Slowly she reaches over, as if I might be a wild animal
about to bolt, and pats my arm gingerly.

—You know where I live, right? Down there about a mile
through the woods, bottom of the hill. Big hickory tree in
front of my cabin. You ever need someplace to go, you can
come stay by me.

Tears spring to my eyes, and I turn my head as if to see
what Joshua is doing. I wait until my eyes are dry before I
look at her. She nods at me, and we both lie back on the
sand. After about an hour, the children are soaked through
and tired of playing. I motion for Joshua to follow me, and
wave goodbye to Yellow Scarf and her children. She grasps
my hand gently before she goes. All the way back to the
house, I think about her words.

When we get home, Aaron is sitting in the kitchen nursing his head with chicory coffee. I send Joshua out into the yard and, seeing that Aaron's cup is empty, pour him a refill from the boiling water on the oven. Aaron takes the cup silently and drains it in four gulps. He stands up and comes close to me. I try to edge away, but he holds my arm firmly and pulls my dressfront away from my neck. His eyes widen. I can see from his expression that he has no recollection of what he did to me last night, but he knows that he is viewing his own handiwork.

—Cora, I— Better put something on that, he says. —Want me to go to the store for some ice?

I turn away and shake my head, no. At moments like this I feel I am living with two men; one the Aaron I knew before I ran off with him, the other a demon who has overtaken the former's body. I know that drink can transform a person's nature; I also sense that Aaron's deprivations as a child have contributed much to the individual he has become. But still it is puzzling to me that someone can be so depraved in drink and then at times seem so sincerely sorry for it afterward.

I feel the vibration of his feet on the floor, and look up to see him go outside and disappear down the path that cuts through the woods.

In the afternoon, I go out to feed the chicken. We usually let her forage for whatever she can get, unless there are slops, and after last night's meeting there are. The chicken pecks up the cold leavings eagerly and circles, hoping for more. Joshua tries to pet her head, and I grab his hand to keep him from getting pecked. I try to discourage him from getting too attached to any of the few animals we've had, since most of them wind up on our table. There had been a little cat he'd liked at the place where we used to live, but one day she stopped showing up and I had a time making him understand that she wasn't coming back. Finally he'd repeat, —She goed to heaven, pointing to the sky, and I'd tell him, yes. We moved shortly thereafter.

I'd always felt close to animals growing up, maybe because I didn't have many humans to feel fond of. It was always hard when one of the animals I'd made a pet of had to be killed for food. I remember being at the barn one morning as the sun came up, the mule and the brown-and-white cow standing nearby with her calf. The cow turned to face the sun as it crept up over the trees, and the mule turned too. Together we watched the brilliant golden orb spill over the tops of the trees like a broken egg. In that moment I felt at one with them, like I was an animal myself.

Then that next week Father killed the calf, and we had to listen to the cow lowing for her baby, day in and day out. Even Mother agreed it was a pitiful thing. She knew how upset we were, and chose particularly soothing passages that week from the Bible for our nightly readings. Sibby and I made a secret vow not to eat beef after that. I think she kept her promise for about a month, and I for a few months after that.

Often, Mother recited Bible verses to us during our daily chores, as well. Her favorites were from Psalms and the Book of Matthew, the story of Jesus' birth. We'd sit shelling butterbeans on the sagging back porch, and she'd prop the Bible up in the seat of a broken chair. There'd be no sound but her voice and the pinging of the beans in the tin pail. We'd sit there for hours, until WillieEd brought the cows in from the pasture for me and Sibby to milk. Mother would get up slowly and sigh, sensing that Father was close behind, wanting his dinner. Even if he'd spent the afternoon sleeping off a spell of drink, he'd eat like he'd been ploughing in the fields since sunrise. And if dinner wasn't exactly to his liking, Mother would be the one to pay.

I know that the Bible was Mother's source of strength. She used it to bolster herself, to get through yet another day. I wish I could find the same solace in reading it, but somehow I cannot. Still, it is the only book Aaron allows in the house, so I retreat into it whenever I can.

Sibby and I used to wonder why Mother put up with Father's meanness, but at least we had food most of the time. Others who didn't have fathers didn't even have that. It was a necessity of survival, and she was probably afraid of what would happen if she ever did try to leave. How do you walk out of your house with four children and nothing to feed them, no place to go? I feel ashamed, now, of all the times Sibby and I criticized Mother for putting up with him. Now I understand only too well why she did.

Chapter Thirteen

Once in a while when Aaron has work that I know will take him away from the house for a while, I screw up my nerve and walk the mile and a half into town with Joshua. Although I am leery of it, Joshua loves seeing the farmers strolling around with their mangy dogs, the farmers' wives followed by hordes of their barefoot children, imploring their mothers for this or that. He loves to stand outside the feed store watching the workers haul the bags of corn and oats and seed, and to look into the windows of the general store, smeary with the wishful breath and sweaty palms of others who've peered into the panes. So on rare occasions I take him into town, whenever Aaron is sure to be out of the house and I'm able to retrieve a nickel from his overalls without his knowing it.

Today Aaron announces that he has a job to tend to. He hitches up Nettie and self-importantly leads her down the road. I know what this means; he will work for the farmer who's hired him maybe until noon or one, then start drinking with one of the other hands and never make it back to the field. He'll turn up here around three, stinking drunk and ornery as an old goat. But that's enough time for my purposes. I motion to Joshua that we are going down the road too, but in the other direction, and he skips along beside me excitedly. It absolutely delights him to go into town, and I feel I should take him, although if Aaron ever found out he'd make me suffer for my waywardness.

The sun shines in such a fine way that I feel like skipping too. As Joshua grows bigger, at times it is hard for me to keep up with him, and I am happy about that. I envision one day when he is taller than me and Aaron, and when he will take his father down a notch or two. But that is a long time off, and until then it will be up to me to do the protecting.

—We gonna buy something in town? Joshua asks, squinting up at me.

I smile and nod, catch his hand and swing it. I can feel his happiness flowing into me.

—What we gonna get? Can I have a whistle? he asks.

I make an elaborate I-don't-know gesture. The nickel in my pocket probably isn't enough for a toy, but I'll get him some kind of treat. Joshua interprets this in a positive way and hops about, swooping in to give me hugs around the knees that hobble me. I kneel and squeeze him back, then motion that we need to get on down the road. I want to be home well before Aaron returns.

—He not gonna be to town? Joshua wants to know.

I shake my head. Joshua grins in relief and lunges forward.

After an hour or so we enter the town square, me lagging behind Joshua, who is now pulling at my arm to get me to hurry over to the general store. But first I gesture that I want to sit with him in the shade to rest and to eat the lunch I have packed for us in a clean rag. He follows me unhappily to the bench under some big oaks in the center of town, a little plot of green amid the dusty streets.

Several farmers are talking over by the post office, and three horses tied to the rail switch their tails at flies. A colored woman leads her two girls into the post office, to exit five minutes later with a package wrapped in brown paper. One of the farmer's dogs begins to bark at the children, and they cower against their mother's skirt until the farmer cuffs it sharply and pulls it back down beside him.

I unwrap our lunch, dried peas and two apples, and hand Joshua his. I unscrew the cap of an old flask and give him a deep drink of water before I take a swig. The water from the flask is cool and sweet on the back of my throat. I always give Joshua lunch when we first arrive in town to keep him from hounding me for bought food from the diner. He still keeps after me for a sweet, but not as much after we've eaten.

Once in a while a car drives by, spewing brown smoke and dust and making us cough. Although most of the farmers in our area have an automobile, poor people like us don't, and a car is still enough of a sensation to Joshua to make him sit up excitedly whenever one passes.

I chew my peas slowly, savoring each one. The apple is a little peffy, gone past its prime, but it nourishes the growling in my gut and I am grateful for it. Joshua has gobbled his peas practically whole, and is jumping about while he chews his apple into a cud. He loves to keep the mauled bits in his cheeks until they puff up like a squirrel's, sucking on the juices until the last bit of sweetness is pulled out of them. Only then will he swallow the pulp and take more voracious bites. He comes over and tugs at my hand.

—Come on, let's go, he says excitedly.

I sigh and rouse myself, brushing pea husks off my apron.

We walk across the road, holding our hands over our noses to keep from inhaling the dust from a car that has just passed. A few farmers are sitting on a bench outside the entrance to the store, talking and poking big plugs of tobacco into their cheeks. One of them speaks to Joshua as we pass, but I do not catch what he says, and Joshua knows better than to reply. I carefully step around the brown puddles of spit, avoiding their eyes, and we enter the cool dry expanse of the store's interior.

My sight adjusts to the darkness after the brilliant sunshine. The smells of the assorted dry goods are tantalizing— a straw smell from the stack of hats, a clean-washed scent from the oilcloths for table coverings, with a faint, sweet odor underlying everything. It has been months since we were last here. The clerk is new to me, a balding young man with big patches of sweat under his shirtsleeves. He is talking to two women, bowing over a bolt of colored cloth. I am glad that his attention is taken. I hold Joshua's hand tightly so he doesn't dart away from me and do the unthinkable and break something I can't pay for. He squirms but lets me grip him as we head toward the candy counter.

Joshua stops just short of the glass shelves and stares up in awe. I smile at his slack-jawed look of wonder, remembering the times Sibby and I would go into Job's store and practically slobber until he served us a penny's worth of licorice or peppermint. Joshua's favorite is lemon twist, and I see that they have it in a big jar behind the pinwheels. I lift him up so he can see what is there. His eyes grow big and he points.

—Can I have some? Please? he asks, pointing to the twists.

I put him down, smiling, and nod. I tug on his arm to indicate that we must wait for the clerk. I look back and see that he is still gesturing over the bolt of cloth. Slowly I lead

Joshua around the stacks of sewing baskets and carefully folded aprons and reduced-price chipped china until we come to where the women are, finally deciding to purchase their piece of material.

The clerk nods to indicate he's seen me, and begins tying up their parcel with a piece of white twine. Joshua watches, fascinated, as he winds and winds the twine around the printed blue fabric. He looks up at me, eyes wide, wanting an explanation. I cannot attempt one here with my spurious gestures and hums, so I simply shrug. Joshua accepts this for now and hops from foot to foot, impatiently awaiting his treat.

The women step aside so the clerk can help me, and I see that one of them is from our church, although I do not know her name. She smiles at me in recognition and pats Joshua on the head. Wanly I smile back and draw Joshua to me; I don't want her attentions. The clerk looks at me in a friendly way and says

—Ma'am. What can I help you with?

This is the moment I hate, another reason I don't come to town but every so often. I feel my face darken as I motion mutely toward the candy. I look sideways at the clerk to see if he has understood. Joshua is pointing too.

—Candy! Want some lemon candy, please.

The clerk looks at him and me, then glances at the ladies uncertainly. The one who knows me from church angles her head slightly and says

—She's a deaf-mute.

His eyes widen, he nods and motions to me to follow him. Ducking my head in shame, I lead Joshua back to the candy counter, point to the lemon twists, gesture as he scoops out too many, dig out my nickel and hold it up in my sweaty palm. He slides more back into the jar until he has a nickel's

worth, five pieces, then he plucks two more out of the jar
and adds them to the lot. He opens a paper bag smartly,
tucks the mouth of the scoop into the bag and slides the
candy in, hands it to Joshua, and takes the damp nickel that
I am still offering.

Joshua plugs his mouth with the pieces like a little savage. I try to get him to wait until we have left the store, but
he is patently unable. As we are leaving, the colored woman
from the post office enters with her two girls, shyly avoiding my eyes, seeming to want to appear invisible. *I know how
you feel,* I wish I could tell her. I hurry by the farmers, conscious of my limp, and indicate to Joshua that we must go
home now. He wants to stay and sit on the bench in the
shade and eat his candy, but we don't have time for that;
Aaron may well be back early, for all I know.

Joshua stubbornly refuses to walk in the direction I need
him to go, so finally I pick him up and limp with him on
my hip until we are out of town. He is almost too big for
me to do this anymore; his weight sits heavily on my body
like a sack of meal. Close up, his teeth and lips are yellow
with foam from the twists, and he smiles the happiest smile
I've seen in weeks. I wish I could buy him sacks and sacks
of the twists, a mountainous pile of candy that would fill
the entire yard, enough to see that dazed happy look on his
face every morning of the world.

Chapter Fourteen

I am bringing the wash up from the spring. I have wrung every bit of water that I can out of it, but even so it weighs down the pail so heavily that I cannot carry it. I have to drag it along on the ground, stopping every few yards or so. I used to be able to carry a pail full of wet clothes all the way up the hill, but this past year it seems much of my strength has vanished.

Joshua has run ahead of me. When he is four or five he will be able to help me with such onerous chores, but at three he lacks the stamina or concentration to do so. And that is fine for now. Most children in these parts start working as soon as they can walk without falling, bringing in kindling wood and such, but I'd like him to have at least another year or two before I ask him to do much.

Sibby and I used to swear, when we were hauling in buckets of water and chopping wood for cookfires, that we wouldn't let our children work like dogs. Sibby was going to marry a city fellow and never see a farm again, she used to say. And I was going to be a single career woman and be independent. I wonder if she wound up marrying Charlie. They had just met when I left with Aaron, but she seemed gone over him already. I realize that I might never find out what became of her, and it leaves me with a hollow aching sadness.

As I am musing over this, I come out into the clearing of our yard. I look up and see that Joshua is talking to a man on our back step. Something in the burly shape of his shoulders is familiar, but I can't name him until I come closer and see that it is Sam Jones. A cold tingle of fear streams down my spine, but I tell myself that Aaron must be home, he must be here to see Aaron about something. When I come closer he turns and smiles, showing his blocky teeth. His bristly blond hair is thin in patches over his sunburned scalp.

—Just catchin up here with your son, he says, opening his mouth exaggeratedly. I can tell from Joshua's expression that he is shouting. It is odd that people who know I can't hear often still try to shout at me, as if the loudness will somehow help. Joshua looks at me expectantly.

—I explained to your boy that I'm an old friend of his daddy's, Sam Jones continues.

I try to indicate that Aaron is not here. Joshua knows what I am trying to do.

—He not here, he tells the man. But Jones doesn't seem interested in this piece of news.

—Waal, I'll just wait a bit. I 'magine he'll be comin home shortly, he says, and my spirits sink. How long does he think he can hang about?

—Here, let me he'p you get this washbucket in, he says, going for the pail.

I try to hang on to it, but he lifts it out of my hands and carries it over to the line I've strung up between two trees. I look down and realize that my whole dressfront is wet through. I cannot go upstairs and change with Jones here, so I cross my arms in front of me until he sets the bucket down. Then I begin hanging the clothes at the far end of the line, holding them up before my chest as I work. Joshua is playing right in sight like a good boy. I keep thinking that Jones will leave, seeing that Aaron isn't here, but he leans back against a tree, casually watching me hang the laundry. He seems to have no harmful intentions. Maybe his grabbing me in the kitchen was just a drunken act that he's long forgotten, I tell myself.

I lay the last of Aaron's tattered shirts over the line and pick up the pail to go indoors. I motion that Jones can wait here under the tree until Aaron comes; at least that's my intention. But he seems to misunderstand and follows me back to the house. I don't want to go inside with this man, but if Aaron comes home and his dinner isn't started, he'll be furious. I stand at the kitchen door, debating what to do. Jones squints up at the sky and seems to make up his mind.

—Waal, I'm gonna leave you now. You let that husband of yours know I was here, he shouts, leaning toward me.

I nod and watch him lumber off toward the road. I tap Joshua on the shoulder and gesture for him to stay in the yard while I'm cooking supper. I put some water on to boil and notice that we have only about two dippersfull left in the bucket. Sighing, I realize that I will have to go back to the spring and fetch more water if there is to be anything on the table tonight. I pour the remaining water into a jug and pick up the bucket.

Joshua has found a nest of ladybugs and is carefully holding a stick for them to climb onto before they take off into the air. I kneel down beside him and show him the bucket. He nods, knowing where I'm going, and again I motion for him to stay where he is. Dreamily he goes back to his ladybugs.

I start down the path to the spring. The late-afternoon sun

burns a bright hole in the edge of the sky, inflaming the horizon. From somewhere comes the cloying scent of honeysuckle, and past it the silty smell of mud. I stand for a moment looking at the little whirlpools that form in the water, then hike up my skirt and wade in to dip my bucket.

As I draw the water in, I see the reflection of a big white bird swooping overhead. Then a hand clamps around my mouth. I almost retch in disgust at my stupidity, imagining Sam Jones harmless. I thrum my elbows into his belly as he tries to drag me to the bank. I can feel his voice vibrating in his chest, saying I cannot imagine what. We struggle to the muddy bank, and I am thrown down on it, hard. He stands over me, calmly unbuttoning the front of his pants.

—thought you'd got rid of me, he is saying, laughing. —You little she-cat.

I try to roll away in the mud but he grabs me by the ankles and drags me uphill. My skirt gets caught on a root and is pulled up to my waist. Jones throws himself on me, his heavy arm across my neck. I can hardly breathe, and his legs thwart my efforts at kicking. Suddenly I realize that I do have a weapon. I open my mouth wide and scream,

—Let go — me! Aaron! Help! Aaron!

My throat pulses with the effort. Jones pushes up to his feet and stands there staring, breathing hard, his member dwindling to a limp dangle.

—You—you spoke! he gasps, looking as if he's seen a haint.

I sit up.

—Yessss, I hiss, baring my teeth.

—I didn't mean nothin by it, he says, backing away from me. —Don't say nothin to Aaron. Then he turns and runs off through the woods.

Dazed, I stand up, try to brush the mud off of my clothes,

gather my pail and walk home. I keep looking over my shoulder, thinking that he will surprise me again, that this is some horrible game he is playing. But he does not appear. I would feel exhilarated about using my voice again were it not for the circumstances. As it is, I only feel weary, dirty. I make it back to our yard, where Joshua is running about after fireflies, and grab his hand and lead him inside.

Thank the Lord, Aaron never does come home that night. Numbly I give Joshua his dinner, and I gesture that I fell when he asks about my muddy housedress. I get him to bed and then wash myself furiously with a wet rag, scrubbing until my skin is raw.

Chapter Fifteen

It has been several days since Sam Jones's appearance, and I realize that he will not dare to come here again. He is a coward, and now that he knows I can tell Aaron what he did, he will not dare to bother me again. Little does he guess that I would not dream of telling Aaron; if I did, I'd merely be beaten for my unwilling participation, as well as for speaking. But that secret is safe with me.

Today is Thursday, a day Yellow Scarf often comes to the creek with her children to let them bathe, and I look forward to these days when I will see her with an intensity that results in deep disappointment when she is not there. Aaron leaves after he eats his breakfast, around eleven, and I wait awhile to make sure he is really gone. Then I motion for Joshua to come along with me to the path through the woods. Joshua leaps up excitedly, exclaiming,

—to the creek, Mama? We gonna bathe?

I nod my head, hum, and smile. He grabs my apron and flips it up delightedly. I catch hold of his hand and swing it as we walk along. But soon he grows impatient with the hand-holding and is off to try to catch a grasshopper.

Even with my slow gait I have to pause every once in a

while on the path, as Joshua finds a stick he wants to draw lines in the dirt with; rolls over a big rock to see the grubs uncurling underneath; thrashes his stick into a bush, scattering its pretty purple flowers; and stops to pull some wild crocuses for me. He hands them to me with a big grin.

—I pick them for you, Mama!

I accept his gift happily. These times that we are alone are paradise. I breathe in the minty scent of the narrow pines as we walk along. The shade from the trees keeps us cool even though the sun is already high. It is the perfect morning for a bathe, and I hope mightily that Yellow Scarf will be there. Somehow it seems to me that she is my friend. I find comfort in the thought that at least I do have one friend, even if she might not consider me one.

Before we begin the descent to the creek, Joshua stops his darting about and listens.

—Mama, Yvonne and Tyree there! They comed!

I pat him on the head, motioning that he can run ahead of me. As I pick my way through the last stretch of underbrush there they are, already spread out on the creek bank, Yvonne and Tyree rolling up their pants legs. Yellow Scarf looks up from fixing one of Yvonne's braids and her face breaks into a smile. I wave and negotiate the sandy bank and help Joshua roll up his pants. The children go splashing and laughing into the creek.

—How you this mornin? Yellow Scarf asks.

I pantomime being tired.

—Me, too. Yvonne was up cryin with nightmares again. I tell you, that chile has more imagination than is good for her. She tells me she's dreamin about a monster with green hair! I never heard suchlike from any four-year-old in my life. I'm gonna remember that green-headed monster next time she won't sit still for her hair to be braided. That monster could come in kinda useful at times, she laughs.

I glance out at the children, who are dragging branches into the water to make a dam. Finger-length minnows follow the current, and waterbugs dimple the surface. When I look back at Yellow Scarf, she is reaching behind her toward a covered basket she has brought.

—Made up some biscuit this mornin, she is saying, reaching back—

I see a sizzle of movement near her hand. Before I can think I cry out

—Snake!

Yellow Scarf jumps almost straight up from where she is sitting, and I get up and move back slowly. There, behind the basket, is the light-brown curl of water moccasin. Yellow Scarf dashes up the creek and returns holding a big rock.

—Stand back! she orders me.

The children are coming up from the creek, and I herd them away from her. I want to urge her to be careful, but she has a gleam in her eyes that tells me to let her alone. She kicks away the basket, and the snake begins to move quickly toward the water. Yellow Scarf drops! the rock squarely on its back, stunning it. She picks the rock up again and chops! it down on the snake's head. Now the snake is still, but she lifts the rock back up and chop chop chop chop chop chop chop chop chop, she bends and humps at her waist, until the snake is a smashed tan pulp. Finally she stands up straight and throws the rock down. The children crowd around the snake's carcass and she looks up at me, wiping sweat from her face.

—That devil almost got me, she says, shaking her head. She goes to pick up a stick and lifts the crumpled snake on the forked branch. Joshua comes to hold on to my skirt, afraid it will come back to life.

—It aint gonna hurt anyone now, Yellow Scarf tells him. —I'ma take this thing home and let John dry it for Tyree. He likes to collect snakeskins. We've got about eight of 'em tacked up on a tree outside our cabin. You all have a biscuit and go on back and play.

The children take their bread and go back into the water, strafing the surface with branches to make sure no more snakes are around. Yellow Scarf and I seat ourselves again, after carefully looking around in the sand.

—I was just about to offer you a biscuit, she says. —Whew.

She hands me one still warm from its cloth covering. I bite into it and savor the flaky outer crust and the surprise of the tartly sweet interior. Yellow Scarf smiles when she sees my expression.

—You ever have persimmon jam before? she asks. I shake my head.

—Nice, aint it?

I nod and chew. Perhaps, in the excitement, she has forgotten that I cried out.

—Want another? she asks. She hands me the basket. As I meet her hand to take it, she says,

—So you can talk after all. Can you hear, too?

I flush, heat creeping up my neck and throat. What to tell her? I look at the children to make sure they aren't paying attention to us, then I open my mouth and croak out the first thing I can think of to say.

—My name — Cora, I say, my voice cracking. —My —sband doesn't — me to talk.

I am skipping whole words, but I don't care. It is so good to be using my voice again. I feel as if I am unwrapping myself from a long winding sheet that has embalmed my voice and hearing, my whole being.

—Oh, he don't like it. Well. And can you hear?

I shake my head, no. It is true, I cannot hear with these things in my ears. And she need not know about them. I cannot bring myself to recount that horror to her, at least not now.

—So you can't hear, but you can talk. But your old man won't let you talk, right?

—ight, I say, trying out my voice again. My own words sound strange inside my head. I can hear that I am making a noise, but it is indistinct, distorted. And of course I cannot hear Yellow Scarf, since the blockade of wax prevents that.

—What —ur name? I ask.

—Nita, she says, enunciating so I can see it clearly. —Nita Raines. And you know my kids are Yvonne and Tyree.

—Mine's Josh—a, I say, feeling my voice resonate inside my throat.

—Yes, I know his name. So—Joshua don't know you can talk?

I shake my head, no.

—Since when?

—Since we moved here, —most a year —go.

—Before then, you could talk? In your old place?

—Hmmhmmm. Husband got upset when we moved. No talking here.

I look up at Joshua again, playing with Tyree and Yvonne. I have to make sure he doesn't see me talking to Yellow Scarf; Nita, I correct myself. If he forgets and says something to Aaron about me talking, there will be hell to pay. Joshua is just too young to be trusted with a secret. Maybe when he's older, but not now.

—Well, I'm glad I found out, even if it took a snake to get you to speak. Nita smiles. —Thank you for shoutin. I hate to think what'd happened if I'd gotten bit. Those old moccasins can kill you right dead.

She shivers, then sees me watching Joshua. —You don't want your boy to see you talkin, she says.

—can't — him tell Aaron. Husband.

—Let me sit a little in front of you. That way he can't see you.

She scoots forward on the sand and indicates the basket again.

—Have some more biscuit, they's plenty there. I made up a big batch for John to take to the field this mornin. They gettin in Mr. Odell's tobacco for the next month. Then they got to work for Mr. Soames. Sometimes it seem like tobacco never end.

She wipes the moisture from her forehead. —Your man do tobacco work?

—When he can get it, I say, my voice becoming more fluid. —Lately it's been hard to find.

Nita chews the side of her lip, obviously thinking what I know, that any man who wants to work hard during tobacco season, particularly any white man, can certainly do so. Unless there's something wrong with him, or word has gotten around that he's not a good field hand.

—How old — Tyree and Yvonne? I ask. —She's about four?

—Be five next April. And Tyree is six. I had a little baby that died, before Tyree was born. Took me a long time to get over that.

Nita scoops up a handful of white creek sand and sifts it through her fingers. The sand is startlingly white against the darkness of her hands. She shakes the sand from the cracks of her fingers and scoops up another handful. The mound of sand disappears slowly through her fingers, as if a strong wind is blowing it over the roots of an old oak.

—Then I met John, and ev'ything got better. My family's from around Cheatham. I met him at my friend Sally's family reunion. He was there as a friend of her cousin. We moved here, I had Tyree and Yvonne, and we've been here ever since. Though I told you I want to move to Dry Fork, she added.

—Did you get all that, last time?

—Yes, I can read lips well. Learned from watching people in church. And Joshua knows to look — me when he talks. Do you see your folks very often?

—Naw, I don't. It's not that far, but we don't get to see them much. I'd like to see my mama, all of them. They aint seen Yvonne since she was two. John just works so hard, and I don't want to make the trip by myself. Where your peoples from?

I think for a moment. Am I telling her too much? But there is no way Aaron will find out I am talking to Nita. This isn't like what happened before, with the government lady. And it feels so good to be able to talk to someone, to be able to use words again.

Nita notices my hesitation. —Tell me if I'm gettin too nosy. John say I can talk a person's ear off.

—No, I just can't believe we're talking. Feels good. My family lives on a farm in Gower County. Not that far from Cheatham. My father died a while back of stroke. My mother lives on the farm with my brothers. WillieEd and Luke. Luke's just little, and WillieEd — about sixteen. My older sister is probably married by now. I haven't spoken to them since I left with Aaron, about four years ago. We haven't — able to travel, either, I add.

I have to catch my breath from this long speech. It is so

odd to use my voice again. I feel as if I have to relearn how
to cadence my words and breath. And it is hard to tell how
loudly I am talking since I can hear my voice inside, but not
outside of my body.

—Am I talking too loud? I ask.

—No, I can't hardly hear you, Nita replies. —Don't worry,
Joshua aint goin to see you. They busy dammin up the creek
again.

I look around her and they are still at it, piling up more
branches. Their clothes are sopping wet, but will dry off
quickly on the way home in this heat.

—Where you live? Nita asks.

—Just up the path through those woods. There's a clearing at the end of it, and we're down the road half a mile. I
don't even know who owns the house; Aaron found it when
we came. To Tarville. I hope the owner knows we're there,
I laugh. —Maybe he doesn't.

—We in the Bottoms. I b'lieve I told you. It'd be fine if
it wasn't for them skeeters. They like to eat you up alive at
night. I put nettin over the windows and doors, but still they
find a way in. You hear 'em whine and before you can cover
yourself, you've got yourself a skeetabite. John was all broke
out in whelps this mornin before he left.

—Our house is too hot. Where we are, we never seem to
catch — breeze. I'm not much of a cook, but when I do
make dinner, I just about burn up in that kitchen. I wish I
could make biscuits like yours. How'd you get them so flaky?
The best I've ever had, I say sincerely.

—Aw, they won't nothin special. You just can't mess with
the dough too much. That's the secret, not foolin with the
dough. Then when you roll it out, just do it once or twice.
You know how some women keep rollin and rollin their
dough? Don't do that, or it'll come out tough as shoe leather.

Just roll it a couple of times, then cut your biscuits. That'll make 'em flaky as can be. That, and a little dab of buttermilk. After I churn my butter I allus skim off the buttermilk right before it gets hard. Then I've got my milk for my biscuits.

I can't think how long it's been since I've had cream to churn for butter.

—Who taught you how to cook?

Nita laughs. —Didn't have no choice. My mama was workin in the fields, and we had nine comin in for dinner and supper. By the time I was eight, I had to get food on the table for all of us.

—I wish I'd learned. My mother wasn't that big a cook, and what little she did, she didn't pass along to us. My sister Sibby can cook when she puts her mind to it. Anything with a nut in it, she'll cook it and eat it. She used to love to make candied sweet potatoes with crushed hickory nuts on top. And pecan pie, when she could get pecans. We didn't have a lot growing up. We rented land to farm, but my father wasn't very reliable.

—My daddy worked hisself to death, Nita says, a frown on her face. —That old peckawood he worked for—'scuse me, but he was a mean old man, no two ways around it— just drove him and drove him til he died of it. One winter he was out breakin ground for that farmer, hadn't even paid him in a month, and still he went out ploughin. He had a bad cold and it got into his chest and that was the end of him. Broke hisself ploughin.

She frowns and looks up at the children. —Tyree, do not drag Yvonne like that! Do you hear? I'll warm up your behind good!

Nita looks at me and shrugs. —I wish they'da known my

daddy, specially Tyree. Daddy would've gotten such a kick out of him.

I can't say the same for my father, so I don't comment. I wonder what Mother and Sibby would say about Joshua. Certainly they'd love him, wouldn't they? Or would the fact that I wasn't married ruin everything for them? Sighing, I realize that this is probably true.

—I guess I'd better go back home, I say, beginning to rise. —Could you call Joshua for me?

—I'm glad I found out your secret, Nita says. —I'll see you next time.

—Next time, I say, and she calls Joshua and all three come thrashing out of the water, dripping wet, broad grins on their faces.

—Your mama's got to go, Nita says to Joshua. —And we'd best be headin home too, chirren. Tyree, you can hold that snake on the stick, but no scarin your sister, you hear?

Tyree runs to get the snake, and Nita faces me.

—You take care of yourself, and I'll see you both soon, all right?

Joshua tells her goodbye and I nod, humming to Joshua to come along. We move into the woods and uphill on the path. I take it slowly and Joshua stays with me, tired from all his playing. The sunlight through the trees dapples our skin and clothes. All the way home I alternate between joy at having a friend, someone I can safely talk to, and concern about having spoken to Nita. But through all my worry I keep reminding myself that there is no one who knows Aaron who knows her. There can be no way for him to find out that I have broken his prohibition on speaking, or that I am friendly with a colored woman.

Chapter Sixteen

I have noticed that there are different kinds of pain. Some are worse than others. There is the pain that doesn't start until three days after the blow, then hurts like the devil for a solid week. There's the nagging ache that you want to fool with, like a throbbing tooth that your tongue goes to, over and over. Then there are the soft areas with the sharp point of tension in the middle. This leaves the worst bruise, turning from deep purple to black to green to the color of tallow, but oddly enough does not hurt nearly as much as some of the other thumps and cuts.

There is the kind of pain that echoes in your brain and causes a ringing that goes on for days. I do not know if this is from my ears being plugged up, or if it is the reverberation of the blows to my head. It is horrible to have the only thing you hear to be this ringing. It goes on and on in the silence, and seems louder in the dark. Oddly enough, when I am frightened, the ringing stops, or else perhaps I just do not notice it.

The worst pain so far is the echoing ache in my heart, seeing my own son try to talk to me and not being able to respond. Unlike the other kinds, that pain does not ever lessen or go away. And the fact that now I have spoken to Nita makes it even more tempting to say something to my child.

Tonight, Aaron comes in after I've fed Joshua supper. Joshua is playing with some dried gourds that I'd given him; I know from his delighted expression that the seeds make a noise like a rattle when he shakes them. Aaron stops for a minute, takes one of the gourds out of Joshua's hand, and looks at it. He says something to Joshua, but I cannot tell what, since his back is turned to me. I watch him carefully. Although he has never tried to hurt Joshua, I don't know where his temper will lead him. Joshua glances up expectantly, knowing not to protest about his taking the gourd.

—You can have, he says, watching Aaron.

—I used to play with gourds when I was little, Aaron says, turning so I can see his lips. —Be careful not to crack them.

Joshua nods his head energetically, and it saddens me to see the wariness in his eyes. I hope that Aaron will continue the conversation, but he merely puts the gourd handle into his back pocket and goes upstairs. Joshua is so thirsty for a father, and at times I think it might help Aaron if he spent more time with Joshua. But I am so afraid of something happening when he is drunk that I quickly let that idea dissolve.

After a while I take Joshua up to bed. I notice that he has bitten holes in his covering; little ratted edges gnawed loose at various places. I hope he is doing this in his sleep, not as he is lying there awake, listening. I change him into his nightshirt.

—like the gourds, he tells me. —Me have a ball?

I nod and smile, thinking surely I can get into town at some point and buy him a rubber ball.

—a big blue one?

I nod again, stretching my arms wide to indicate how big it will be. He smiles happily.

—thank you, Mama! thank you!

I gather him in my arms and hold him, humming, until he goes to sleep. His eyes droop, flutter, then close at last. He leans back against me, his sleep so deep and innocent, his mouth open, small even white teeth showing above his still-babyish-looking lower lip, delicate blue veins scattering across his eyelids. I hold him like that for a while, smelling his boy-smell from the top of his head, feeling him breathe. It is a moment of utter peace, and I feel happy.

I ease Joshua off my lap and onto the bed without waking him. I hold my breath and go into our bedroom. The smell of wet ashes from the fireplace hits me; Aaron has poured something on them, whether water or liquor or his own urine, I cannot tell. The poker sprawls askew in the plashed soot. I should clean out the fireplace, but so far I have lacked the energy to do it all summer long.

I look at Aaron, breathing deeply on the bed. Thank God he is asleep. He has thrown his overalls on the floor on top of his mud-caked boots. A few hairs sprout from his otherwise bare chest, and his underdrawers are stained yellow. No matter how hard I scrub them, I cannot get the stains out. Luckily he doesn't seem to notice my failings with the laundry.

I ease out of my shift and try to lie down on the pallet without making a stir. Just as I think I am safely in, Aaron sits up. He reaches over to the floor and rummages in his overalls, pulling the gourd out of his pocket by its long handle.

He looks at it for a moment, musing, tapping it into his palm, running his hands up the side of the stem. Suddenly he pushes up and is over me, breathing into my face. A sharpness is pushing into my bottom. At first I think I have laid on a knife he has dropped in the bedcovers, but then I realize that one of his hands is below me, thrusting. He is pushing the stem of the gourd into my anus.

I try to squirm away, but he catches my shoulder hard with his other hand. I look up into his face, pleading.

—You hold still, you, he says, his teeth flashing in the moonlight.

Something in me gives way and the handle is sliding up into my nether parts, tearing me as it goes. Aaron pushes it hard and then slides it out a little ways, then in again, hard. I cannot help gasping as it hurts me. He takes his hand from the gourd and pushes his erect member into me. He has entered my anus with the gourd and my vagina with himself. I gasp at the evilness of it, hurting. As Aaron pushes himself into me, he reaches around again and pokes me with the gourd. I shut my eyes in humiliation, hoping he will hurry up. It seems the invasion of my body will never end.

Finally I feel him burst into me and he collapses, knocking the wind out of my lungs. He lies there, panting, as I try to get my breath back. After a few minutes he sloughs off of me and yanks the gourd out of my body. I squeeze my eyes shut but he grabs my jaw and forces me to look. The handle is rusty with my blood.

—Wash this thing off. You disgust me, he says. He shakes his head and laughs. —The things you make me do, woman.

He makes me take the gourd, then cuffs me in the head as I get out of bed to go downstairs to get cleaned up.

I tried to run away once, right after we moved here. Ever since my mistake with the government lady, Aaron's temper had spun out of control. Whereas before, when he'd have days where he was at least civil or merely ignored me, when

I could gauge his moods and avoid him when drunk; now he had become sadistic, relentlessly cruel, whether sober or intoxicated. Now he was either stopping up my ears with the painful hot candle wax or hitting me, hard. There were no more reprieves for me, and since we'd come to Tarville, he'd paid no more attention to Joshua than he would a gnat.

Finally I decided I couldn't stand it anymore. I'd long lost the anger I'd harbored against Mother and Sibby after receiving their letters, and yearned for the day I could return home to them. I merely had to muster enough courage to go, as the thought of Aaron's fury if he caught us was very frightening to me. On one hand, I found it hard to believe he'd object to our leaving, as he complained almost constantly about me—my lack of domestic abilities, my bad cooking, my ugliness—and how much upkeep the two of us required. Given all this, you'd imagine that he'd be happy to see us go, but somehow I sensed it wouldn't be as easy as all that.

I gathered up Joshua and a bundle of his clothes and walked out one day when I knew Aaron was going to be working in a neighboring farmer's field all day. I made it about four miles down the road by late afternoon, and then I had to rest. I had no idea where I was going, but I had to get away. He had hit me so hard the night before, I thought I was going to die. I really thought I wouldn't live to see my son the next morning.

When I did wake up, blood matted in my hair and my lip split and swollen, all I could think of was to escape. By the time I was four miles down the road, I was struggling, but still determined to go on. I knew he'd look for me at my mother's farm, so I couldn't go there immediately. I figured maybe some kindhearted farmer's wife would take us in when it got to be nighttime, or I'd find a barn to shelter us, as I'd done so many times when I was first with Aaron.

I sat resting by the side of the road, Joshua asleep on my lap. My legs ached from carrying him so far. I must have been in a daze, staring at my cracked shoes, when suddenly a shadow fell across my legs. I looked up and it was Aaron. I started and tried to edge away from his boots, eyeing his face to see what he would say.

—Get up and come on back, he cried. —You think you're going somewhere? You're crazy as you look. You aren't going anywhere I don't want you to go. You'd better get back home if you know what's good for you.

I wanted to ask him why he wanted us back, when all he ever did was hit me and ignore our son. I wanted to ask him why he treated me this way, what I'd ever done to him. But I knew if I tried to speak, I'd infuriate him even more. I laid Joshua on the ground and struggled to my feet, tears coursing down my face. Aaron smiled at me evilly, grabbed Joshua, and set off on the road toward home. I could see Joshua screaming in his grasp, his mouth wide open in a wail, but I couldn't keep up to save my soul.

When I got home it was pitch-dark. I went upstairs, my legs burning with the fiery pain shooting through them. My heart pounding, I looked into Joshua's room. Thank God he was there, asleep on his pallet. I examined him in the lamp-light and saw that he was not torn or bruised. Wearily I went into our room. Aaron had left the house that night, but he took it out on me later. I never had the fortitude to try to leave again, for fear of what he'd do to Joshua if he caught us.

Chapter Seventeen

Aaron has been in the field behind the house all this morning, trying to break ground for a few rows of corn. I imagine he thinks that if he does this, he will be able to make his own squeezins and not always be in need of money for drink. It is a good idea for a man more organized than Aaron, but I know that even if the corn manages to send up green shoots from the scorched earth, he will not have the time or patience to see that they are watered and cared for so they grow to maturity. Aaron is impatient, dyspeptic, choleric. He hates anything that tries his patience, and everything does try it—me, Joshua, the dry barren earth, the farmer he works for occasionally, and Nettie, our broken old mule.

The sun beats down on the parched field. The reddish mud has crusted over many times, and is very hard ground to break. Nettie is feeble and tired and does not want to be pulling the plough through this tough clay under the merciless sun this hot morning. She pitches her head from side to side, trying to rid herself of the blinders that Aaron thinks she needs. I believe they only make her worse about staying in the row, but he always puts them on her, hot as it is. Sweat makes dark runnels down her sides; I can see them

all the way from the backyard where I am hanging up laundry that I've just pounded clean at the creek. If I wash Joshua's
shirts once more they will fall apart in my hands, they are
so old and frayed. I sewed them out of Aaron's old shirts,
so they were already worn when he got them. Now they are
almost transparent from wear.

Joshua races around the yard happily. At least I can be
thankful that living with Aaron hasn't ruined his spirits yet.
He leaps and bobs, brandishing a crooked tobacco stick, now
riding it as if it's a horse, now using it as a spear. His brown
curls fly free in the air as he chases and whirls. He has just
learned how to jump, and he does it over and over, gleefully. He looks up at the sky and shouts, proclaiming his
own wild energy. I wish I could hear his cries.

I look toward the field again to see Aaron pick up a big
rock from the ground and start clubbing Nettie about the
face with it. She is tossing her head and kicking, and I see
she has stepped out of the traces at the end of the row. Aaron
hits her repeatedly, and blood starts to flow from a cut above
her huge brow. Now he drops the rock and strides off into
the woods. I hope he is going away for several hours. Perhaps he will drink enough to pass out and be gone until the
wee hours of the morning. He has been doing that lately,
once a month or so, and it is a blessed relief when he does.

I go over and take Joshua's arm as he is whirling around
with his stick, and motion for him to stay in the yard. I pick
my way through the brambles and clumsily walk across the
burnt earth to where Nettie is standing in a stupor, the cut
on her head bleeding profusely. I pull off the halter with the
blinders and her big brown eye rolls up at me, blood dripping into it. I take the corner of my apron and try to sponge
it off, then unhook her harness from the plough traces and
lead her back to the yard. Joshua runs up and says,

—wrong with Nettie, Mama?

but I just indicate for him to stay there. I go inside and get a bowl of water and a rag and come back out and clean Nettie's wound. Then I change the dressing on her hind leg where Aaron kicked her last week. The cut on her leg is still oozing pus. I worry that the infection will worsen in the heat with the horseflies and bluebottles feasting on it, and that she will die. We will be in serious trouble if she doesn't survive because Aaron has been using the fact that he has his own mule to get work. The farmers like it when you show up with your own work animal, he says. Besides all this, I like Nettie, and feel we are comrades in our suffering.

I take off the rope that I have led her with and remove the harness from her back. She kneels slowly and rolls in the dirt of our yard as Joshua and I stand there and watch. Then she gets to her feet and shakes the dust off her body. Joshua and I are covered in a red film, but we don't care. I motion to him that we will take her to the creek, and we head down the shaded path to the water.

I remember Mother watching a farmhorse roll after having been hitched to a plough all day. They took off her harness and she rolled in the dirt and Mother laughed and said, —That must be how Bessie Myers feels when she takes her girdle off after church.

It was one of the few jokes my mother ever made, and Sibby and I nearly died laughing from it.

The creekwater is blessedly cool. Nettie wades in fetlock-deep and takes long, thirsty slurps with her rubbery lips. I drop her lead rope and let her graze on the grass on the far bank while Joshua rolls his pants legs up and wades in. He splashes a little water at me and I smile and splash him back. Joshua thrusts both hands in and up and I am soaking wet. The water dripping down my face and dressfront feels heavenly in the heat. I wade in farther and we splash each other until we both are drenched. Nettie stands gazing placidly at us as if she thinks we've both lost our minds. I point at her and Joshua giggles—I can see his shoulders shake as he laughs. He splashes Nettie too, and the poor old thing stands there and lets the water trickle down her sides.

Finally the horseflies set upon us in earnest and we must go. When we get back to the house with Nettie, Joshua helps me look for a patch in the yard where there is a little grass, and we tie her up. The yard is nearly grazed out, the grass so short she can hardly get any up, but still she tries, for hours on end.

We have a new hen, which I imagine Aaron stole from a neighboring farm, but I don't ask. I catch Joshua's shirtsleeve as he hurtles past and motion to him that it's time to check for eggs. He leaps in excitement, and I indicate for him to walk toward her quietly.

The hen always sleeps on the drooping branch of a struggling oak that provides us with a pitiful bit of shade for the yard. I keep hoping she will drop an egg, although what she would use to sustain such a production I cannot imagine, other than the insects she manages to swoop down on. She certainly isn't being fed cracked corn the way she must have been at her former residence, and Aaron doesn't show any signs of buying any for her. Nettie's ribs are more obvious every day, and I worry that unless we get some feed for her she will die of starvation, much less from the infection. But Aaron isn't one to believe in coddling the animals.

We sneak up on the hen as she is roosting, her scat spattered all over the tree branch and ground beneath. Her head remains tucked upon her breast and I see, wonder to behold, an egg peeking out beneath her dirty lower feathers. Carefully I place my hands on either side so it cannot roll

off, and shake the limb. The hen flutters up and I capture
the egg, still warm from its nesting place. I wave it at Joshua,
who of course wants to carry it, and he follows me into the
house. Aaron is nowhere to be seen, so perhaps I will have
time to boil it for Joshua so he can have a rare treat.

Just as I am placing the cut-up egg on the table to cool,
I see a flash of color through the window, in the corner of
the yard. I go to the doorway and it is Nita, holding a cro-
ker sack in each hand. I step outside and she drops the sacks
and smiles at me.

—Got some fine 'maters and squash, too much for us, she
says, speaking nice and slow and looking straight at me.
—Thought you might could use some.

I nod and smile, nod and smile, indicating that Joshua is
in the kitchen behind me and I cannot speak to her. I will
thank her the next time I see her at the creek. No one in
this community has brought us a meal or a sack of anything,
so this is a rare kindness. But perhaps I can blame that on
Aaron; he is capable of telling people we lack for nothing,
out of pride. Or perhaps he has told them all I'm crazy and
to stay away from me.

—You makin out okay? she asks.

I nod again. I wave my arms to indicate how much I appreciate the bounty. The tomatoes have heated up in the sun
and smell deliciously red.

—I'ma be goin. See you down at the waterhole, Nita says,
and waves her arm as she walks off.

Only after she is gone does it occur to me that I didn't
warn her about coming here. The thought of what Aaron
might do if he saw a colored person in our yard is too frightening to contemplate for long. The next time I see her at
the creek, I will tell her not to come here, ever again.

I touch the egg to see if it has cooled enough for Joshua

to eat, then motion to him that it is fine. He sits at the table and scoops half of it into his mouth, hastily chewing, then an expression of remorse comes into his eyes.

—Want some, Mama? he asks.

I shake my head, no.

—Can I have one 'morrow?

I smile a hopeful yes. Maybe I can find a way to get a little feed for the hen so that she will produce more. I dip a cup into the bucket and give him water, which he gulps, spilling it down his shirt. As I go to clear away the plate, he asks,

—Why Tyree's mama can talk?

I hesitate, then take the plate to the sink and pour some water from the pail over it. Wiping my hands on my apron, I turn to meet Joshua's questioning eyes. I put my hands on his shoulders and kiss the top of his head, his forehead, his nose, his silky-soft cheek. Someday I will make it up to you, I tell him silently.

To my dismay, Aaron comes stomping back in around dusk. At least he hasn't been drinking, as far as I can tell. Luckily I have gotten dinner started, just in case he showed up. A pot of spoonbread is heating on the stove, and I have boiled some creasey salad with a dab of lard we had left. I have sliced some of Nita's beautiful tomatoes, hoping Aaron will not ask where they came from. This is all we have for supper, unless he's brought something home, and it doesn't look like he has. Lately he's been stealing from the local farmers, a few ears of corn, a head of cabbage. I dread the day he's caught. Not for his sake, nor for my embarrassment, but for the way he'll take it out on me, long after the self-satisfied farmer has gone to sleep.

Aaron pulls out a chair as I set the plates on the table.

Joshua is playing with some sticks on the floor, and I pull him up and gesture for him to sit on his stool. Aaron dishes out spoonbread, wincing as his thumb touches the hot side of the pot. He serves himself over half of it, leaving small dribs and drabs behind for me and Joshua. Then he dumps creasey salad on his plate.

The sight of him gnawing at his food like a hungry animal sickens me. I serve Joshua and then take a spoon of each for myself. I don't feel hungry now, even though I could feel my stomach rumbling while I was cooking it. Aaron finishes his last gulp and rears back in his chair. I look at him expectantly. He seems to be in an expansive mood, but I know that can change in an instant.

—Old man Peel's barn burned down last night, he announces, pulling a straw out of his overalls bib and poking at his teeth. —Two of his kids were rolling cigarettes and caught the place on fire. Like to have burnt up all his cows. Every bit of his equipment is gone, new haymow, tractor.

I stare at him, wondering why he is telling me this. I haven't met any of the Peels; they don't go to our church and I haven't been by their place. It's unlike Aaron to make idle conversation with me.

—Old man Peel hasn't whipped his kids yet, Aaron says, chewing hard on the straw. —Burnt up his whole livelihood, and they aint got beat. Everybody feels it's a bad example to the children around here. If it was mine, you'd best believe their hindends would be tanned.

I gulp and look sidelong at Joshua, who is cringing on his stool, eyes wide. I hate for him to have to hear Aaron talk like this. Aaron knows it, and that's why he's doing it. I rise slowly from my chair and shrug. I gesture at the bowls, to ask if he wants more. Aaron stands up abruptly.

—No, I don't want more of your slop, he says.

I watch him carefully as he goes out of the kitchen and into the backyard. At times like this I can't read his mood. It's hard to tell what he's up to when he isn't drunk; in fact, since we've moved here, I've received some of my worst beatings when he was sober. His aim is a lot better then, and he doesn't fall asleep in the middle of it, the way he sometimes does when he's drinking. I'd better try to get Joshua to bed early tonight in case the worm turns in him. There's no telling what our child has heard from his little room upstairs, what he's imagined. But I want to keep him from actually witnessing it for as long as possible.

I wash out the dishes. The spoonbread sticks to the bottom of the pot and leaves a scum in the sink that is hard to scrub off. Aaron is sitting on a rock in the yard, whittling a stick. The bark falls away in long curls, and I can imagine the wood whining with every stroke of the knife. I wish he would use his carving skills to make a pull toy for Joshua, but I haven't steeled myself to ask for this yet. It would be so easy for him to do for Joshua, to give him a word, make him a gewgaw, take him fishing occasionally. Once Joshua asked him to play chase with him in the yard, and Aaron actually ran around in circles with him for a while. But ever since my transgression with the government lady he largely ignores the boy, only commenting to me on what I'm doing wrong with his upbringing.

I gather Joshua in my arms, pointing upstairs. He kicks a little in protest, but not too much. My boy is such a good little fellow. I kiss the top of his head as I blunder up the narrow, tilting steps with him. He hugs me tight, his breath warm on my neck. I breathe in the scent of his hair, the fresh outdoors smell clinging to it. I wish I could protect him from everything bad in the world.

I put him down and strip off his clothes, changing him

into his nightshirt. He clasps his hands together and says a prayer, a garbled version of what they teach the children at church.

—Now I layme, downa sleep, praytha lorda, soula keep.

His eyes are open over his folded hands, looking for my approval. I smile at him and hold him close. I feel his little heart beating wildly in his chest. I never realized children's hearts beat so fast, until I had him. I allow myself one more kiss and then lift him onto his pallet. Even in the heat, he likes to have something over him. He pulls the ragged quilt up to his chin and smiles at me sleepily.

—Good night, Mama.

I pat him on the arm and go back down the steps.

I hope so, baby.

Aaron is still somewhere outside when I get to the kitchen. I stir the ashes in the stove to get rid of any remaining cinders and take the Bible off the shelf. It is the only book Aaron allows in the house. Funny how, way back when, I had a vision of him and me reading the same books, then discussing them afterward in a genteel, intellectual manner. I guess this went along with the gingham-dress-three-children-sitting-around-the-kitchen-table notion. I almost have to laugh at that now.

I open to Corinthians, to the passage for tomorrow's sermon, which they post the Sunday before:

Even unto this present hour we both hunger, and thirst,
and are naked, and are buffeted,
and have no certain dwellingplace;
And labour, working with our own hands

I feel so sleepy I can barely keep my eyes open. The light from the window is dying and Aaron doesn't let me use the kerosene lamp unless he is here; he says why waste oil if you don't need it. I'm squinting at the words and they blur together. I tell myself I will shut my eyes only for a few minutes.

I have a curious dream. I'm in a pasture, and there are two horses, a white mare and a roan. The roan approaches the mare and I see his member protruding from its furry sheath, a long slithery thing, shockingly pink. As he rears up on the mare's hindquarters it grows even longer, until it hangs almost to the ground. The mare whinnies but I cannot hear it, I just see her mouth open and her long teeth extend. The roan manipulates his legs somehow to get the mare to accommodate him. She whinnies again, whether in pain or in pleasure, I cannot tell. Then she falls writhing on the ground, and I wake up.

The Bible has slipped down between my legs and a piece of paper is hanging out of the seam of the cover. I wonder what this could be. I stand up and look out the window. I don't see Aaron in the failing light, so I unfold the paper.

M. Coombs	1st group	
S. Jones	Secd grp	
Tho. Jones	Secd grp	
C. Wellridge	First	maybe
T. Wellridge	2	
Cat. Jones	2	
L. Thrush	first	may be
Ed Bean	first	
L. Willis	lst	maybe
P. Bailey	lst	
H. Teeter	2nd	

lst group—11 pm. Meet at Boggs Rd.
2nd—11:30 Under Bridge.

I puzzle over the list. These are the names of the men he meets with, but they seem to be planning something beyond their usual drinking party. It doesn't make much sense, but I am too tired to think about it anymore. I slip the paper back into the Bible's seam and clump upstairs to sleep.

Chapter Eighteen

The spoken language is a lovely thing. The way an *r* curls off your tongue, a languishing *l*. I used to love the word *ripe*, saying it. Ripe tomatoes. Ripening corn. Lovely lilting words. How I miss them. I never appreciated being able to talk, back when I could. I took it for granted. I think I miss the talking more than the hearing. What I heard was so often ugly and mean. But talking, you can express what you are thinking. You can explain. You can read out loud. You can whisper. It was heavenly to talk to Nita the other day at the creek, but how often will I be able to do that? When the warm weather passes, it will be too cold to go there. Perhaps there is a barn where we can meet and let the children play.

The hardest thing is not being able to speak to Joshua. I see as he gets older that there are so many questions he will have that I won't be able to answer. And I worry about his speech. He seems to be learning to talk, but will he have problems later on? Just this morning as I was getting him dressed for church, he said,

—why sun come up ina sky, Mama?

I tried to show him the sun and the moon with my hands,

how one comes up when the other goes down, but I don't know if he understood. It is frustrating not to be able to talk to him. But if I speak to him in private, I fear that Joshua would say something about it to Aaron, not realizing the consequences. After all, he is only three years old. So I gesture and hum, and do not speak to my child.

I lift my arms to pull on my worn shift, and grimace. Aaron came home drunk last night and lit into me with a fury. It turns out he'd been at another of those meetings; I pieced this together from his mumblings. Then he began ranting about something involving his mother, calling her names and hitting me all the while. Often now when he is drunk, he seems to believe that I am she. I used to feel sorry for him, but now he is so wicked to us that I cannot.

This morning I have bruises the color of squashed pokeberries up and down my ribs, and a sharp ache in the middle of my back. I remember him leaning all his weight into me with his knee, so that must be why I'm hurting there. I manage to pull the dress over my aching body, and see in dismay that it is torn down the front. I'll have to wear my apron over it; there is nothing else to do. This is the only outfit I have that can pass muster in church, and that only barely.

Despite his condition last night, Aaron manages to pull himself out of bed and dress in time for this morning's service. I follow him down the road, holding Joshua's hand, wondering at the mind of a man who would beat the mother of his child to a pulp on a Saturday evening, then march off to Sunday services the following morning. But he is probably more like the others than I would imagine.

The sun is already high in the sky, and the bright light makes little needles of pain behind my eyes. Aaron is always careful not to bruise my face on Saturdays, so I assume that if he hit me about the eyes, it doesn't show. I doubt he'd let me go to church if my bruises weren't hidden from view.

My father used to hit and kick me and Sibby, but he took the worst of it out on Mother. He used to hit her with his fists, then swear at her because he was out of breath from the exertion of beating her. As a child, I never had the strength to fight him. But I often wondered why Mother never fought back, since she was an adult, and stronger and bigger than we were.

Now I know why. For one thing, you get hit harder if you fight back. The slightest resistance to the blows brings them raining down even more fast and furious. And with Aaron, I'm afraid to infuriate him more because I'm afraid he will kill me, and then who would take care of Joshua? I have to survive for my child. I can't bear to think what would happen to him if I weren't around.

We make slow progress down the road, with my bad foot and aches and pains. Aaron strides ahead of us, looking fresh as a daisy. It is amazing, the transformation in him on Sundays. When he sings the hymns, at times he looks almost angelic.

We reach the church, go up the stairs and into our pew. Two women seated in front of us turn to look, then smile and whisper among themselves. I doubt my own perceptions lately, but I have a feeling they are saying something about me. I duck my head in shame. In the past, I never had new clothes to wear, but at least I was always clean and neat. Now I cannot even lay claim to those attributes.

Joshua wiggles and squirms throughout the opening devotions and hymns. I seat him on the other side of me, away from Aaron, but Aaron still glares at him across me. I give Joshua one of the funeral parlor fans to play with, and he amuses himself with it for the time being. Aaron sings out lustily, his mouth opening widely with the words.

> —how sweet the sound, that saved a wretch like me
> I once was lost, but now am found
> Was blind, but now I see

The singing is so loud that I can hear a faint echo of it. I used to love the singing in our church at home. Esther Richardson used to warble the most beautiful solos, and the men's choir would sing a rollicking version of *Oh When the Saints* about every other Sunday night. Then I recall the hymns we sang with the colored women, handing tobacco under the huge old oaks. I glance over at Aaron again, settling himself on the pew for the offering prayer. His Bible is on his lap. Suddenly I remember the piece of paper folded into the seam. What on earth is he up to?

The women on the pew in front of us turn and glance back at me again during the prayer. Then one whispers something to the other. Now I'm sure they are talking about me. Tears spring to my eyes, and I swipe at them quickly so they don't leak down my face. Why do I suddenly care about them, when I've gone so long without caring what anyone thinks? I'm so far away from any other human being, except Joshua. Why should I care if some nervy women want to whisper about me?

The prayer is finally over and the offering plate is passed. No one has much to put in it; a penny here, a nickel there. Aaron doesn't even take the plate this Sunday; I guess he spent his last red cent on his liquor last night. It's almost getting to where I resent anything he gives the Lord, anyway; why should He get our few pennies instead of our having food to eat?

There is a disturbance in the front pew, and a woman drags a little boy screaming wide-mouthed out of the church. This is one time I'm glad I cannot hear, because it would grate on my nerves to have to listen to his screams as she lights into him outside. The women of this congregation seem to thump on their children as hard as the men do.

Now comes the time for the announcements. I watch closely so I can comprehend what is being said. Preacher Moody reads from a list: Betty Atkinson is still doing poorly, Maybelle Walmsley is on the mend. Carl DeWitt has thrown out his back, let's pray he gets better soon. Clem and Myra Franks have just had a baby, seven pounds, eight ounces, delivered Saturday morning. Baby and mother are doing well, praise the Lord.

With this announcement, heads turn and tongues start wagging. Mrs. Peale at the piano stares straight ahead with her hand barely covering her wide open mouth. I know what they are saying: Clem and Myra just got married seven months ago. On the pew ahead of me, the women are counting on their fingers. Seven months and a seven-pound baby. That means Myra was in the family way before they got married.

Preacher Moody launches into his sermon, which I try to focus on but without much luck. Too much commotion is going on in the pews, too much whispering, for me to be able to watch his lips carefully enough. Heads bob together and then spring apart, blocking my view of the preacher's mouth. It is a lesson about the Sermon on the Mount, which I'd like to see, but I cannot follow it. They are all gabbling about poor Myra Franks.

I know what is going to happen next Sunday. The preacher will announce with a posture of great regret that Clem and Myra are moving their church membership to a fellowship in another part of the county. This is how things are done around here; they shame people into skulking and hiding. Even though they got married in time to right their wrong, that is not enough for this congregation. Myra and Clem will have to leave the community to be let alone in peace. I don't know the Frankses; I have only seen them coming and going in church, but they seem nice enough. I think it is a shame that this young woman is going to have to start a whole new life because of one mistake.

At last the sermon is over and a final hymn, *Bringing in the Sheaves*, is sung. This used to be one of Mother's and my favorites, and I move my toes inside my shoes in time to what I perceive as the music. Joshua is about to squirm out of his seat, so I let him stand beside me and hold on to my skirt. Finally it ends and Aaron bustles up to the front of the church to stand with the other men, where he will shake hands with each and every member of the church, smiling like the cat that got the cream. You'd think he'd have given up on this church idea when he didn't get any fine job offers, but he's come to like the pat-on-the-back, you're-one-of-us business with the other men. I can tell that it makes him feel important.

I slink out the back with Joshua and get along home to fix some dinner. I spy some purple-and-white turnips poking up out of a field on the way, and Lord forgive me, I pull them up and bring them home in my apron to round out our meal. Walking with the heavy knobs jouncing in my skirt, I remember how Sibby and I used to love to eat them raw. We'd dig up a few turnips, scrape off the tough outer skin with her pocketknife, and eat them just like that. If I had something to cut with, I'd peel me one right now. When we get home, I'll give Joshua a piece of one raw before I boil them. The thought makes me feel a connection with Sibby. I wonder if she is now home after church, cooking dinner for Mother, WillieEd, and Luke. Or maybe they are at Charlie's mama's house sitting down to a big dinner with all their in-laws and cousins.

A wave of self-pity washes over me. Why couldn't I have found a normal husband, like every other girl seemed to find? I'd long ago concluded that Aaron had sought me out because he perceived that I was naive and weak. I must have seemed like easy pickings to someone like him. And I hadn't asked for much—I never wanted someone handsome or rich; I'd just wanted someone to care for me, someone to love me back. The injustice of it stings me until I look down at Joshua, escorting me like a little man. At least one good thing has come of this union, I remind myself. The thought is some comfort to me as we walk home.

Chapter Nineteen

Joshua and I walk down the woods path to the creek. My anticipation is that of a giddy girl; the thought of conversing with Nita has been like a lifeline to me all week long. I am tempted to try to remove my earplugs to see if I can hear her, but Aaron checks them every so often, and he'd be able to tell if I had taken them out. It is another Thursday, the day I can usually count on seeing her.

But when we descend the bank, my heart sinks. The creek has shrunk to a tiny trickle in the heat. Dry brambles stick up like spindly arms where once cool water swirled around them. Wondering, Joshua and I walk along what was the creekbed, our bare feet making swirling lines in the loamy sand. Joshua is speechless at this change of events. I point to the ground and motion that the water has gone away, trying to indicate that it has dried out in the sun. When he looks up at me, tears are streaming down his cheeks.

—Why it go? Why the creek go away? he cries, and buries his head in my skirt.

I kneel down and hold him, feeling the sobs shake his little body. I breathe into his hair and wish I could soothe him with words. Maybe if I dared just this once . . . but this is dangerous thinking. I am on the verge of murmuring to him when he turns around in my arms. I look up and see Nita and her children, the same look of amazement on their faces, standing on the opposite bank.

Tyree and Yvonne jump down into the sandy bed, and Joshua runs to join them. Soon they are all kicking up dust and kneeling to examine the rocks that once were covered with water. Nita picks her way through the brambles and vines and approaches me.

—Looks like our bathin come to a stop for a while, til this drought breaks, she says. —Whyn't we take the chirren over to that big field behind the tree stand over there? They can play in the grass and not get so dusty.

I nod and motion for Joshua to follow us. The children are loath to leave the creekbed, but the lure of a new place to play entices them. Soon they are running ahead of us down the path. I have never been on Nita's side of the bank, and I am interested to see it. When the children are far enough ahead of us, I say,

—I was hoping you come. Today.

My throat feels dusty and dry, unused to speaking, since I haven't had the chance to for a whole week. For a moment I think she hasn't heard me, or that perhaps I merely whispered when I thought I spoke aloud. But then she looks at me and says,

—I was hopin you'd be here, too. But I wondered if you'd talk today. I thought maybe you'd be too spooked about it to talk to me again.

I smile. —It's all I've thought about, all week long.

I am about to say more, but Tyree comes running back to us, holding a tiny frog in his hand.

—A frog! He peepeed on me! he laughs, holding the creature up for us to see.

—You better wipe your hand off if you don't want to get a wart, Nita tells him.

Tyree quickly drops the frog and wipes his hand on his pants. Joshua and Yvonne squat down to watch as it hops into the underbrush. We wait to speak until they are satisfied with the frog's progress and go hurtling down the path again.

—I've never been over on this side before, I say.

—This a big old pretty field. Somebody cut it down so the grass aint so chiggery. I take 'em here sometimes when I don't want them to get wet. There's an old train trestle back of that field I keep them away from, but other than that it's a nice place to play. Lessus see if we can find some blackberries. Last time we picked enough for a cobbler, but they might be dried up with all this parchin heat.

—I love blackberry cobbler, but I never knew how to make it.

—Oh, that's easy. You just do a reg'lar pie crust, put it in a square pan if you want, with extra pieces for the top. Dump in the blackberries, sugar, butter and some milk. It's better with cream, if you have it, but milk'll do in a pinch. It's real good with some homemade ice cream.

—Do you have an ice cream crank?

—John's mama do. Boy, your hand gets tired turnin that thing. That old rock salt is hard to churn with those big lumps of ice. But then once it gets creamy you can spin it right along. I usually let John do the first few cranks til it gets goin. Tyree can take a good turn now too. It's hard work, but worth it when you taste that vanilla ice cream meltin on that old blackberry cobbler.

—You're making me hungry, I say. —Thank you again for those tomatoes and squash.

I start to warn her about coming to our house, but then I hesitate. The moment seems too nice to spoil.

—Oh, it won't nothin, Nita replies. —We had lots extra. I'm makin my own self hungry, talkin about cobbler. What you want to bet they aint a berry to be found in this heat?

We reach the clearing and step out into the big open field. It is indeed beautiful; tall green grass standing high, yellowing on the ends from the lack of rain; wild honeysuckle along the edges of the trees; curled-up blue and purple-and-white cornflowers waiting for nightfall to open. The children are playing tag, tickling each other with pieces of long grass.

—Here's the berry bushes. Looks like maybe they are some berries that aint dried up.

We walk over to the bushes that stand in the shade of a few oaks bordering the clearing.

—Not enough for no cobbler, but enough to pick and eat, Nita says.

Sure enough, there are some berries that haven't dried up. They are huge, larger than hickory nuts, and full to bursting with juice. Several collapse in my hand as I pluck them, and I eat them on the spot. The sweet berries warm my tongue with their ripeness. We motion the children over and they come galloping and prancing, pretending to be horses. We feed them from our hands. Joshua's bluestained smile is one of pure happiness. I show him how to pick the berries without getting pricked by the thorns, and he goes about rapidly picking and popping them into his mouth.

Nita begins collecting some berries in her apron, holding a corner of it up with one hand while she picks, and I do the same. Tyree bolts off to explore the far edges of the field, and Joshua soon follows. Yvonne eats awhile longer and then goes to join them. I am hungry for more exchange, eager to continue my conversation with Nita.

—Aint they good? Nita says when Yvonne is out of earshot. —Nothin like berries right off the bush. Why don't we sit down in this shade and rest awhile?

We ease down to the ground, careful not to spill our bounty.

—I used to pick them with my sister, I volunteer. —We never made cobbler though; we'd just be greedy and eat everything we picked ourselves. Sibby's big weakness was hickory nuts and walnuts. I could get her to do anything if I'd promise to help her crack hickory nuts. She did a week's worth of my woodchopping once in return for a five-pound bag I'd stored up all summer.

Nita laughs. —Lawd, we use to fight over our chores. My sisters and I hated to carry water up from the spring, and my brothers hated to slop the hogs. Once in a while we'd trade with them, but come a time, we'd always decide the other ones had it the worst.

—Sibby used to try to get out of washing dishes. She'd leave soap on them or not dry them all the way, then I'd have to go behind her and make sure they were done right. My mother had enough on her hands without us causing her more work, I explained. —And I didn't mind doing dishes. I was better at the things where I could stand or sit to do them. Bringing wood in was one of the hardest things to do, with my leg. I just don't have good balance when I go up and down steps with something heavy in my arms.

Nita glances over at my foot. —You got a clubfoot, right?

She says it so naturally that somehow I do not feel embarrassed or ashamed.

—Yes, that's right. I was born with it.

—Does it bother you much? I've noticed you limpin once in a while, she says with a sympathetic look.

—It hurts at the end of the day. Makes me tired more

than anything. I can't walk as fast as most people. But I'm
used to it, I say, hoping my intonation is light. I don't want
Nita to think I'm a crybaby.

—That musta been hard growin up. Chirren aint long on
sympathy, that I've noticed.

I think for a moment, and decide to be honest. —It was
kind of hard. The kids in school picked on me, but then
they picked on others, too, for being fat, or slow, or poorer
than anyone else. When I was little I remember grown-ups
saying how easy children have it, but I never could figure
out what they were talking about.

Nita makes a motion that looks like she is snorting.
—Can say that again. Pickin cotton, ooh is that hard work.
That made housechores seem like nothin. They started us
pickin when we were eight or nine, I reckon. I never worked
so hard before or since.

—How long were you doing that? Until what age?

—Oh, I want to say til I was 'bout sixteen, seventeen.
Then I had my troubles with a boy I met, then my baby
died. All those years were bad uns.

I'm not sure if I am supposed to ask about her boyfriend,
or not. Nita is being so open with me that it makes me feel
I can tell her things about my life, too.

—It must have been horrible to have a baby to die, I say.
—I can't even imagine how hard that must have been.

—It was, Nita says, staring off across the field. —I never
thought I'd get over it. The boy, his daddy, was long gone.
It was just me and the baby alone for a while. She got a
fever one night and in the mornin she was gone. I still dream
about her sometimes, her little hands and feet. They had to
shut me up for a while after that. I went stark ravin mad
for about a year.

We sit in silence for a few minutes, Nita remembering.

Anything I can think of to say would be wrong. Finally she continues,

—I tried to hurt myself a few times, things like that. My mama did for me as much as she could, but when she was out workin she had to lock me up in a room with nothin in it so I wouldn't do nothin to myself. I 'bout went stir-crazy in there. An old lady who lived near us would check on me once in a while during the day, try to get me to eat. She'd sit and read the Bible to me, lick her fingers to turn the pages. I 'member the sound of her quavery voice in that hot room, the pages raspin. But a lot of it I can't recollect, and prob'ly a good thing too. Mama said I'd scream and fight her, tryin to break things or get to the knife. Finally after about a year I got better and they could let me out.

—How old were you then? I ask.

—Twenty. I was twenty years old, and I felt like I'd lived three lifetimes.

—You met John after that?

—'Bout six months later, she says, shaking her head. —He the best thing that ever happened to me, I can tell you that. No tellin where I'd be if he hadn't come along.

Her words make me think about my situation. Aaron was probably the worst thing that had happened to me, like the boy who'd come and gone when Nita was seventeen. But maybe there was hope for me yet. Maybe at some point in the future I'd be telling a friend like Nita about my past life with Aaron, and saying about a new man, *no telling where I'd be if he hadn't come along*. It gave me hope to know that Nita, too, had once been in the depths of despair and had made her way out. Maybe there was a way out for me, too.

—You said you met him at your friend's family reunion?

—Yeah, my friend Sally. She and I go way on back. She kept tellin me she had someone she wanted me to meet. I won't in no mood to meet anybody, after what I done been through. I was just gettin to the point where I could wake up and get out of bed without havin thoughts of doin away with myself. I won't in no frame of mind to meet any man. But Sally kept insistin, sayin, Come on, just come. Just meet him and see. So I went to her daggone family reunion.

Nita smiles, shakes her head, and tucks her hair up under her scarf.

—There was John, sittin with Sally's cousin. They was friends. He come over the minute Sally and I got there. It was an outdoor picnic, and it was workin alive with family from three states there. Some of 'em, like me and John, won't relatives, but just friends invited along. But most of 'em were related some kind of way. John come over with a big smile on his face, looks right at me and says, You must be Nita. Just like that. Not, Here's how I know Sally's cousin and here's how I sorta know Sally and know about you. Naw, none of that. Just, You must be Nita, with a smile on his face. At first I thought he might be laughin at me. You know, maybe he'd heard I was the crazy gal they shut up on accounta her baby died. But after we started talkin I knew he wasn't laughin. He was serious as sin. We talked all through that reunion, never even bothered to eat. And you should see the food at some of them family wingdings! I got home and my mama ask me whose pickled peaches and fried chicken I done et, and when I told her I didn't eat a thing, she was fit to be tied.

I laugh with her, the eerie sound echoing in my head.

—My family didn't have reunions, but I went to one of Sibby's friends' reunions once. I remember I ate until I was sore.

—Well, I would have, if it hadn't been for John. He took up all my attention. I told my mama I was goin to marry him, and she looked at me like I needed to spend a little mo time shut up. I said, No, you wait and see. This the man I'ma s'posed to marry.

—And John felt the same way.

—Reckon he did. We upped and ran off and got married by a j.p. a month later. We didn't have but a one-room cabin to live in, a shack really, but we was just like two lovebirds. We had Tyree a couple of years later and you would think he was the only baby born in the world, the way John carried on. Same thing with Yvonne. I was afraid he'd be let down after havin a boy, but he was tickled to have a girl. She a real daddy's girl, too. She know if she want anything, she jus' has to ask him real pretty and he'll do his darndest to get it for her.

Nita looks at me carefully, her face serious now.

—Reason I'm goin into all this is, I've been down and low, about as low as anybody can get. And then I was lucky enough to meet someone made me happy. It has nothing to do with who you are, it's just chance and luck. I was lucky, an' that's all there is to it. When you're down low, it seems like you'll never get out. But then something can happen and your luck can change. You just have to be open to helpin your luck along. If I hadn't of gone to Sally's reunion, I never would've met John, and no tellin who I'd have hooked up with after that. Maybe no one, maybe someone worse than that first boy. But I did, and I met John, and here I am. And if I can get us moved out of that skeeterhole we livin in, my life will be complete.

She leans back as if to rest, then pops up.

—Lawsy mercy, we done forgot to check on the chirren. Where they at? Ty-reeee! Yvonne! Joshua! Where you all?

I pull myself up and look across the field. There's not a child in sight, but then I see the tall grass in the middle of the field waving and I know that they are there. Finally their forms are visible above the grass as they walk toward us. They are holding their hands out in front of them, clutching something. As they get closer I see the weathered brown husks of cicada shells.

—We finded these locusts! Yvonne shouts at Nita. —Look! We finded lots of them!

Joshua runs up, clutching his shells in his hands. He's held them so tightly that he's crunched some of the fragile bodies. They have collected dozens of cicada shells that the creatures have shed on the trees lining the clearing. Boys in my school used to scare girls with those shells, putting them in their hair. They never bothered me, but some girls pretended as if they were terrified of them; an act to goad the boys on, I always suspected. Joshua crams them into my apron pocket, crushing them further, and Tyree and Yvonne pile their shells up on the ground. Then they run off to find more.

—You all stay round close! We gonna have to be goin home soon, Nita calls to their retreating backs. —Locust shells, she says, fingering one. —Them cicadas sure kick up a racket down by us. They bothersome near your house? she asks.

I look down. She has forgotten. I look up and say,

—I can't hear them, but I imagine they do.

—Oh, I'm sorry. I forgot. We was talkin along so good, I forgot you can't hear me. You must be a natural lipreader.

—I've gotten used to it, I say.

—So it's been a year since you . . . couldn't talk?

I nod.

—And you wasn't born deaf? she asks, a worried look on her face, as if she is afraid of what I will tell her.

—No, but I am now.

I cannot tell her about the earplugs, the indignity of it.

She would not understand why I put up with it. For her to understand, I'd have to tell her everything about what Aaron does to me, how afraid of him I am. I just don't feel ready for that revelation yet.

—It is good to talk to you, I say. —If my husband was any different, I'd be able to talk all the time. But he is . . . angry. And he drinks, and—

Suddenly to my horror I am crying. Nita comes and puts her arms around me. I stand there for a few moments, her arms lightly embracing me. Then we pull back and I dab at my eyes.

—Sorry, I—

—That's all right. You gonna be all right, Cora. Whatever mess you in now, I believe you can find a way out of it. I just do. You too smart not to figure something out. That's just what I believe, after talkin to you.

Nita squints up at the sky.

—'Pears to me it's around one o'clock, she says. —I tole John's mama I'd help her shell some beans this afternoon. I guess we mought to be goin. Tyreee! Yvonne! You all come on, we got to go.

—Maybe we can meet here next week, I say in a rush before the children approach.

—I'll be here, Nita says. —I sure will. You have a good couple of days til I see you again.

—You too, Nita.

Tyree and Yvonne are tussling over something, and she goes to separate them. Joshua looks up at me and wails,

—we stay longer? Please? We havin fun, Mama. Can't we stay?

—Hmmhmm, I say, and shake my head.

Nita turns and waves, the children tell Joshua goodbye, and we part. I have gotten so used to talking in the last hour

that I almost ask Joshua about the cicada shells. I stop myself, fretting. How long will I be able to go on like this? It
is as if talking to Nita has opened a door that has been closed
for too long. The door swells, being unconfined by its frame,
and is almost impossible to shut again.

All the way home on the path, Joshua chatters happily
about Tyree and Yvonne and how they played. I worry that
he will say something about them to Aaron, and decide to
watch what Joshua says carefully tonight. Maybe I can keep
him away from Aaron altogether.

All afternoon as I play in the yard with Joshua, I run
through imaginary scenes in my mind in which I am defi-
ant of Aaron. I picture him stomping into the kitchen, and
me yelling back at him when he starts to shout about dinner. Or me simply not cooking dinner, just feeding myself
and Joshua and letting Aaron fend for himself when he gets
home. I imagine myself explaining that half the time when
I cook he never shows up anyway, off drinking or doing God
knows what somewhere.

What if I waited until he was seated at the table and
grabbed up the iron skillet and cracked him in the head?
I imagine this several times and in several different ways:
me confronting him, screaming at him that I'm not going
to endure his treatment anymore, stabbing him with a paring knife or hitting him in the head with the skillet. Every
time I imagine it, I am stronger and more lithe than he,
can move faster around the kitchen table and can aim better. Each time in my mind I conquer him, have him begging for forgiveness on his knees as I make him cower.
Then I grab Joshua, threaten Aaron once more, and make
my escape out the door forever. Every time I picture it, I
feel better.

By evening, I am almost looking forward to Aaron's return

from wherever he has spent the day. It is curing season again, a time when there is plenty of work, but Aaron seems to be the only man in Tarville without steady employment. He has taken Nettie with him, so he must have done some plough-ing somewhere. Unless he just ties her in the woods while he's drinking, so he can pretend he's been working. But this is one of those nights, usually so longed-for, that he does not return home until very late. I start humming Joshua to sleep in his bed, fall into a deep slumber myself, and do not wake up until the sun finds its way through a chink in the wall.

Chapter Twenty

The mailman rarely comes by our house; in fact it's been months since Aaron got any mail. But this morning he trudges up the dusty dirt road and hands me a letter that looks like it got rained on, stomped on, and mauled by a tomcat.

—This'n got for'arded from your last place of res'dence, the mailman says. —Reckon I could have a glass of water? I'm parched.

I nod and let the rawnecked young man in. Normally he merely leaves the letters tucked in our screen door; this is the first time he's spoken to me. He looks around the kitchen while I dip out a cup of water from the bucket. He drinks deeply and hands me the cup for more. I give it to him and wait impatiently for him to finish. I want him to leave so I can read the letter before Aaron comes in. From what I can tell, it's in Sibby's handwriting; it has to be from her.

—Thankee, ma'am, the man says, wiping his mouth with the back of his hand. —Mighty hot, and goin to get hotter, if you can believe the papers.

He waits for an answer. I nod, take the cup, and stand there looking at the door.

—Well, goodbye then. He leaves the house awkwardly and trudges down the hill.

Joshua is running around outside, chasing a cloud of blue-white butterflies. I sit at the kitchen table and open the letter carefully. A corner is ripped off the top, but part of the date is visible. It is four months old.

Dear Cora:

It's been so long since we've heard from you, it's like you dropped off the face of the earth. I'm writing to you at the last address I had, even though I heard you moved. The last few letters I sent came back with Addressee Moved Away stamped on it. I hope this one won't come back to me. Won't you write to me, if you get this?

First of all, there's been a lot of news. One of our old cows died having her calf and we've had a real struggle to keep the little one going. Charlie rigged up a bottle from Daniel's old one and is feeding the calf every three hours. I don't know how long we can keep it up, but so far it seems to be thriving. Mary Jane Markley had her fourth baby in five years. For someone who used to pretend she didn't know where they came from, that's quite a record, don't you think? Charlie says her husband is no-count, but I don't know why he says that. Probably because he got a better price for his tobacco than Charlie did last fall. Ha!

May and Willa Smith still live with their Daddy. Seems like nobody who came a-courtin was good enough for them. Some boys did come around, but I imagine it was more for their Dad's three hundred acres than for their acre apiece of fat behind.

My knee baby Carol is now two, can you believe it? Daniel is going to be one next month. Where has the time gone? I hope you and that fellow are doing well. Have you settled into a town where you will stay yet? Land sakes, it seems you all did a lot of moving around, from what I can tell. Charlie has asked around about you as far as Shoah, but he lost track of you a few years ago. I would love to see you and your husband. Maybe you even have children by now. Please do write and let me know how we can get in touch with you.

Charlie is still growing tobacco with his cousin Tom, that's working out all right. We lost half the last crop to hail, but this one looks like it's going to turn out. It's something to keep the kids in clothes with them shooting up like weeds, but at least I get some hand-me-downs from the neighbors. I dressed Daniel in Carol's outfits until a month ago, and then Charlie said enough, you've got to put him in pants now. So I try to sew things out of old gunnysacks. At least he's at the age where he doesn't mind what he has on yet. Maybe he never will, since he's a boy. He'd be happy if I let him run around naked, little savage that he is.

Mother, WillieEd and Luke are doing all right. Her health is still not good, but since WillieEd turned sixteen, he's finally taken on some responsibility and does a right smart turn at farming. They have a truck patch and some hay, and WillieEd's helping Man Murfree with his tobacco. He does a sight better than Father ever did. To hear Mother speak, you'd think she rues the day Father left here, but I believe that's just for show. You know she can't possibly wish him back here. You and I bear the marks still, don't we? I'm glad the old devil went to his due. He's probably roasting nice and hot down below.

Luke has grown into a sweet little boy. His eyes are the same pretty blue as yours.

Are you farming, or is your husband working in a town? I'm dying to know. Please do write me and get in touch.

I miss you a lot, we went through so much growing up and now we're all grown up and having children on our own (at least I do) so we have a lot to catch up on. I can't believe it's been almost four years since I saw you last. Write me soon.

Love,
Sibby

P.S. That awful Alicia Farnsworth got married eight months after her husband died. You probably didn't even know he'd died, well he did. And eight months later she ups and remarries. Don't that take all?

I read the letter through again, the words reverberating in my head. Despite her entreaties, I can't write to Sibby now. What would I say? That my husband (who wasn't even that) drinks all the time, beats me, and barely keeps us in clothing? And what if Sibby insisted on coming to see me? How would I explain that I couldn't talk or hear? Aaron wouldn't allow it, anyway. He'd never let me have a visitor from home.

Maybe if things improve somewhere down the line, I'll get in touch with her. Or better yet, maybe I'll manage somehow to get away from Aaron for good and go back home.

Amazing that she has two children I haven't even seen. Joshua would have so much fun playing with his cousins. I could just imagine the good times they'd have, running about the yard, catching fireflies in mason jars, playing tag and kick the can. Sibby and I would sit and watch them from the back porch of her farmhouse, sipping iced tea and commenting on their silliness. Charlie sounded like such a nice fellow, too. And with Father out of the picture, maybe Mother could enjoy herself more, spend time with her little grandchildren. With WillieEd almost grown and Luke not a baby anymore, things had to be easier. A strong craving to see them all hits me hard, and tears well up in my eyes.

Maybe I could get up my courage to try to leave again, I think. If I could predict when Aaron will be away on one of his drinking spells, that would be a safe time to go. Maybe I could get away from him this time, just run away with Joshua, go back home. Surely Charlie would protect us if Aaron came looking for us. And even if people back home found out I had never been married, what did that matter at this point? Sibby was safely married to Charlie, mother of two children herself. What did I care what other people thought, anyway?

I look out the window to see Aaron coming across the yard. Despite Nita's encouragements, with the ponderous reality of his presence, all my previous bravado about my imagined escape leaves me. Just the sight of him reminds me of how slowly I move with my bad foot, of the fact that I do not have a cent to my name, of the memory of his fury the one time I did try to get away. I can feel his fists pounding into me, his huge hands around my neck. I think of what those hands could do to Joshua, and fear sends shivers circling around my back like pins and needles. What seems so easy in his absence becomes impossible when face to face.

Aaron is carrying something heavy in a tin pail. He seems oblivious to the flies buzzing around it, and I wonder if he has gone fishing with Merris Coombs. If so, he has caught a mighty catch, because it appears he cannot hold the bucket without staggering. Joshua trots over to look, then runs back to play.

Aaron approaches, and I can feel the vibrations of his feet coming up the steps. He enters the kitchen and drops the bucket on the floor. For a minute I can't tell what it is, with the flies buzzing around and water sloshing. Then the water settles down and I lean in for a better look, thinking it is perhaps a huge catfish. A fetid smell hits me. It is a pig's head. There is a deep gash on its forehead, and long red tendrils uncoil slowly from the cut into the water.

I straighten up and look at Aaron. He gestures toward the bucket.

—My momma used to have a way with pig's head, he says. —Tell you what you do. You wash it down good with some water. Then boil it in this pot—

he grabs the biggest pot we have and sets it on the oven

—for about two–three hours. Then after it's boiled to a turn, you put it in a pan and cook it in the oven with some lard and salt. It's a devilish good meal.

I glance at the head, holding my breath against its smell. I cannot imagine eating something like that, but maybe people do, where he comes from. People develop tastes for all kinds of things when they're hungry. I turn around and pour off some of the water from the bucket into a pot. Aaron gets set to leave, then turns around at the door and grins.

—It's a mighty tasty treat, some might say a delicacy, he says, articulating carefully so I catch every word. —Be careful not to ruin it.

After he leaves, I think of a dozen retorts I could have made, if I had dared to speak. Somehow my defiance has petered out. It is hot, and I feel tired. I suppose I will have to try to cook this to his liking.

I stare at the thing in the bucket. Finally, when the water is boiling, I make myself lay hands on it. It is slippery, and a sharp bristle cuts my finger. I try to wrestle it out of the pail, which is hard because its skin is so slimy that my fingers easily lose purchase. The flies are still swarming around it, and one lands on my lip. I blow it off, hating to think where it had been. Finally I get the dripping mess into the sink and examine it. Should I try to clean it out before I boil it? I cannot imagine that he would want the innards left intact. A wave of nausea makes my stomach flip for a moment, but I go to the door and breathe fresh air and it calms down. Joshua is now digging doodlebugs out of the dirt with a long stick. Good.

I take a fork and try to stab the thing so I can flip it over, but the skin is too tough. Holding my breath against the smell, I put my hands on it again and turn it upside down. The snout rubs against the metal sides of the sink in a way that looks particularly uncomfortable. Poor old sow, I think. What did you ever do to anybody? I resolve to get rid of the mess inside the head before I boil it. I take a tin cup and begin scooping the innards into the pail. The brains stink, and come out in long drooling strands. Finally I get most of it out and pour more water into the head. Then I lift it and put it into the boiling water on the oven. I dump some salt on it and cover it up.

I carry the pail to the edge of the yard where the sunburnt weeds begin, my right foot dragging as I walk. By the time I dump out the contents and head back to the house, two wild cats are already eating the brains. At least they'll get something out of this, I think. I leave the pail by the back stoop and go inside and wash my hands three times, but it seems I still can't get the stink off of them. This is a delicacy that I hope he won't be in the mood for often. I wonder where on earth he found the head.

As I bend down to wipe up the mess on the floor, Aaron comes running into the house. I look up at him.

—You threw out the brains! That's the best part, you idiot! he shouts, kicking me in the behind. I go sprawling on the filthy floor, skinning my elbows on the cracked linoleum.

The pig slime gets all over me, in my hair, down my dress-front. Aaron laughs, and nudges me in the ribs with his boot.

—Next time ask me if you're supposed to throw something away, he says, and walks out.

Slowly I get up on my hands and knees and finish wiping the floor. When I am sure he is gone, I poke my head out the kitchen door and motion for Joshua to stay in the yard. Then I strip right there in the kitchen and go upstairs to find something clean to put on.

While I am changing, I curse myself for my inaction. All my big ideas seem to have drained out of me. Was my courage only a momentary mental revolt, the result of Nita's kind words? I tell myself I have to have some backbone. I have been under Aaron's oppressive thumb for too long. I don't want my son to grow up this way. I long to cry out, to scream back at Aaron, to tell him he cannot treat me in that manner. Somehow I will have to find a way to leave him.

Chapter Twenty-One

All this fuss over the pig's head is for another meeting that's being held tonight in our yard. Aaron didn't tell me this until late this afternoon, when the head lay leaking into its pan of black juices. I have never seen anything so vile in my life; the eyes caved in upon themselves, flabby gray cheeks squashed senseless, one ear charred dark from touching the side of the stove. But Aaron seems happy with the way it turned out.

—Company coming tonight, he says, and from that I assume it is his group of men, since no one else ever comes to our house. The church people stay away, probably believing every lie Aaron has told them about me.

I feed Joshua his supper, a little corn pudding and a quivering piece of cooked flesh I scraped from the pig's inner cheek so Aaron wouldn't notice it was missing. If there is meat in the house, you can be sure my boy is going to get some. Joshua is very still tonight eating his meal, making me wonder if Aaron said anything to him.

—Those mens coming tonight? he finally asks me. His wispy eyebrows meet in a frown over his bright brown eyes.

I nod and pat down his hair, trying to make him sense

that he has nothing to worry about. He slept through the last meeting that was held here, didn't he? I give him a tight hug and get him upstairs to bed. He has almost gnawed through his chewing stick. I'll have to remember to find him another smooth one to bring up to bed tomorrow. I'll dye this one purple if I can find some pokeberries. Joshua likes the pretty colors.

After I'm sure he's asleep, I go back down to the kitchen to peel some potatoes. I spent so much time on the pig that they'll just have to make do with it and some boiled potatoes and their squeezins. They can't expect me to make a meal out of thin air, and the pantry is pretty empty right now.

As I peel the potatoes, carefully scoring out the eyes, I start to think again about the paper I found hidden in Aaron's Bible. Maybe tonight they'd be talking about whatever it was they were planning. I decide that I want to know. If they are planning some nasty business, I want early warning. If Aaron is getting set to go somewhere, I want to know that. Maybe he is planning to just get up and leave in the night.

If Aaron left, I'd be free to go where I wanted. I wouldn't have to worry about him trying to come find me, or about his harming Joshua in retaliation. A great relief washes through me at the thought. I could move back home. Maybe I could try to sew, or else grow and sell vegetables for necessaries, so I wouldn't have to tax Mother's tightened circumstances. Joshua would be in school in three years, and maybe then I could get some kind of work for someone from church, or help Mrs. Whitmell at her house.

If only it weren't for my bad leg! This leg has brought me down so in life. I wonder if I would have wound up with someone like Aaron if my leg had been regular. Maybe not; maybe I would have had beaux coming out of the woodwork. I try to imagine it, but cannot. I'd seen other boys buzzing around girls like Mary Jane Markley like bees around honey, but I can't imagine what that would feel like.

Then it occurs to me that if Aaron leaves, I can take these plugs out of my ears. I would be a normal mother again; I could talk to Joshua. I could do so many things that I can't do now. The thought excites me, and I resolve to spy on the men at the meeting. I'll serve them the pig, cut it up whichever way you cut up a pig's head, serve them the potatoes with a smile.

I decide to try to find some greens for creasey salad, and go out by the road to pull a few handfuls. It won't take much to fill their bellies, with all the liquor they'll be swilling. I hurry back inside with the greens, wash the grit out of them, and boil them alongside the potatoes. This gives me three dishes to bring out and serve. Maybe that will be enough time to try to figure out what they're up to.

About dusk Aaron comes back into the yard with two other men whom I haven't seen before. Soon the yard is filling with men, faces I wish I'd never have to see again. Merris Coombs with his fishhooks, beet-red already from drink. Perkinson Bailey with his big cauliflower ears. Larry Thrush, Ed Bean, and the others. So far Sam Jones hasn't shown up, and I hope to God he doesn't. Although I can't imagine that, given our last encounter, he would dare to show his face here again.

The men sit around the yard and open their jars. The clear liquid glints in the sun as they tip the containers back to their lips. Their mouths are wide and red, laughing, black hollows of carious teeth making gaps in their smiles. I brace myself for a minute and then carry out the pot of potatoes. I can feel their eyes crawling on me as I go to the plank bench, where I lay the food. It makes me more awkward to know they are watching me, but I take my time so I can watch for their words. For once I don't look down at the ground, but at their faces. I want to see what this plan of theirs is.

I go back inside for the creasey salad. I bring it out with a glass of vinegar for them to sprinkle over it. I'd love to have some myself; I haven't eaten since a crust of bread this morning. But I won't. There isn't enough to go around, as it is.

I make one more trip back to the kitchen for the pig's head. The huge pan is heavy, and grease drips onto my sleeve and down my dress as I carry it, tilting, to the plank. I lean over to put it down and then go back inside to get a carving knife and a fork.

When I come out, Aaron is standing at the plank, gesturing and laughing. The men have roused themselves to come over and they, too, are laughing at what he is saying. I approach to carve up the pig and I see his lips smiling, his eyes bristling at me.

—See this slop she gives me? It's a sight for sore eyes, aint it! This is the kind of thing I have to put up with.

I freeze in my tracks, horrified. What is he saying? Aaron sees me stop, whirls around, and points, and the whole group turns to stare. They burst out laughing at my expression.

—Woman, you call this food? I wouldn't serve this to a dog! Who ever heard of cooking a pig's head! Do you expect me to eat this? I tell you, boys, she's cuckoo!

He twirls his finger around his head twice. I cannot move; my feet are planted in the earth like Lot's wife turning to a pillar of salt. My face feels like it is on fire. I turn and hobble back into the house, tripping on a clod of earth that almost sends me to the ground. When I manage to get my balance and dust off my skirt, Ed Bean is there, holding me by the elbow.

—There now, he's just having some fun, he says, mouthing the words emphatically. —None of us here would hurt you. Come on out and serve your meal. Them potatoes look mighty nice.

I get up warily, ready to go back inside, but the rest of the men are telling me to come on and serve. Aaron gestures angrily for me to come, and I'm afraid he will walk over and hit me right in front of all these men if I don't. In these parts, the right to hit your woman is sacred, and no man had better interfere if he values his life. It's right up there with the liberty to clobber your kids.

I clump over to the plank and pick up the spoon for the potatoes. My face feels as if it's turned to firewood, it's so stiff and flaming. Hot and cold thrills of shame run up my arms as I serve the men. They hold out their plates for the potatoes and salad, none meeting my eyes except Ed Bean. Somehow I force myself to serve the whole group before I sidle back to the safety of the kitchen.

Still shaking, I pull up a stool and watch the men from the window. Aaron, Timothy Wellridge, and Perkinson Bailey seem to be leading the discussion. I catch snatches of lip movement, but it is impossible to tell exactly what they are saying. I go to look out the kitchen door, but again the angles of their faces are wrong and I cannot tell more than a few words. I smack my hands together in frustration. Now Perkinson Bailey is getting up in front of them for what looks like a big speech.

Suddenly I feel a whisper of movement at my elbow. I look down in surprise to see Joshua dart past me and out into the yard. I hurry down the steps and try to get him before he reaches the men. What on earth could have possessed him to run out there? I know he is afraid of them. I click my tongue, trying to get his attention. Joshua stops and begins to walk back toward the house, then stops again, confusedly turning around. I see that the entire bottom of his nightshirt is wet. He hasn't wet his bed in a long time, but obviously that is what has awakened him now. Maybe the noises of the men frightened him in his sleep.

I glance at Aaron, who like the other men is too transfixed by Bailey's words to turn around and notice his son, and hurry over to where Joshua is. He sees me, flails his arms, and bolts over to me, but he doesn't slow down and the impact knocks me to the ground. I feel a searing pain in my ear as my shoulder hits the hard clay. A roaring fills my head. Then as I sit up and gather Joshua to me, I hear a loud voice. I look down and there in the dirt lies the piece of hardened brown wax that Aaron poured into my ear a month earlier. I look up toward the men and see that Perkinson Bailey is still talking.

—on, now, you know they's been asking for it for a long time. I say we go in and hit 'em hard and fast. They won't know what's hit 'em if we go in the middle of the night. We go in, roust 'em out, set fires to them hovels and in the morning there won't be a single nigger left in the county!

The men roar their approval, raising their jars in the air. Joshua quivers in my arms. I pick up the wax plug, then make him stand. Slowly I get up too. I push him toward the kitchen, and he runs inside. I hobble behind him, wanting to hear the rest of it. Aaron chimes in next.

—I agree with the whole plan, except one thing, he says. —The roustin part. I say let 'em burn with their shitty huts. Who needs the niggers around at all? Personally, I can't stand 'em. They take good jobs from decent working men. If we

burn down their houses, they'll just rebuild somewhere
nearby. I say let's get rid of 'em once and for all!

An even more frenzied groan comes from the crowd. I
turn back to look, and see Merris Coombs getting ready to
speak.

—So it's goin to be this Sat'day night, eleven o'clock at
the Bottoms. They'll never know what hit 'em.

As I watch in horror, a cry emanates from the open mouths
of the men. The sound vibrates in my head with a strange
swooshing echo, making my head feel as if it is going to
split open. I go into the kitchen to find Joshua cowering at
the bottom of the stairs.

—Mama, wet my pants, he cries. —Couldn't woke up.

The sound of my son's voice is miraculous to me, but I
cannot linger over it now. It isn't safe. I only hope that Aaron
didn't see him in the yard. I hurry him up the stairs and
change him into another shirt. Not a breeze stirs in the close
upper rooms; the heat stored from the afternoon sun is
weighted and motionless. I can hear agitated shouts from the
yard. No wonder he wet himself. I motion for him to stay
in his bed, no matter what, and go back downstairs as fast
as I can.

I look out the window again, but now the swooshing in
my ear has become so loud that I can't tell what they are
saying. I run over their speeches in my mind, my earlier
shame forgotten. I cannot believe that they plan to set fire
to the colored people's cabins. I think of Nita and her children, of the others I'd seen walking past on the road or
working in the fields. How could they do it? But I knew it
was possible. I had heard of similar things in other parts of
the South when I was growing up.

Since I cannot hear any more of their conversation, I wash
out the pots and go upstairs. I pull the odd-shaped wax out

of my apron pocket and work it back into my ear, hoping it will stay there at least until Aaron checks it again. When he sees it is loose, he'll be sure to replace it. I'd rather have that than the beating I'd get if he thought I'd prized it out. I lie in bed, tossing and turning in the breathless heat, trying to decide what I am going to do.

Chapter Twenty-Two

I awaken at dawn to find Aaron's side of the bed empty. Cautiously I go downstairs, where I don't find him, and look out in the yard, where he is not. I guess that he has gone off with some of his cronies to find another still in the middle of some cornfield. I hope for the hundredth time that he will fall afoul of someone in a bloody liquor-inflamed knife fight, or catch pneumonia sleeping in a ditch in a drunken stupor. I used to ask God's forgiveness for having such vivid imaginings, but I don't bother anymore.

Then I remember what I heard last night, and it hits me like a bolt from the blue. They are actually planning to immolate Nita and her children, along with their cousins, aunts, and uncles; set them all aflame in their cabins just like they would burn dry husks to clear off a field. I should get Joshua up, go down to the creek, and wait for her, this very morning. I should tell her what they plan to do, warn her so she can summon her children and relatives and leave in the night.

But somehow I cannot move. I sit and stare at the filthy dishes piled up in the sink and imagine what he would do to me, or to Joshua, if he ever found out I'd fouled his plans. Finally I get up and start heating water for the dishes, and slowly I wash and dry each one. Joshua comes downstairs, and I feed him and take him back up to get him dressed. Then I sit outside in the dust and watch him play and stack pinecones for several hours.

Every time I think of what I should do, an enormous exhaustion overcomes me. I cannot bring myself to go anywhere, to do anything. My whole body feels tired, my shoulder aches, and even though my ear is plugged up again, I still hear echoes of the swooshing noises in my brain. I know I should rouse myself, take Joshua to the creek, and tell Nita what has happened. But a vision of Aaron's furious face if he finds out keeps me immobile.

Just as I've begun to hope Aaron won't be coming home at all tonight, he shows up, dirty and reeking. He tromps in and heaves himself into the kitchen chair with an enormous belch. I have been giving Joshua his supper, but I know he will not take another bite now. Joshua slides off his stool and backs toward the door. I am watching Aaron and do not catch what Joshua says, but Aaron's face contorts in fury.

—you say now? What's that you said?

He goes over to Joshua, grips his tiny shoulders with his hammy palms, and shakes him, hard. I get up to try to stop him, but a blow I didn't see coming knocks me into the wall. Aaron grabs the table and flips it over so the bowls and plates go crashing to the floor, the reheated spoonbread so dry it cracks open. A runnel of lard puddles where the table meets the linoleum. Joshua stands trembling, his eyes darting around the room for an escape.

—What you say, boy? You asking me to explain myself? What do you know about them people?

—N-nothin, Joshua stammers out.

—Nothin! Why you asking about my meeting then? You

think I have to explain myself to you, you pulin, pukin little goodfornothin?

Joshua bursts into tears, and Aaron gestures drunkenly at him and laughs. I push off from the wall, grab a pot from the stove, and swing it at Aaron's back. It falls short and clatters to the floor. Aaron turns around and stares at me, surprised. Then he narrows his eyes and grabs my wrists, clamping down hard.

—not gonna hurt your little miss-priss, he taunts. —I heard what he said. He's been listenin to things he shouldn't hear. I guess little jugs do have big ears, just like they say.

I try to get past him to Joshua, but he pushes me away again roughly.

—We'll have to see about that, he says, leering at me now. —We'll just have to see.

He purses his lips to whistle, and gets ready to go out into the yard.

—I've got a little errand to do, he says when he turns back to look at me. —I want this mess cleaned up by the time I get back.

Joshua runs up the stairs, and I follow him. I wish I had seen what he said, but I can deduce that he heard something the men said last night and was asking Aaron about it. I hold Joshua tight on his bed until he forgets his fright and begins arranging his new stick on the pallet with his pinecones. Finally I get him to say his prayers. It seems like it takes forever for him to go to sleep.

Once his eyes are shut, I go back downstairs and fall to work setting the table aright and wiping up the mess on the floor. Aaron comes back inside just as I have finished. He is carrying a little cloth parcel tied up in a white string. I can't imagine what he has bought, but he grins at me and takes it upstairs with him to our room. I shudder to think what new torture he might have devised for me as punishment for Joshua's transgression. But at least he seems to be planning to let the boy alone, which is all I really care about.

I steel myself and climb up the stairs. It seems I can barely force myself up each step. I have the horrible urge to bark like a dog, to soil myself, anything to make him stay away from me tonight. But I keep climbing the steps, one after another.

When I go into the room, the little parcel is lying on the floor, still tied up with its string. Maybe he's bought store tobacco for some reason. I go into a corner and pull on my nightshift. The thought of lying next to him in bed makes my skin crawl, but I am afraid to stay downstairs longer with Joshua alone with him up here.

When I am finished changing, I look over at him. He has unzipped his member, and it is protruding from his pants. I wonder if he wants me to undress him now, but he motions for me to come over to him. Laughing at my puzzled expression, he pushes me down to the floor by my shoulders. My knees hit the pine boards hard, and I hope Joshua is still asleep.

Aaron drags me closer to the pallet. I stare at the horrible engorgement with its single eye. Just as I am wondering what new humiliation is in store for me, he grabs my jaw and wrenches it open, then thrusts his member into my mouth, strangling me. I choke and start to fall back, but he forces it upon me again, holding my head hard, his hot hands covering my ears, thrusting and thrusting deep into my mouth. Each time I think I can get a breath of air, he pushes into the back of my throat again.

Now I understand what he is doing, and the perversion of it sickens me and convinces me that I am living with an individual uniquely evil on the face of the earth. He continues until a hot stream of foul-tasting liquid pours into my throat and spills out the side of my mouth. Aaron falls back onto the pallet as I gag and cough. I feel as if I am going to throw up, but somehow I keep my dinner down. If I throw up, there's no telling what he'll make me do. I am afraid in his new twist of meanness he might try to make me eat it.

I sit by the side of the pallet, holding as still as I can. At last, when his breathing appears even, I get into the other side of the bed, trying to lie as close to the edge as I can without falling off. I lie awake for half the night, wondering if I will go to hell for what he has made me do. Surely he has to have had a whisper from the devil to dream up something as disgusting as this act he has forced upon me. As the first rays of sun streak the dusty windowpane, I decide that I am in hell already. There can be nothing worse than how I am living now.

In the morning he is not there. My throat feels raspy, as if I have the croup, and my mouth has a foul taste and odor. I struggle into my dress and apron and go down to the kitchen for a dipper of cold water. The buckets are low; I'll have to make two trips to the creek and back to fill them. As I sit down at the table to drink the water, I see the parcel he'd brought in last night. Wax has dripped all over the table, and lying on the bag is a small brown candle, melted and misshapen. Lying next to the candle are two soft waxen earplugs, about half the size of mine.

My heart stops, and time seems to suspend. An image of Joshua leaping about in the meadow, giggling as he chases a flurry of yellow butterflies, enters my mind. I see him hugging Nettie's flea-bitten neck, splashing about in the creek with Yvonne and Tyree, his entire life ahead of him like an unbroken shining chain. My thoughts return to the objects on the table. I will keep that creature from laying hands on him if it is the last thing I do. I scoop up the candle and the earplugs and maul them so they are unrecognizable, then with a wave of revulsion I plunge them deep into my apron pocket.

I walk up the steps and get Joshua out of bed, dress him hurriedly, and take him downstairs half-unbuttoned. I give him a piece of bread to chew on the way to the creek. I go along as fast as I can, my skirt catching in the hateful briars along the way. I don't know what day it is or if Nita will be there or at the field, but if she isn't I'll just take my chances and look for her in the Bottoms, in her cabin near the hickory tree she described.

Joshua is excited about a trip to the creek, not understanding that we aren't going here to play today. I let him think he's going for fun because he runs along more quickly that way. When we reach the dry creekbed, I take the mangled wax from my pocket and throw it into the bushes. Then we sit on the bank for a moment so I can catch my breath. I pull Joshua close to me so I can feel his beating heart. As I hold him, determination courses through me. I will not let Aaron hurt my child.

After a few minutes I nudge Joshua off my lap, stand, and indicate that we're going farther. Joshua's eyes widen.

—Where goin, Mama?

I point up the far bank and into the woods. Joshua jumps up and exclaims,

—We goin to the big field? Get some more locusts? Maybe Tyree and Yvonne be there!

I nod and try to show him that we are going even farther than the field, but he is now chattering about seeing Tyree.

—We gonna see them, Mama?

I nod yes, and he grabs my skirt and swings it in excitement. We continue on the path until it becomes overgrown with brambles. We are heading down a steep hill. I have no idea which way Nita's cabin is. I assume if it's called the Bottoms it will be at the bottom of this hill, but I don't know in which direction.

It has grown very hot, and Joshua is asking for water. Horseflies plague us, and he stops to swat at them futilely. I indicate that we must keep walking, and we head down the slope again. My foot is aching from walking on uneven ground, and my throat feels as if I have caught a bad fever. Every time I think of last night, I flush with shame.

Finally we reach what seems to be the bottom of the ravine. The ground levels off and is very swampy. I can see what looks to be a clearing up ahead through the thick brush. We push on through and come out into a muddy field with several cabins built close together. I look for the big hickory tree that Nita described, then I see it at the far edge of the clearing. I point to it, and Joshua, whining now about the heat and his thirst, follows me through the mud. It is very hard going with my leg, and halfway across the field Joshua sinks to the ground and I have to carry him.

Faces appear at some of the open doors as we pass the cabins, but no one offers to help me. It occurs to me that I am not welcome here, that none of these people know me. I try to hurry, but it is slow going. Mosquitoes buzz around us in the fetid heat, and Joshua cries out as he is bit. I try to swing my arm at them, but it is too hard to do so while holding him. With the last bit of my strength I manage to get him to the hickory tree, then I put him down and show him that we are going to the cabin directly behind it.

I limp up to the door, which is open, and peer inside. Yvonne and Tyree are playing hopscotch on the swept dirt floor. The children open their mouths in a scream when they first glimpse me, but then they recognize us and smile.

Yvonne goes running into the other room, and out comes Nita. She is surprised to see me here, but she quickly beckons us in out of the sun and gets us a dipper of water to drink. Joshua gulps down the whole dipper and asks for more, which she brings. He wipes his mouth on his arm and joins the children in their game. Then I drink, the cool water soothing my mouth like a miracle. Once I am done drinking, Nita indicates for me to sit on a rag rug on the floor. She settles opposite me.

—So you finally decided to leave him, she says slowly. She reaches out and pats my arm. —Are you all right?

—I have to tell you something, I say, trying to gauge my voice low so Joshua won't hear me.

Nita begins to speak, but she is talking so quickly I cannot tell what she is saying. I have no time to waste. I have to get back home before Aaron discovers that I've been away half the day. I have no idea where he is, and no idea when he will come back. I stick my finger into my ear and dig. Nita looks at me curiously.

—Gnat in your ear? she asks sympathetically. —Want me to look?

I shake my head, digging harder, pain shooting into my jaw. Finally a bloody brown kernel comes out in my hand. She stares at it. I push my finger into my other ear, and a ringing starts. With the ringing is a dizzying ache. I poke deeper, and the other one pops out onto the dirt floor. Nita looks at it in horror.

There is a swooshing in one ear, a ringing in the other. In the closeness of the hot cabin and with the eerie noises and pain, I feel as if I might faint. I shake my head to try to clear the sound away, but the motion makes it swoop and expand. She is now standing near me in concern, but I motion for her to sit again and let me be still for a few minutes. Gradually the noises quieten. I cannot hear at all out of my left ear, but I can hear out of the right one, the one that Joshua knocked the plug out of at the meeting.

—What were them things in your ears? Nita asks, her eyes wide.

—He put them there, I say. —He melted candles into my ears. — wasn't supposed to talk, and I couldn't hear with the wax plugs. He did it to me out of meanness. A whole year, I couldn't talk or hear.

Joshua sees me talking. He stops playing and runs over.

—Mama! You talked! he cries, watching me expectantly.

Hearing my son's voice again is like a wave breaking over me. I listen to its echo in my head for a while, trying to memorize it.

—Hello, sweetheart, I say. He comes over to sit next to me, staring. I put my arm around him.

—I have something — tell Nita now. Honey, play some. Talk to you on the way home, promise.

Reluctantly he rejoins Yvonne and Tyree in their noisy game. Nita's intake of breath sets off more swooshing in my ears.

—You done put up with enough of that, chile, she says, again patting my arm. —You made the right decision to cut loose a' him.

—I have something — tell you. He and these men—they meet every month. They're planning to set fire to your houses. All of you. I found out—by accident the other night. You have to get away.

I am gasping in the close air of the cabin. It strains my breath to say so much.

Nita sits back. She looks at me for a long time. —And you came here to tell me this? she asks.

I nod. —They're coming Saturday night, eleven. They'll burn you alive if they can. You have to get out. All of you.

Nita sits thinking for a moment. —Let me go get a few peoples. John's away workin, but I want some other folks to hear you. You can tell them what you just told me. Chirren, go on out and play awhile. Show Joshua how you can do skin the cat on that old hickory tree.

The children scramble outside, and she leaves the cabin. I sit in the airless room, sweat dripping down my back and neck. If I hold my head very still, I can make the swooshing stop for a while. When I breathe, it seems I can hear every intake of air. My stomach gurgles, and I hear that. I can hear the children playing in the back. Birds sing out in the sun, then stop. At one point everything is quiet, and I fear my hearing has gone again, but then a cicada starts its drone. I never heard such a good sound in my entire life.

I decide that I am not going to put these things back into my ears ever again, no matter what.

Nita comes back with two men and a heavy older woman with her head tied up in a red-and-white-checkered bandanna. They stand in front of me, arms folded. The woman speaks.

—You sayin your man and others are gonna burn us down this Saturday evenin? she says, as if it were an accusation.

—I just found out. Last night. He belongs to a group that meets. I heard them planning it; you have to get away.

The older of the two men looks at me suspiciously. —Why you tellin us this? he says. —Why should we believe you? You white yourself, it appears to me.

—More water? I ask Nita. My mouth is horribly dry, my

tongue cleaving to its roof. She brings me another full dipper and I drink.

—I'm going to get away from him too. He plans — hurt my boy. He hurt me, bad, several years. But I'm not going to let him hurt my son. I don't know when or how—I'm going to leave as soon as I can.

The younger man spits in the dust. —You got proof of these plans?

—I saw a piece of paper, notes from one of his meetings. When the men came to our house, I heard them talking. They want to burn you all.

—Aint no end to white folkses' devilment if they got their minds set on it, the older woman says. She heaves a sigh. —I aint takin any chances. I'ma go clear out and stay with my Aunt Clarisse down by Clearwater.

—I think we should stay and fight, says the younger man. —Why should we just let 'em burn down our homes? And then we got to uproot and look for work again?

—We try to fight, we'll wind up in jail ourselves, says the older man. —You know how that be. Come to the law, nothin the white man do is wrong. It all be on our backs.

—What if we went to the sheriff? the younger man says. —That new man they got in there seems better than a lotta those good ole boys. He just gonna ignore us?

—Boy, you aint lived long enough, have you? He laugh you out of his office, then come by the next mawnin tell you he's sorry your house caught on fire, says the woman.

Nita heaves a sigh. —I aint one for runnin, but this time I think we'd best clear out. I can't see anything good comin out of this. I got two chirren to see after. I can't take no chances. Seems to me, one place about as bad as the other. I was gettin tired of this old skeeter-infested swamp. Seems like now's the time for us to make a move to where my cousin live, down to Dry Fork. One thing I do know, this lady's tellin us the truth. I can vouch for that. I know her.

—Where you gonna go? the older woman asks me. —You want to just stay here with us until we leave?

—I have to go back to the house so he doesn't suspect anything. I don't have any money with me—haven't had time to think about where I'm going to go.

—You got family you can go to? she asks.

—Not right now. Too afraid he'd find me. My mama's farm would be the first place he'd look.

The older man looks at me, considering. —California supposed to be a good place for people got nowhere to go, he says finally. —Bein white, nobody would bother you on the train.

I think about it. —He keeps a little money hidden for liquor. Not much. I doubt it would even pay for my ticket.

—Tell you what, honey, the older woman says. —Whatever you can beg, borrow, or steal, you do it. You go on and protect your boy.

Numbly, I nod. Maybe Aaron will go off on a drinking spell, and I can slip away with Joshua before he knows the difference. Maybe if I could get to North Carolina or West Virginia, and make do until some time goes by, then I could come back to live with Mother. Maybe if I waited awhile, he'd go to Mother's farm, see we weren't there, then give up and never come back.

I turn to go. —Whatever you all do, be careful. These are dangerous people. You won't be able to reason with them.

The older woman laughs. —Honey, reasonin aint even been thought of. It's fight 'em or run, far as I can see.

Nita touches my arm. —Are you gonna be all right? she asks. —You could stay here with me til we can all get out of here.

I think about it for a moment. If Aaron caught me with
Nita, it would be even worse for me and Joshua than if he
caught us running off alone. And it would be much worse
for Nita and her people.

—I'll figure something out, I reply. —I have to.

—Lawd be with you, Nita says, her eyes wet with tears.

Joshua and I walk all the way back to the house. The heat
and horseflies are torturous, but I barely feel their stings.
Joshua pelts me with questions about why I can now talk,
but I decide to act as if I can't respond. If he talks to me
when Aaron is in the room, he may become suspicious, and
then it will all be over. It hurts me to do it, but I pretend
that I can't hear Joshua. I grunt and hum the way I've always done, and eventually he grows silent. If I can just keep
things the way they were until we get away, then no one will
ever be able to keep me from talking to him again.

Chapter Twenty-Three

For two days now I have watched Aaron like a hawk, hoping for some clue as to when he might be gone from the house for more than half a day. Often if he's not back by early afternoon, that means he won't return until late at night because he's found something to drink. I figure I'll need at least three hours to walk with Joshua to the train station, situated as far out of town as it is.

Yesterday I searched and searched until I found Aaron's hidden money, wadded up in a filthy handkerchief in a chink in the fireplace in our bedroom. I picked up the poker, still lying in its bed of ashes, and prized it out. He has saved almost four dollars, enough for us to get out of the state, at least over the North Carolina line, I imagine. Then I'll just have to pray no one sees us on the train or tells Aaron where we have gone to, if he thinks to ask after us there.

My hearing has become a little better since I removed the wax plugs at Nita's. I still cannot hear much out of my left ear, and the swooshing sounds come and go, but I seem to be hearing more out of my right ear now. Sometimes the sounds startle me, like the noises Joshua makes when he is playing. It is wonderful to be able to hear my son, even if I cannot respond to him yet. But soon I will, soon.

Aaron has not asked about the earplugs I threw away; those meant for Joshua. Perhaps he was so drunk he has forgotten about them. I know that he can easily make more, so I take care to keep Joshua as far away from Aaron as possible so that nothing sets him off until we can leave.

Today Aaron awakens unusually early for him, and I have to scramble to get Joshua out of the house before he comes downstairs. Joshua whines because he is playing with some creek pebbles on the floor and does not want to go outside at that moment. Finally I lift him up and set him outside by the step, indicating that he isn't to come back indoors until Aaron has left the house.

Aaron's face is a ghastly yellowish hue when he descends to the kitchen. He pokes at the frybread I've got ready in the pan and covers the pot back up gingerly. I sense that he has another massive, roiling headache from drinking and is unable to eat, as he is many mornings. I watch out of the corner of my eye as he tries to lift his cup of chicory that I have poured for him. His hands shake too much for him to be able to hold the cup, and he sets it down on the table quickly, sloshing the coffee over the rim. His eyes are bloodshot, and it looks as if he has a cut or bruise high up on one cheekbone. Worse for the wear, I tell myself.

At times I look at him and cannot believe I once thought him attractive or that he was a person of any qualities whatsoever. He catches me watching him, grimaces, starts to speak, then holds his head in his hands. I resist the impulse to clatter the dishes in the sink, to make his head ache more. In this weakened state he will not hit me, but I might pay for it later, as well I know. So I just stand there quietly as if I am looking out the window, and shortly I hear him get up and go outside. I watch the back of him walking across the yard and out to the dirt road. The morning sun seems to glow with a promise, and I think, Maybe this will be the day we will get away.

I do the dishes, then go outside to join Joshua. If Aaron is not back by early afternoon, I will start walking down the road with Joshua and see what happens. Maybe we will make it to the train station by nightfall without his noticing we are gone. My mind races, imagining our progress down the road. Perhaps we will take the route through the woods and stop at the Bottoms to see if anyone there is going in that direction today, although a white woman and child riding with a Negro would be sure to attract notice. Perhaps we will see a farmer with a wagon who will give us a ride, making the distance into no obstacle at all.

If only that had been the case, things would have turned out so differently.

I make two secret bundles under Joshua's pallet, two changes of clothes for us both. I pace the yard all morning, watching Joshua play.

I am about to bring him inside to feed him at midday when Nita comes around the corner of the house. My mouth drops open in surprise. Somehow seeing her here instead of our usual meeting place astonishes me, even though this is the second time it has happened. She smiles wide.

—We fixin to leave, but I wanted to see you one more time. I saw your man goin up the road earlier. I've got something for you. We took up a collection, see—

She hands me a packet of brown paper. I can feel coins through it, and some bills. I put it into my apron pocket.

—Oh, thank you, I breathe, quietly so Joshua won't hear. —You didn't have to do that.

—We all wanted to. We wanted to thank you for tellin

us. Now we're gonna have a chance to get away. There's an address in with the money, somebody who's helped our peoples before, if you can make it that far. When are you goin? she asks, frowning.

I shake my head. —Soon. I have to wait until I think he's going to stay gone at least half a day. I figure that's how long it'll take me to get to the train. I may even try to get out of here today if he stays away a little while longer.

—Whyn't you hook up with us tonight? Nita asks, mopping her brow with a rag she pulls from her bosom. —We leavin for Dry Fork soon as the sun sets, a bunch of us. We could give you a ride as far as the train. It's in the direction we're goin. We figure nobody'll much notice us in the dark.

I start to speak, but then out of the corner of my eye I see Aaron standing at the edge of the yard, arms crossed, looking at me hard. I start, and think, How long has he been here? When he sees me see him he begins moving, and I mutter to Nita,

—Go on, go home. Get away quick. It'll go better for me if you're gone. I'll try to come tonight if I can at all.

—You sure? Nita asks, watching over my shoulder as he approaches.

—Sure. Go.

She looks into my eyes and turns to leave. As I watch her cross the road, I am swung around hard by a heavy hand on my shoulder.

—What were you talking to that nigger about? he shouts into my face. —Who was she? Did that little brat say something to you about our plans?

—Hmm*hmm*ahm, I mumble, shaking my head.

Aaron shakes my shoulders til my head rattles. —You tell me, you bitch! What were you tellin her? Why you havin a long *conversation* with that niggerwoman!

I clear my throat to speak. —wanted a job, I say, my words jolting out as he continues to shake me. My neck snaps back from his blow.

—You're lyin! You lyin little bitch! I'm gonna find out, you know! You and your little tenderbait aint goin to ruin our plans!

He pushes me back and heads over to where Joshua has been watching, transfixed. I motion for Joshua to get up and run, but he is too afraid to move. Aaron picks him up by the arms and holds him high, screaming into his face.

—You little bastard! What did you tell her! What did you tell her, I said!

By now I have reached him and hang on his arm so he has to drop Joshua. He swings around to club me again but misses, losing his footing.

—Goddammit! See what you made me do! You're gonna be sorry for this! he screams as he gets up from the ground.

I stand right over him and scream back. —She was looking for work! She has five children and not a speck of food in the house! That's all! I let her know we didn't have anything — give her! That was it! I never saw her before in my life!

Aaron stands unevenly, his mouth gaping open, and I smell the liquor on his breath. He looks astonished, I suppose having forgotten that I could talk at all. I hope that Joshua has taken the opportunity to run far into the woods by now, but I can't risk looking around or it might draw attention to his absence.

—I never saw her before, I say again. —She was looking for work.

—You shut up now, he says, eyes narrowing. —You've done said enough.

He pushes past me, knocking hard against my body as he

goes by, and heads down the road. I watch him until he is out of sight, then hightail it out of the yard and go into the woods to look for Joshua.

Finally I find him sitting on the path, sobbing. I rush over to him and put my arms around his quaking body.

—Honey, we're going to get away from here. Tonight. Nita told me we can go with them. We're going to be safe where he can never find us.

Joshua looks up at me, tears streaking his face.

—Really, Mama? he says in disbelief. —He can't find us?

—No, I say with a firmness I don't feel. —He won't. We'll have a whole new life, once we get out of here.

—You keep talking to me? he asks, and my heart breaks. —You said you would, but then you didn't.

—Yes, I'll keep talking to you. I'll never stop talking again. He made me, but he won't be able to anymore, I say, unable to keep back my own tears.

Joshua climbs into my lap and holds on to me. We sit like that for some time, and I see that he has fallen asleep. I let him rest while I stare into the trees, watching the birds fly, listening to their calls. It is still a surprise to be able to hear, and every birdnote is a particular joy. When I notice that the sun is much lower in the sky, I rouse him. We stand up, and I feel for the packet of money in my apron pocket. It isn't there. I stoop down and scrabble through the leaves we'd been sitting on, but it isn't there, either.

—What you lookin for? Joshua asks.

—Nita gave me some money in a brown piece of paper. I need it to help us go far away. I put it in my pocket but it isn't here, I say frantically, my eyes searching the ground.

—I saw it, Joshua says. —It fall onna groun when he push you. I watchin from the tall grass.

—Are you sure? I ask, kneeling down to look into his face. —You're sure you saw it fall?

—I sure, he says proudly. —It fall right onna groun.

Inwardly I groan. —We're going to have to go back to get it. We can't go far enough away without that money.

—What if he there? Joshua asks.

—He was walking down the road when I left to find you. I doubt he's back yet.

—But what if he there? Joshua insists.

—Then we'll just stay in the woods until he leaves, I say. As quickly as we can, we go back along the path. When we get to the clearing, I tell Joshua to stay in the underbrush until I am sure Aaron isn't in the house. I creep out of the woods and crouch. No sign of Aaron, but there is the packet of money, laying in the dirt near the kitchen steps. I motion for Joshua to stay low, and I walk into the yard.

My heart pounding, I swoop down on the money, stuff it into my dressfront and then peek into the kitchen door. No one. Straining to listen, wishing my hearing were clear instead of congested with this gurgling and swooshing, I step inside and look up the stairs. Somehow I feel that he is not there, and I dearly wish to get the money I took from Aaron and a change of clothes. I start up the steps quietly. When I get to the top, I see the two empty bedrooms and sigh in relief. Quickly I hurry to the pallet and get the bundles I'd hidden, find the money, and pry it out of my shoe. I put that into my dressfront and start down the stairs.

My heart stops. Aaron is standing at the bottom of the steps, smiling wickedly up at me.

—Thought you'd go off gallivanting? he says, starting up the stairs.

The only thing I can think to do is to go back up.

—Stupid bitch! he calls to me. —Where were you? Did

you go off to meet your niggerwoman friend? he cries out as he climbs.

Suddenly Joshua is hurtling toward him, attacking him from behind.

—Get away! I shout, but it is too late. Aaron kicks out and Joshua is thrown back, hitting his head on the steps as he falls.

—Joshua! I scream, and run downstairs. Aaron catches a hank of my hair as I try to get by and yanks me to my knees, then grabs my arm and drags me back up. I claw at him, screaming, frantic to see to Joshua, but am unable to gain my footing.

—Joshua! Joshua! Are you all right? I cry out as I fight Aaron, but Joshua lies still at the bottom of the steps and does not answer.

Aaron gets me to the top of the stairs, throws me down, and kicks me about the head until I feel blood pouring from my ears. I scream Joshua's name over and over, until after a particularly brutal kick, I see black.

When I come to, I feel limp as a dishrag thrown onto the floor. The kerosene lamp casts a dim light around our bedroom. Aaron is not there, and for a moment I hope that he has gone. Then I hear Joshua whimpering in the next room, and Aaron's grunted commands. I hurry in and find Aaron wrestling with him. He is trying to hold Joshua's head down so that he can push something into his ear.

—Hold still or I'll knock you still! Aaron shouts, yanking him across the pallet.

—Nonono! cries Joshua. —Mama!

A powerful rage overtakes me. Quietly, so Aaron does not know I am revived, I leave them. Shaking inside, I rush back to our bedroom. I grab the poker from the fireplace and

hurry across the doorway. Aaron is about to hit Joshua with
his fist when I say,

—Stop it! Don't you touch him!

Aaron turns, an evil leer on his face, and I bring the poker
crashing down on his head. He looks at me dazedly for a
moment, then falls heavily to the floor. Joshua gets up from
the pallet and runs to me, crying. I hold him for a minute,
wary that Aaron may awaken.

—Shh, I whisper. We're going right now. Going away. Wait
for me outside.

Joshua doesn't want to leave me, but his fear of Aaron
spurs him on, and he runs downstairs.

I glance wildly around the room. If I leave Aaron like this,
he might arouse and come after us. I have to get out of here
with Joshua. I go into our room and grab the lantern and
carry it to where Aaron lays sprawled across the pallet. With
trembling hands I drip kerosene onto the bedclothes, then
light it with the flame. Then I turn, and without a backward
glance, I clump down the stairs.

Joshua is shivering outside on the steps.

—Mama, he hurted me, he cries, pushing his head into
my legs.

—Oh baby, I know. Let me see your face.

I examine the bruises and cuts, and feel a big lump on
the back of his head.

—How bad does that hurt? I ask when he winces.

—It hurted a lot.

—Can you walk with me? We need to go find Nita. They
are going to help us get to the train, I say, hoping they haven't
gone yet. I wonder if we will be able to make it all the way
to the Bottoms in our sorry state.

—He not find us?

—No, not where we're going. Come on, honey.

I take his hand, and we walk into the woods. I keep touching my chest to feel the comforting crackle of the money in my dressfront. Luckily the moon is bright, so we can see our way on the path. We are both so sore and weak that it takes an interminable time to reach the creekbed. Whenever I start to think of what I have done to Aaron, I push it out of my mind. I have to concentrate on getting away with all my being.

When we arrive, Nita, the older woman, and the older man are waiting there. They are a sight for sore eyes.

—I'm glad you made it, says Nita. —We figgered we'd meet you halfway, seein as you had so far to come. Gerald's got a buggy up the hill to drop you two off at the train. One's coming through at eleven. If you hurry, you'll catch it. Then we're all gonna go to Dry Fork. John's already there with Tyree and Yvonne. Guess I'll finally get that house I told you about.

The man carries Joshua, and I follow along as quickly as I can to the buggy. I feel I am walking in a fog, so much has happened. They put Joshua in back of the buggy, wrapped in blankets, and I sit up front with the younger man, who is driving.

—Good luck, says the woman.

—God bless you, says Nita.

—Oh, thank you, I say, tears coming to my eyes. —Good luck, Nita. Thank you so much.

She gives me a tight hug, and we are off.

As we head down the dirt road, I look back and shudder. Beyond the roof of the trees I can see tongues of flame licking higher, higher into the sky.

Chapter Twenty-Four

Every morning I wake up, bathe, put on my severe gray dress and white blouse, and eat with the other women at the long tables. There are no mirrors here, which is fine with me. When the time comes, I will look at myself and see the reflection of what I have done in my eyes. For now, I am glad not to have to face myself in such a direct manner.

I wonder what the other women think about me. I know little of their circumstances, the reasons they ended up here. I do not want to know. Whatever they have done, it cannot be worse than what I have done with my own two hands. Since I set Aaron on fire, the guilt at times has been crippling. At times I cannot breathe for contemplating what I have done. The thought of Joshua, alive and unharmed, is the only thing that keeps me going in such moments.

The food they serve us for breakfast is bland, either whey-like oatmeal or wheat crackers with milk. The other women do not say much, nor do I, as we are not encouraged to talk during meals here. There is a long prayer at the beginning of breakfast, then another at the end of the meal. Every meal is monotonous and repetitive, as are all my daily ablutions and movements. I have found sanctuary in the regularity and order of this place. Where many of the women complain, I find it gives me peace.

The children eat at several smaller tables on the other side of the room. When the meal is finished, we all joyfully find our own. Joshua runs to me, heaving himself at me. He has been growing like chickweed, with the better diet and milk he gets twice a day.

For a while, he constantly asked me where his father was, and if he was coming back. I couldn't tell if Joshua wanted to see Aaron again, or if he was asking out of fear, as opposed to concern. But I simply replied, as Adelaide, the director of the Home told me to, that his father had gone away and would not be returning. Eventually that seemed to satisfy him, and the questions have ceased.

Director Adelaide has been very nice to me, ever since the night we showed up at her door. She listened to my story with nary a sign of horror or blame. I imagine she's heard even worse since she started the Society of Friends Home for Women and Children here in San Francisco. At times I have visited her in the middle of the night, racked by conscience. But she always reminds me of the trials I went through, and of the fact that we have a very forgiving God.

In addition, she has helped me search for jobs, comforted me when I came back from interview after interview with no luck, and expressed great satisfaction when I finally got hired as a secretary for an import-export firm on Market Street, just last week.

I am coming along well in my stenography and typing lessons. The teacher, another Quaker, tells me I am quite skilled at it. It is nice to hear encouraging words after being told I was stupid for so long. I had begun to believe I was dumb—not only not able to hear or speak, but intellectually lacking as well. Now I see that it was Aaron who was insane.

Joshua attends the Society of Friends school five days a week. This week, he is learning his colors. Yesterday he learned blue. He likes the girls and boys in his class, and his teacher. I hope that I can keep him in this school for a while longer after we move out of the Home.

I have rented an apartment that we will move into next month. It is tiny but clean, and has a nice view of the hills with their quaintly colored rows of houses, one after another. I have never lived in a city, and thought I might not like it, but I see that for a person with a deformity such as mine, it is just the right place to be. People are too busy rushing about to pay much notice to someone with a bad foot, and there are many people so much worse off than me.

Just the other day, someone sent me a clipping from the Tarville newspaper. It was mildewed and tattered, and there was no note inside or return address, but I know it came from Nita. The first clipping described a raid on the Negro community in the Bottoms. Fire was set to two cabins, but the sheriff had been tipped off, and his men came to put out the blaze before it could spread. The article said that luckily all the inhabitants were attending a revival in a neighboring town, and no one was hurt in the flames.

So the sheriff helped them after all, I thought. I was glad of that, although I knew none of Nita's friends would ever feel safe in the Bottoms again.

The second clipping concerned the burning of a cabin on the other side of the creek. The article said that Aaron Melville had burned to death in his bed, his remains so charred they were barely recognizable. His wife, a deaf-mute, and child were presumed burnt up in the fire, but their remains could not be found.

I have written a long letter to Nita, thanking her for everything she did to help me and asking her to come to visit me whenever she can. I hope she will be able to live in the house with five acres that her cousin told her about. I have no idea if my letter got to her, since I simply addressed it to Nita Raines—Dry Fork.

Soon after I arrived here, I wrote to Mother and to Sibby. I did not go into detailed explanations about Aaron in my letter to Mother, but simply said he had died in an accident and that I was starting a new life here in San Francisco. In my letter to Sibby, I told everything. I had to let her know what had happened to me, why I had been so out of reach. I told both Mother and Sibby about Joshua, and invited them to come visit us.

I have not heard back yet from Mother, but Sibby actually showed up at the Home a few weeks ago. I was sitting in my little room with Joshua in my lap, reading a book to him, when there came a knock at the door and whispered admonishments.

—Cora, you have a visitor, came the voice of Joan, one of the women who helps run the place.

I slid Joshua off my lap and went to the door, trying to tidy my wrinkled skirt. Imagine my surprise to see Sibby and her two children standing there!

—Cora, I had to come, Sibby said, and stepped into my room holding out her arms. I fell into them and stood there sobbing with her for several minutes.

—I'll leave you alone, I heard Joan say as she shut the door.

When I could see through my tear-blurred eyes, I told the children to sit on my bed and for Sibby to take the only chair in the room. I stood, Joshua clinging shyly to my skirts. Sibby was still very pretty, only slightly older and with a pleasant roundness to her figure that made her look womanly.

—This is Daniel, my two-year-old, and Carol here is three, Sibby said.

The little boy was the spitting image of Sibby, with her dark eyes and hair, and the girl was lighter-complected like Charlie. They sat close together on the bed, eyeing me cautiously.

—Land sakes, Cora, you're living like a nun here! Sibby continued, looking around the room. —Is this a Catholic convent? You're not thinking of joining a monastery, are you? She rolled her eyes, indicating the severe decor.

Our little room has only a sink and a bed and chair—no ornamentation whatsoever—but I love it. I sighed and smiled.

—It's so good to see you, I can't believe it, I said. —No, I'm not going to be a nun. These people are Quakers. I'm hoping to find an apartment to move into in a month or so. As soon as I get a job, we'll be out of here. But they've been so good to me, Sibby, you have no idea—

The tears came again. Sibby jumped up and hugged me tight, her children's eyes following us from the bed.

—Your children are going to think their aunt isn't glad to see them, I said, sniffling. —Joshua, can you say hello to your cousins?

Joshua managed to say hello, then ducked his head back into my skirt.

—How did you get here? When did you come? I asked Sibby.

—Late last night. We took the train, same as you did. I told Charlie I wasn't going to wait no three more years for you to decide to come visit. He said, Go on and see her, you won't be satisfied til you do. So here I am. Great God, that train ride was long! And Daniel here just about worried

me to death wanting to run up and down the cars. I thought
he'd gotten off somewhere in Kansas and I'd never find him
again.

—It is a long ride, I said, remembering my terrifying ex-
odus with Joshua four months back. At every stop, I'd thought
each man in a suit who got on our car was a detective looking to catch me for killing Aaron. I shuddered at the memory.

Sibby watched my face closely.

—You've been through a lot, girl, she said softly. —I
couldn't believe your letter.

She glanced down at Joshua, and I shook my head in
warning. I didn't want to bring up any more questions from
him, as he'd finally settled down a little about things.

—We'll talk later, I said. —Let's go out and walk to the
park. It's beautiful here. Do you have someplace to stay? I
can ask Joan if there are any extra rooms.

—Oh, we're all set, Sibby replied. —Charlie had a good
year with his tobacco, so we're staying in a hotel for the first
time, aren't we, chirren? We're at the Pacific Hotel down the
street. Do you want to stay with us tonight? We could order
us up some room service, stay up late and talk.

—Maybe we can. It would be a treat for Joshua, I said,
who regarded me questioningly. He was still wary of new
things, and didn't know what a hotel was, I imagined.

We walked to the park, and while the children were playing, Sibby and I caught up on our lives. Charlie had done
well with his tobacco and was also raising dairy cattle. He
still did some farming with his cousin Tom, and they were
very close to that side of his family. Mother and WillieEd
had managed to make a go of things with Man Murfree's
help, and little Luke was in school and doing well. Mother

looked ten years younger, Sibby said, and had started going to church socials and ladies' circle meetings again.

—And now, Cora Mae, I want to hear about you, she said quietly, raising her eyebrow. —I got your letter, and cried and cried. I told Charlie what he'd done to you—I hope that was all right, but I just had to talk to him about it. I didn't tell him you started the fire, she said in a low voice, noting my agitation. —But I'm glad you did. If you'd stayed there, he'd have kilt you.

—I lie awake at night thinking I could have got away from him without doing what I did. I've agonized over it.

—You had to get away, Cora. If you hadn't, he would've hurt Joshua. I wish you'da knocked him into tomorrow a long time ago. If I'd had any idea you were in trouble all that time you were away, I would have come running. I just thought you didn't want to see us, were ashamed of us or something. I had no idea you were in bad circumstances until I heard about the fire and some rumors started going around that reached us. At first I read in the newspapers that you died in the fire, and I just about went crazy. Then when I got your letter and you told me what you'd been through—

She stopped speaking, tears filling her dark eyes. I looked out at our three children, romping around on the grass.

—I know you would have come, would have helped me, I said. —Part of it was pride; at first, I just didn't want to admit I'd made such a big mistake with Aaron. He turned out to be so different from what he seemed. Then I became afraid of what he'd do to me if I tried to leave him, or if anyone from home showed up. I was afraid of what he'd do to Joshua. I've thought over and over about why I stayed with someone like that, and I can't come up with any good answers, except I was just plain scared.

—Well, you're here now, that's what counts, Sibby commented, taking my hand and squeezing it.

—You know, you could come back home and live with me and Charlie, she continued. —I talked it over with him before we left. There's a separate two-room house in back we could fix up real nice; you wouldn't have to stay under the same roof as us. But you'd be welcome any time you wanted to come for dinner or whatever. Think about it, Cora, she said when I shook my head. —I feel like we have so many years to make up for. And our children could have so much fun together. Listen to them now.

Their laughter rang out as they played under the big trees.

—It's not that I don't appreciate it, I said. —I do. I may take you up on your offer sometime. But for now I think I need to be in a new place, away from all the memories. It's been so good to be in new surroundings, where no one knows me or my past. I feel like I'm starting everything new.

—I can understand that, Sibby replied. —I can see how you'd need to do that. But if you ever change your mind, you know you can stay with us. At least I hope you'll come back home to visit.

—I will, as soon as I get settled in here. I want to find a job and get a place for us to live. I have a second interview at an import-export firm that Director Adelaide set up for me—she knows one of the owners of the company. I'm hoping I'll get taken on as a secretary.

—Cora Mae Slaughter, working in an office in the big city of San Francisco. That sounds real exciting. Maybe I'll leave Carol and Daniel with Charlie and come shack up with you instead of going back to podunk holler, she laughed.

We rounded up the children and went back to her hotel, where Joshua and I spent the night. Sibby and I stayed up until three o'clock in the morning, laughing and crying and reminiscing. We visited for two more days, and then they had to go home. But Sibby and I write each other every week, and once a month she calls me on her brand-new telephone that Charlie has installed. In December I will have one week's vacation, and I imagine Joshua and I will take the train to see them. By then it will be good to be back home.

Joshua bursts into our room from the hall, where he has been playing with some of his friends. I take him down to his classroom and kiss him goodbye. Then I step out into the cool October air and catch a trolley to my new job.

Now that I've been coming here for three weeks, I feel less trepidation when I walk into the huge portals of the company. My boss seems kind, and the other secretaries are too busy to pay much notice to my foot. One of them, Mary, invited me out to lunch the other day, but I told her I would have to wait until payday. She laughed and said she knew what that was like, and that she'd look forward to next Tuesday so we could have our lunch.

My hearing has come all the way back in my right ear. I am still partially deaf in my left ear; the doctor who comes to the Home said he'd never seen an eardrum that had been burst so many times. He pressed me to tell him what had happened to me, but I could not. I just could not bring myself to relive it. He says that I am lucky to have any hearing left at all in either ear, and I agree wholeheartedly. I am lucky, period.

Every day I wake up and realize I am free, and I rejoice.

Author's Note

Women and children who are in violent domestic situations need a safe refuge. Please contact your local women's shelter to find out how you can help.

The author supports:

The Retreat
P.O. Box 988
Wainscott, New York 11975

Acknowledgments

My endless gratitude goes to my agent, Julie Rubenstein, whose brilliant editorial insights helped me to make this novel complete. Without her, this book never would have seen the light of day.

A multitude of thanks to Amy Einhorn, whose skillful editing was a wonderful gift. I feel blessed to have been able to work with such a caring, enthusiastic, and talented editor.

Much appreciation to Linda Chester for her invaluable support, and to Meredith Phelan for her thoughtful suggestions.

Thanks to Pat Mulcahy for an early read and encouraging words, and to April Sinclair for friendship and support in this endeavor.

Thanks to Bob and Martha for letting me work at home. Love and gratitude to my good friends Richard and Kris; and to Patti.

Grateful thanks to Phil for his support.

Appreciation and love go to Jane and Janet for many years of conversation and advice; to Monica for listening to my plot ideas, and for being such a good pal; and to Karen and Mimi for longtime friendship.

Thanks to Papa Paul for all the time, love, and care you've

given all of us—and for being the best grandfather anyone could ask for.

Thanks to Paul Scott and Tammy, Eric and Gloria, Kevin, Keith, and Janice for being such great family.

Thanks to Sheri for years of listening and sharing, and for being a true friend through thick and thin.

Huge appreciation to Jennifer and Emily, who couldn't be nicer, closer, or more supportive.

The love of my husband and son sustains me. You are the light of my life.